GW01158952

# THE CURSE GROWS STRONGER STILL

K.M.Bishop

—Shellville Press—

Shellville Press

Printed by Shellville Press in the United States of America

Cover illustration by Natalie Qualmann, @nats.mcgats with figure element AI-generated

ISBN: 979-8-9886954-2-4

Shellville Press
a division of Shellville Design LLC
www.shellvillepress.com

10 9 8 7 6 5 4 3 2 1

# PREFACE

THE WOMAN LET OUT AN ANGUISHED WAIL AS THE JUDGE announced the verdict, falling to the floor as he pronounced a sentence of death.

"No! No! I be innocent! I beg thee!" she hollered, fighting against the bailiffs as they tried pulling her away. "I've cast no spell! I've hurt no one!"

"Take the witch away!" cried the spectators in the courtroom.

"Hang the witch!"

"Devil worshipper!"

"'Twas not me!" the woman continued to cry as she was dragged out of the building. "I be no witch! I beg ye tuh let me go!"

She tried pulling against the men who held her, but she was weak from spending months in a dingy cell with meager provisions. Exhausted, she gave up and allowed them to drag her limp body through the dirt-filled streets to the temporary gallows in the middle of the square.

She sobbed as she was dragged up the stairs and dropped under a rope being prepared by the executioner. She shakily pushed herself to her knees and brushed back her graying hair tumbling from her yellowing cap. She gulped and faced the crowd gathering to witness her death.

"I beg ye to spare me!" she cried, clasping her hands together. "I be a child o' God as ye be! I say me prayers! I've ne'er hurt no one!"

Boos and hissing rang out from the crowd as pebbles were thrown at her. The woman shielded herself, letting out cries of terror and pain as they bounced off her. She scanned the crowd through her hands, looking for a friendly face, but she stopped when she saw him.

"You!" she called out pointing at the man.

Startled, the crowd stopped in their jeering.

"You! You lied! 'Tis because of you I be here!" she continued. "Tell 'em! Tell 'em ye lied and spare me!"

The crowd shifted, looking for the person she was speaking to. They stepped away, creating a circle around a man who stood stiffly, awkward in what appeared to be new, fancy clothes.

"Did ya buy them rags with yer thir'y pieces o' silver?" The woman spat in disgust. "Tell 'em! Tell 'em ye lied!"

The man remained silent and turned to walk away.

The woman was dragged to her feet and the noose was fitted around her throat.

"I curse ye!" she shouted, almost growling, causing the executioner to flinch.

Gasps rang through the crowd, and the man stopped in his tracks.

"I curse ye an' yer family!" the woman continued. "I shall allow ye to profit from the thir'y pieces o' silver gained by me death. But know, no one in yer family shall live older than me. No one in yer family shall live past the age o' for'y-five. Pain an' suff'rin' shall befall yer family until yer name dies

2

*out with thee comin' o' a new century!"*

*She spit again, and struggled against the executioner as he helped her onto a stool. Her body trembled in fear, but her words continued to convey the anger boiling in her veins.*

*"I curse ye!" she screeched. "Everythin' ye sacrificed for will turn tuh ash and ye family with it!"*

*The executioner kicked the stool from under her and she fell.*

"BUT SHE MUST HAVE BEEN A WITCH!" THE YOUNG BOY PONdered, shaking his head. "If she was not guilty, surely God would have saved her."

"God has nothing to do with it," replied the young girl sitting at the desk beside him. "Men and their free will, which he made the mistake of bestowing on us, do."

"That is blasphemous!" cried the boy. "God does not make mistakes."

She sighed and rolled her eyes. "No, but men do, and as we are his creations our mistakes are God's by default."

"That is enough Agrippina," her uncle chuckled. "Stop antagonizing Master Thomas."

The two children wrinkled their noses at one another.

"In a perfect world, Master Thomas, you would be right. God would not permit an innocent person to be persecuted for a crime they did not commit, but, as our world is no more perfect than a half-built home, innocent people have indeed died for crimes in which they were not guilty."

"But that does not seem fair, Dr. Greystone," Thomas said quietly.

"No, it does not," Dr. Greystone agreed. "But past injustices teach future generations," he turned to the chalk board and began writing, "and from the witch hunts of yore with the sacrifice of hundreds of people, most of them women, we enter a new era of enlightenment. With that, we have the passing of new laws and in 1735, Parliament made it a crime to accuse someone of having magical powers or practicing witchcraft."

Thomas frowned. "But what if someone were a witch? How could someone seek justice for their crimes?"

Agrippina giggled which earned her a raised brow from her uncle. She cleared her throat to regain her composure. "Witches are not real," she informed Thomas. "That is why the law was put into place; it is to protect ordinary people from the superstitious ones."

Thomas shook his head. "But what about the curses and illnesses that surround these men and women? If witches are not real, then what caused them?"

Agrippina opened her mouth to reply but hesitated, her brow furrowing. Her uncle smiled at the frustration that glinted in her eyes; she did not know what to say. He patted her hand lovingly.

"Sometimes, Master Thomas, things in this world happen that we cannot explain—that we have yet to learn how to explain. But the human mind wants to be satisfied, so sometimes, we make things up."

He shook his head. "I don't understand. You are saying that people lied about people being witches to explain away their misfortunes?"

Dr. Greystone nodded slowly. "Yes, and no."

"Perhaps they didn't know they were lying because they truly believed the people they accused were witches," Agrippina suggested.

Dr. Greystone pointed at his niece. "Exactly! And with one accusation comes mass panic."

Thomas shook his head again. "But you said some of the women accused later confessed. If they were not witches,"

4

he shot Agrippina a look, "because you say they don't exist, then why would they confess to it?"

Dr. Greystone sighed as his expression turned a little somber. "There will always be dark corners of history, Master Thomas, and this was one of them. Torture, of the most cruelest imaginable, was sometimes used to elicit a confession from these poor souls and from these false confessions came the false accusations of others."

Thomas sat back in his seat, his brows furrowed in contemplation. "And then that accused would be tortured into confessing and more accusations, over and over," he said in a low voice.

Dr. Greystone nodded. "Unfortunately, yes."

Thomas blinked, looking dejected. "The world is a cruel place, Dr. Greystone, filled with lies."

"Oh, do not let the past bother you, Thomas!" Agrippina told him. "Yes, it is sad that innocent people died as a result of someone else's religious-fueled panic, but you cannot change what has already happened. You can only learn from it and do better."

He looked over at her. "How?"

She blinked to keep from rolling her eyes. "You will be a lord someday! With the power and influence to help people. Do not waste it by being silly. Silly men make big mistakes and act before they think."

"I am not silly!" Thomas retorted sternly. "And one day, when I am a lord in parliament, I will prove it to you."

Agrippina smiled. "Yes, but until then, you will just be a silly boy."

# 1
## 1793 (13 YEARS LATER)

AGRIPPINA GREYSTONE SQUINTED IN THE SPRING SUN AS IT reflected off the River Grant. She blinked for a moment as she listened to the man before her, unsure she was hearing what he had just said.

"My help?" Agrippina repeated the words she just heard, surprise evident in her voice.

Richard Maddox, a student of her uncle's, nodded. "Yes. There have been some sort of mysterious happenings going on in Halstead, a town not far from my uncle's estate."

"The uncle you are to inherit from?"

"Yes, and he is concerned for the locals," he continued. "Particularly, some of the farmers." He sighed. "Anyway, none of the local authorities know what to do, and when I heard about your success in Blindburn, I could not think of anyone else from whom to beseech help."

Agrippina stood a little straighter after that comment and suppressed a triumphant smirk. "Yes, well, I would need to talk to my uncle, of course, and check my availability."

They turned together to return to the City of Cambridge.

"Might I carry your bag for you?" he asked her, indicating the large leather satchel slung over her shoulder.

"Yes, thank you. But please mind its contents. They are papers I was helping Professor Hartley grade." She handed it to him, rolling her shoulders once the weight was off them.

He frowned slightly. "Are you sure there are only papers in here? It weighs a ton."

"I am rather intrigued by these 'disturbing events,'" she went on, ignoring his observation. "Might you be able to elaborate?"

Richard Maddox took a deep breath, gathering his thoughts. "I believe it began almost a year ago. Nine months ago, really. A farmer went out into his fields and found one of his prized cows dead, drained of blood."

Agrippina looked over at him sharply. "All of it?"

He shrugged. "That is the report. I only briefly spoke with the farmer months later. Rumors spread quickly in small towns, and I was not a witness myself."

They paused to allow a carriage to drive through the street before they crossed.

"An exaggeration, I am sure," Agrippina replied as she moved around a pile of horse excrement.

He nodded. "Yes, well," he paused to clear his throat, "the word 'witch' has been thrown around."

"Is blood draining typical of a 'witch' encounter? I have never heard of such a thing."

Richard let out a small laugh. "I suppose anything that you cannot explain can be contributed to a witch."

Agrippina lifted her brows. "Where was the wound?"

He blinked and stuttered for a moment. "I believe the wound was across the neck. Yet, there was no blood in the grass." He held a hand up to stop her from interrupting again. "And it had not rained the night before. It was one of my first questions as well."

"Hmm. Strange, to be sure, but nothing to start hollering for a witch hunt over."

He shook his head. "But that is only the start of it. In the following weeks, the same farmer lost three more cows in the same way. Cows with their throats slit, yet little to no blood on the ground." He cleared his throat. "Not long after the last cow, the farmer's young daughter started exhibiting strange behavior. Saying she was seeing things, dark shadows that followed her. She would go into screaming fits of hysteria, terrified someone was after her." He paused a moment. "She was found dead perhaps a week later, floating in the Colne River."

Agrippina frowned. "How awful."

"She was only fifteen and said to have had a calm, sweet disposition before all of this."

Agrippina pursed her lips together as she listened.

"Soon, following her death, another farmer's fields caught fire and destroyed almost his entire crop of wheat. Three different fields decimated. And like the farmer before him, his eldest daughter also soon began to see things and have fits of hysteria. She tried throwing herself from her bedroom window to make it stop, but her father saved her just before she fell. She is alive but," he let out a huff of air, "a shell of her former self, I am told."

Agrippina nodded as she moved around a puddle. "What is her age?"

He thought for a moment. "Perhaps, fifteen, same age as the other girl. I am not sure."

"Is there more?"

He bobbed his head. "A merchant, well-known and liked, was found dead along the road as he was making his way to the market. He was clutching his chest as if in pain, his eyes

8

wide with terror. When they opened his cargo of silk, they found it to be covered with hundreds of moths, and the silk fabric ruined."

"All of these are rather peculiar," she agreed slowly, "but why do you believe it is the cause of a witch? To me, and to a normal outsider, they appear to be strange misfortunes that have yet to be explained."

He chuckled lightly. "I want to agree with you, but there is still more to this story that I have yet to tell."

"Miss Greystone! Miss Greystone, my dear!"

Agrippina turned to see Professor Hartley walking quickly toward her, waving to get her attention.

"Miss Greystone!"

Richard lifted an amused brow. "He seems rather excited to see you."

"Professor Hartley, what seems to be the hurry?" Agrippina asked.

Professor Hartley, a portly man in his early fifties and usually reeking of port wine, leaned against the archway where Richard and Agrippina had stopped on one of the Cambridge campuses.

"Oh, dear," he exhaled trying to catch his breath. He rubbed the side of his stomach as he huffed and puffed. "I've a cramp now."

Richard turned away to hide a smile.

"If you were chasing after me for your papers, I have them right here," Agrippina told him.

Professor Hartley chuckled. "Chasing after you! My dear, I have been doing that for quite some time, have I not?"

Agrippina blushed, her eyes wide with embarrassment.

Richard slowly turned his head to look at her, both brows raised.

"Well, that is to say—I believe you mean—" She cleared

her throat as she tried to regain her composure. "I am looking for my uncle." She pointed to Richard and then herself. "We are looking for my uncle."

"We?" Professor Hartley repeated, finally noticing Richard's presence. He adjusted the spectacles on his face, his eyes narrowed. "And who is 'we?'"

"Richard Maddox, sir," Richard answered for himself. "I had the pleasure of taking your class last term."

"Hmm. I am sure." He turned back to Agrippina. "Your uncle has gone home. He seemed a little sallow."

Agrippina paled at this, and she let out a small gasp.

"Are you alright, my dear?" Professor Hartley asked, his brows slightly creased.

She forced a small smile and took a deep breath. "Yes, thank you." She indicated the bag Richard was holding. "Here are your papers, Professor."

Richard took the hint and removed the bag, handing it to him.

"Come, Mr. Maddox." She turned and began walking back toward the road that led into the town, Richard following closely behind.

"But, you have not answered my question from this morning!" Professor Hartley called out.

Agrippina looked over her should and gave a little wave. "Same answer as always, I am afraid!"

# 2

THEY WALKED IN SILENCE FOR A FEW MINUTES UNTIL RICHARD could no longer resist the temptation to speak.

"Curiosity might have killed the cat, but I am sure I will survive it."

Agrippina stiffened her back as she walked, knowing what he was going to ask.

"What was the question Professor Hartley ran across campus and risked an apoplexy for?"

"Do you really expect me to answer you?" Agrippina asked in a hard tone.

Richard chortled. "Oh, I already know the answer, but hearing it from you would make it so much more enjoyable."

Her narrow eyes flitted in his direction.

"Has Professor Hartley made an offer of marriage to you?"

Agrippina took a deep breath through her nose. "Do you not have more pressing issues afoot? Must you delve into my private life?"

He laughed. "Come now! Am I not allowed to tease you? We are friends, are we not?"

She raised a brow at him. "Are we? I thought we had more

of a mutual, respectful distaste for one another."

He laughed again unfazed by her harsh tone. "You certainly know how to cut someone with your words. If I thought less of myself, I might be offended."

At this, she smirked. "I was wondering when your usual arrogance would show itself. Do you act this way with all the ladies, or am I just lucky?"

He blushed and scratched the back of his head. "There are no other ladies."

She looked over at him, her brows furrowed. "Really? None at all?" She shrugged lightly. "And I thought you a rake this entire time."

His lips twitched into a little smile. "You sound disappointed."

She shook her head. "Not at all, just surprised."

They walked the rest of the way in silence, crossing the river and leaving the town area until they reached a row of houses. Agrippina opened the door to the small manor house she lived in with her uncle and ushered Mr. Maddox inside.

"Abigail!" she called out to their head maid.

"Yes, miss," Abigail replied walking into the foyer while wiping her hands on her apron. "Oh!" She stopped when she saw Mr. Maddox, her eyes twinkling in familiar delight. "Mr. Maddox, you've returned. I did wonder when we'd see ya again." She held out her hands to take his hat and the bonnet she forced Agrippina to wear. "Hope yer doing well, sir."

Mr. Maddox nodded, smiling kindly at her. "Yes, I thank you."

"Where is my uncle?" Agrippina asked, getting to the point.

Abigail's cheeks flushed as she smiled. "Oh, you would like to talk to Dr. Greystone?" she replied, turning again to Mr. Maddox. "Of course, you would. He is in the parlor."

She held out her free arm showing him the way. "I've just made him some tea, but I can bring ya anything ya like." She opened the door to the parlor and half bowed as Mr. Maddox thanked her and walked in.

Agrippina jumped back as Abigail shut the door in her face. She shot her a confused and surprised look.

"I think it best they talk alone, miss. It might help him get his point across." Abigail nodded singularly.

"What are you talking about, Abigail?" she asked a little angrily. "I would not have asked for my uncle if I did not wish to speak with him as well. It is what I have to say that matters."

"Well, once ya accept him, I suppose it does matter, but let him ask for yer hand first."

Agrippina blinked at her, her lips pursed. "Good God, Abigail! He did not come to propose!" She shook her head as she pushed her maid aside and opened the door to the parlor herself, promptly closing it behind her.

The men looked over at her inquiringly, and she forced a small smile.

"Aggy, my dear," her uncle began, handing Mr. Maddox a cup of tea. "I am not surprised to see you here with Mr. Maddox."

Agrippina walked forward and took the cup her uncle then poured for her. "He told you earlier then about the issues he is having?"

"A curious case of witches!" Dr. Greystone replied, his eyes glittering with excitement.

Agrippina tilted her head. "You know I do not believe it to be a witch." She glanced at Mr. Maddox. "There has to be a logical explanation."

Dr. Greystone chuckled. "Did your adventures up in Blindburn teach you nothing? Sometimes the logical answer is not always the correct one."

"But the logical answer was correct," she told him matter-of-factly. "It might have taken some time to come to that conclusion, but, in the end, it was not a beast who slaughtered those women, but a human. A sad, disturbed human."

Her uncle shook his head, still smiling. "You still have yet to learn how to use your imagination." He coughed into his handkerchief causing Agrippina to step forward in concern, but he waved her away. "I am fine." His smile returned to his face as he hastily tucked his handkerchief back into his pocket.

"You do look a little sallow as Professor Hartley had said," Richard told him. "Are you unwell?"

Dr. Greystone cleared his throat as he took a sip of his tea. "It is nothing but the change in weather, I am sure. We had a cold winter that melted quickly into a warm spring."

Agrippina eyed her uncle suspiciously but said nothing as she sipped from her own cup.

"Now," Dr. Greystone slapped his knee, "back to the interesting topic. What do you think, Aggy? Do you think Mr. Maddox's case worth investigating?"

"It is certainly interesting, uncle, but if your health is indifferent, I would not wish to leave you."

"Oh, pish-posh! My health is not indifferent," Dr. Greystone claimed. "If it is on my account you wish to stay, then I forbid it."

Agrippina looked from Mr. Maddox to her uncle. "Would you not come with me then? I know this is something you would love to explore yourself. Could we not go together as we did in Blindburn?"

He smiled lovingly at her. "As wonderful a time Blindburn was, I cannot. I am bound to my professorial duties this term. Our last quest was at the behest of the king. I doubt

Mr. Maddox, as grand of a student he might be, will be able to keep the wrath of the board at bay." He nodded singularly. "If you wish to go, you should go."

Agrippina regarded her uncle for a few moments. "Uncle, are you sure I should not wait? Perhaps until you are feeling better?"

He chuckled. "If you are to wait for an old man like me to feel better before going anywhere, then you will be waiting for a very long time to go nowhere at all."

"Old? You are barely fifty."

Dr. Greystone shook his head with a smile. "Then leaving me should be no consequence to you."

Agrippina looked like she wanted to object again but refrained. Instead, she turned to Richard with a nod. "When shall we leave?"

3

BLINDBURN HAD BEEN A DIFFERENT EXPERIENCE FOR Agrippina. She, of course, had traveled with her uncle over the years, touring the continent, Edinburgh, London, Bath, and other usual places English society might travel, but Blindburn was beyond either of them.

It is true, Blindburn did not have the art of Paris, or the culture of Italy, but it did something that the other places did not. It challenged her. The mystery that brought her and her uncle to Blindburn was something she had only heard of in one of her uncle's stories.

When they were younger, Uncle Alfred and her father used to investigate strange mysteries all throughout England. Stories of robberies, murders, disappearances. They were the stories Agrippina would fall asleep listening to as a child. The adventures her uncle and father had together. Blindburn was her chance to be a part of one of those stories.

Five women mauled to death during the full moon, a superstitious little town believing they had a werewolf, an overzealous vicar hellbent on seeing someone hanged for heresy. Solving the mystery behind it all and quelling the fears of a town was worth far more than going to a silly masquerade in London, or walking through the flooded streets of Venice.

And, it didn't hurt she met James Mackland while she was there.

She blushed at the mere thought of him. His curious, understanding nature paired with his dark, windblown hair and constant soft smile. His sister Karen had been one of the women that had succumbed to the beast of Blindburn and it was his letter to one of the King's counsel that brought about the investigation.

The few days she spent in Blindburn, a bond grew between Agrippina and Mr. Mackland. Even after she accused him of being the murderer, he still wanted to continue to know her.

Blindburn had challenged her, taught her, saw her in ways she had never experienced, and it certainly left a yearning she hadn't felt before, a restlessness she couldn't explain.

She finally understood what she had been missing all these years, but despite figuring that out, there was something that made her hesitate when another opportunity was laid at her feet.

Her uncle.


"YOU ARE SURE YOU WILL NOT MIND ME BEING AWAY?" Agrippina asked for the fifth time as she sat down to dinner with her uncle. She moved her food about her plate, a knot of guilt suppressing her appetite.

Dr. Greystone, a brilliant mind in possession of an easy sense of humor, laughed and leaned over the table to pat her hand. "My dear, I meant it the first time I said it, and I will mean it still the one hundredth time. I do not mind."

She cleared her throat and put down her fork as she dismissed the servant waiting to attend to them. "Uncle," she began once the servant had left, "You are sick. You can play it off as the change in the weather, but I know that is not the case. Your consumption, though slowly, is progressing and will continue to do so. If something happened while I was away and—"

"I will not be your excuse to hide from the world, Agrippina," he said in a low, stern tone. "I understand your concern. I appreciate it—am gratified by it—but I cannot allow your life to stop all because mine is coming to an end."

Agrippina placed a hand over her mouth and shook her head as she looked away. "Must you refer to it so casually?"

Dr. Greystone sighed. "I understand this is difficult for you, Aggy," he replied softly. "It is not easy for me either." His voice broke and he cleared his throat to regain his composure. "As a human, I want more time. As your uncle, mentor, and parental figure, no amount of time would ever be sufficient."

Agrippina closed her eyes to keep her tears at bay.

"I have had the pleasure of raising you as my own for over seventeen years and I am so proud. I am confident that I shall leave this world having brought up an intelligent and self-sufficient young woman and there is nothing more I could have ever asked for." He paused for a moment. "Well, there is one thing, but," he chuckled softly, "I will not tease you on that subject."

"You are referring to me getting married," Agrippina said. "Or not having married yet being more accurate."

He chuckled again. "No, no! I will not pressure you. You did, however, receive this earlier today!" He reached into his pocket and pulled out a letter. "From you know who." He raised his brows at her.

18

She tried not to blush as she took the proffered letter but could not help the involuntary smile that crept onto her lips when she saw the handwriting.

"That is your third letter from him this week."

She stuttered a moment. "Y-yes, we often write multiple times during the week to each other. It does take almost a fortnight to receive them."

Her uncle nodded knowingly. "Mr. Mackland is a good man."

"Yes," was all she would allow herself in response.

"Go on, read it," he told her, waving his hand. "But please do more than push your food around and eat. You have a long day ahead of you tomorrow. It would be good to be well rested."

"Yes, uncle."


AGRIPPINA WAS NOT SENTIMENTAL; SHE HATED DISORDER OR clutter, but for some reason she could not bring herself to get rid of any of the letters Mr. Mackland had sent her. She even found herself rereading them when she had nothing better to do. By now she could recite her favorite letters from him by memory and found herself doing so when she was out. It was what she had been doing after grading Professor Hartley's papers when Mr. Maddox had found her.

His hand was not particularly even, the lines tilting as the letter went on, but the handwriting itself was neat and almost elegant. At least by man's standards, she thought. It was certainly cleaner and more legible than Professor Hartley's or even her uncle's.

She sighed and shook her head. There she was again, ridiculously comparing Mr. Mackland to any other man. She put his most recent letter in the box where she kept all of his others and slid it under her bed.

There was nothing of actual importance in his recent letter. As always, his words were sweet, but there was no declaration of great feeling. He spoke of updates in Blindburn, his wish to begin farming sheep, and opening a wool mill to help create more work for those who needed it. He asked for her input and guidance, a line that swelled her heart more than how beautiful he thought her ever could.

*I am desirous to create more work for the impoverished of my town. Seeing the squalor they live in while I live alone in my mansion disgusts me. Giving them financial aid is not enough and will not last. I wish to give them the means to support themselves...*

*What do you think, sensible Miss Greystone? I long for your guidance and honesty.*

It was not what most would call a letter between lovers, but love making does not mean the same thing to everyone. Where most girls want to be called beautiful, Agrippina wanted to be acknowledged by what could not be seen. She could look into a mirror and see that she was beautiful; she did not need a man to tell her so.

She laughed to herself as she reread the last two lines, thinking their relationship could have turned out very differently or could have ended there in Blindburn. Most men would have ceased communication after being accused of killing not only their sister but four other women.

She sat at her writing table that faced a window overlooking the street and took a moment to watch the lanterns in the street being lit. She then took out a sheet of paper and began her response.

Mr. Mackland,

Thank you for asking my opinion. I believe with Blindburn's climate and location, a sheep farm is quite sensible, and a mill to process it only more so. With the proceeds from these businesses, you will be able to rebuild the derelict housing in which the poor people of Blindburn live as you have often expressed the desire to do so.

And, it should allow you to maintain your own estate. I know you have been concerned with how you would make up the loss of income after you pulled your support from Mr. Hawkins' illegal whiskey operation. This will help restore the honor you feel your family name has lost because of that connection. Though, I should never say your honor was tainted.

Her cheeks burned at the last line, and she wondered if she should elaborate more. For a moment, she was overtaken with emotional inspiration, adding to her thought.

It has been a long time since I have considered you to be the most honorable man of my acquaintance, a sentiment that your letters continue to increase.

I have a new prospect of my own. I have been asked to investigate mysterious occurrences in Essex. A student of my uncle's believes a witch is roaming among them. I shall leave you an address where you can forward my letters, though, hopefully, by the time you receive this, I will have already solved it. It is, of course, not a witch.

I hesitated to go, but uncle insists. I have touched upon his illness in a previous letter, but I have not been entirely truthful.

*He has the White Death, the same disease that killed both my mother and father all those years ago.*

*He has been doing better, taking daily doses of fermented honey, onion, and garlic, but I fear for him. I fear what might happen if I am not here to help him.*

*Perhaps, I am not so sensible after all.*

*I should have told you when I saw you this past February at the king's court. My uncle forbade me, however. I tell you now because, next to my uncle, there is no one I trust more than you. Forgive me for not having told you before.*

*I shall write again when I am settled in Essex.*

*— A.G.*

Agrippina thought for a moment to tear the paper up and start over, her vulnerability showing more than she cared it to, but she didn't. She addressed and sealed it for the next day's post.

4

RICHARD MADDOX'S CARRIAGE PULLED IN FRONT OF DR. Greystone's house promptly at seven the next morning. The four horses pulling the carriage stamped their feet and shook their heads seemingly annoyed they were made to stop. Richard emerged from the carriage smiling brightly and shook hands with Dr. Greystone.

"Good morning, sir, you are looking better."

Dr. Greystone thanked him, nodding. "A good night's rest does a man wonders, does it not?"

Agrippina stepped forward and adjusted her bonnet which she only put on after Abigail badgered her to do so. "Good morning, Mr. Maddox. About twelve hours of travel, you said?"

He laughed. "Straight to business per usual, Miss Greystone. Yes, with a few stops to refresh our horses and eat, our journey of just over thirty miles should take about twelve hours."

"Ya sure ya won't take Mariah, miss?" Abigail asked again in a low voice as she directed the footman to the luggage. "An unmarried lady shouldn't be travelin' alone with a man."

23

"That is enough, Abigail. I do not need to take a maid with me. Mr. Maddox is quite respectable. I will be perfectly fine."

Her uncle took her hand and pressed it. "You certainly will, my dear," he said, a sparkle of a tear in his eye.

Agrippina opened her mouth to say something, but he squeezed her hand harder, stopping her.

"Besides," he quickly added, "if she needs to take anything, it would be the witch bottle."

Agrippina let out an exasperated sigh.

Richard regarded her with curiosity. "You have a witch bottle? Whatever for if you do not believe in witches?"

"It was a gift from a woman who was, coincidentally, accused of being a witch," her uncle answered for her. "Bertie, sweet, old woman who was quite prophetic." He laughed as he realized. "Aggy dear, do you not see? Bertie predicted you would need the witch bottle over five months ago."

She shook her head. "Bertie is superstitious and uneducated, uncle. Sweet, yes, but prone to mild episodes of hysteria." She turned to Richard. "I took the witch bottle so as not to offend her."

"Where is it?" Richard asked, slightly amused.

She shifted her gaze back to her uncle. "Buried a few feet from our front door to ward off witches, of course."

Richard laughed. "Should we not take it?"

"I am not having a bottle filled with silly little trinkets and urine dug up and packed with my things," Agrippina replied narrowing her eyes.

"Blindburn was a two-week journey, was it not?" Richard pointed out.

"Yes, but it was packed in my uncle's trunk during that journey."

Richard laughed again. "Well, we should get going if we want to make decent time." He held out his hand again for

24

Dr. Greystone.

He took Richard's hand, giving him a firm shake. "Do take care of my niece, Mr. Maddox, she is worth more to me than you could imagine."

"Upon my honor, sir," Mr. Maddox replied with a bow.

Agrippina planted a kiss on her uncle's cheek. "Write, and do be truthful in your letters."

He laughed. "What fibs do you expect I should come up with?"

"You know what I mean." She looked at him crossly.

He nodded. "I am proud of you, my dear." He squeezed her hand. "Now, go! Go solve another mystery!"

Mr. Maddox handed her in before entering behind her. She opened the curtain and smiled at her uncle as the driver pulled off and he faded into the distance.

"You are rather quiet," Agrippina said an hour into their carriage ride. "I expected you to be talking nonstop, but you have barely uttered a word since we left."

Richard glanced over at her from the window.

"You also appear to be more pensive than I believe I have ever seen you before."

He lifted a brow but chuckled despite her comment.

"Must I pry it out of you, or are you going to tell me willingly what is on your mind?"

He took a deep breath in through his nose. "There are a few things I should have mentioned before," he told her as he exhaled, looking a little sheepish.

Agrippina lifted her brows. "Should I be concerned?"

"I suppose that is up to you whether you feel you should be concerned or not."

She regarded him for a moment. "The fact you failed to tell me lets me know that you believe I would not have agreed to come had I known beforehand."

He rolled his shoulders, uncomfortable. "It reveals a lack of honor on my part, but yes."

"Mr. Maddox, I survived an attack from a dog the size of a small horse. The same dog that was partly responsible for the deaths of the young women I investigated last year. Even after being attacked, I did not give up, and I certainly did not run away."

He looked at her questioningly.

"What I am trying to say, is that even after almost becoming a victim of murder at the hands of the very murderer I was pursuing, I did not stop until I brought her justice." She paused for a moment. "Putting it plainly, I do not scare easily."

Richard nodded, laughing softly.

She held out her hand. "So, please. Tell me what you failed to do so before."

He cleared his throat. "It is difficult to know where to begin."

"From the beginning might work," Agrippina replied, folding her hands in her lap.

He rubbed his lips together. "The beginning might sound obvious, but it isn't as simple as you make it sound." He took a deep breath and let it out in a huff.

"Well, why not tell me what specific event prompted your sister to send you the letter which took you from Cambridge in the middle of the night last November?"

Mr. Maddox nodded slowly, his lips pressed together as he gathered his thoughts. "My sister, Cecelia, had been concerned with my uncle's behavior. He seemed paranoid, swore he was seeing and hearing someone watching him, following him."

Agrippina lifted a brow, already skeptical. She remained silent, however.

"I can see what you are thinking. My sister thought it too. That he was losing his mind." He shook his head. "That was until one night she saw someone too. My uncle woke the household screaming. As Cecelia got up to check on him, she saw the figure of someone, a shadow she said, dashing across the back of the property from her bedroom window. When she made it to my uncle's room, he was rolling on the floor in agony and there were strange scratch marks on his back."

"Did you see these scratches?"

He shook his head. "Not for two days. It was after this that she wrote me the letter. They were faint by the time I arrived but in too awkward of a place for him to have done it himself."

She took a slow breath through her nose and let it out with a nod. "And this is what you chose not to tell me?" She brushed back a stray piece of hair, half shrugging. "As if phantom scratches, or whatever you suppose them to be, are going to scare me off."

His lips curled into a half smile. "Perhaps this is more telling of my honor, but it was not your unwillingness to come I feared. It was your uncle's unwillingness to let you go."

She looked up at him sharply for a moment before a brief smile flashed across her own face. "You are more devilish than I ever supposed you to be, Mr. Maddox."

He bowed from his seated position.

"Your uncle and these girls both seemed to see and hear things. Does your uncle know these girls?"

He nodded slightly. "I am sure they know of him. My uncle is the prominent landowner in Halstead. I am sure they attend the same church, but I cannot say to what extent he might know them."

She tapped a finger to her lips as she thought for a few

moments. "Your uncle has been seeing things for months now then? It was over five months ago you received that letter from your sister. How is he now?"

He let out an exasperated sigh. "He has his days of lucidity. There were a few weeks while I was there where he was as normal as ever. Then he would have an episode and the sightings and paranoia would start back up." He shook his head. "When they stop, he is lost. It takes him days to recover."

She nodded as she listened. "We will figure this out. There is always an explanation; it just has to be found before it can be understood."

"I do not believe I have thanked you yet for agreeing to help me," Richard said after a brief pause.

"You have not," Agrippina replied. "But there is no need to thank me until I solve what is going on."

5

THE CARRIAGE ROLLED THROUGH THE TOWN OF HALSTEAD with an hour left of daylight. Agrippina observed it as they went, moving her head to better see as they passed. It was a prettily situated place, much like Cambridge, on a river, its cobblestone streets paralleling it through the town.

"Is the river where the first girl was found?" Agrippina asked, taking a moment to glance at Richard, who nodded.

"She was not found within the town though, but just outside." He pointed out the other window. "The river bends in that direction, but we are headed a little further east. I will take you to all of the locations, of course, starting tomorrow."

Agrippina continued to look out the window as the town slipped from them and the carriage continued further into the countryside. The grass was lush, and the trees were beginning to bloom after a long winter. Finally, after the sky was becoming illuminated in pinks and oranges, the carriage pulled into the drive of a large estate.

For a moment, she had a flashback to her time in Ipswich, the stone façade similar to the grand manor where she was born. As they came around the corner, however, and the front of the house could be seen, the memory and everything that came with it faded away.

The house, though gothic in architecture from the side, was built in the Tudor style in the front. Agrippina blinked at its oddness. In a way, it was intriguing how the two architectural styles clashed. In another, it was strange.

Richard cleared his throat. "Shocking, is it not?"

She silently peered over at him, not wanting to say anything offensive about the home he would one day inherit.

He smirked. "It is alright," he coaxed, "you can go ahead and say it. It is rather gaudy."

"I was going to say *unusual*."

He laughed. "Are you holding your tongue to spare my feelings?" He arched a brow at her. "I believe I am beginning to grow on you."

"I would not jump to conclusions, Mr. Maddox," she said as the door to the carriage was pulled open. "I merely find it distasteful to offend the family who will be hosting me for the next several days." She took the hand of the footman who helped her out of the carriage.

"So, you will not be talking the entire time you are here?" Richard said as he emerged behind her. "How will you ever investigate?"

A shadow of a smile slipped across her face as she arched a brow at him, but she chose not to reply. The door of the house was then opened, and an elegant, broad-shouldered woman walked out, a close-lipped smile highlighting her round face.

"Richard!" the woman said, taking one of his hands and pressing it. "I did not expect you back so quickly."

"Aunt Lucy," Richard replied taking her hand and kissing it. "I told you I would only be gone for a few days."

She sighed with a nod. "You were always a good boy." She turned and looked at Agrippina, seemingly surprised by her presence. "Who is this?"

"Aunt Lucy, this is Miss Agrippina Greystone. Miss Greystone, this is my aunt, Mrs. Lucile Bolten."

The two ladies curtsied to one another.

"Miss Greystone has come to help us," Richard continued. "To help Uncle Eugene."

His aunt shot him a confused look, a hand gently patting at her fair hair. "Help?" she repeated, her tone reserved. "Your uncle needs a doctor, Richard. I am not quite sure what you expect this woman—"

"Miss Greystone," Richard corrected her.

His aunt fluttered her eyes, visibly annoyed. "I am not quite sure what you expect Miss Greystone to do."

Richard stuttered for a moment. "I—I, uh, expect her to solve whatever has been going on."

"That is a very broad statement," his aunt said blandly. "What specifically 'going on' do you expect her to solve?"

Richard took a deep breath in and let it out in a huff. "Perhaps we could discuss this inside?"

"Oh! Yes, how rude of me!" Mrs. Bolten replied pressing a hand to her chest. "Forgive me, Miss Greystone. I have forgotten my manners in the confusion."

She led them both inside where a maid took their hats and gloves, then ushered them into the parlor with a roaring fire. Mrs. Bolten let out a surprised "whew" as the heat of the room hit her.

"Janet!" she called out, causing a young maid to scramble in.

"Yes, mistress?" a young woman with dark, thin hair, and a pockmarked face asked.

"Open the windows in here. It is stifling," Mrs. Bolten

ordered. "And stop feeding this fire! It is a fine spring evening, not the dead of winter."

Janet bounced on her feet a moment, looking unsure.

"Well?" Mrs. Bolten said crossly.

"Beg ya pardon, mistress, but master did request this fire tuh burn through the evenin'. Says the windows are tuh be kept shut too."

Richard glanced at Agrippina who was surveying the scene in silence. "Why, Janet?"

"It does not matter why, Richard," his aunt answered in a warning tone.

"To keep the witch from entering."

They all turned at the sound of the voice as a man rose from an armchair that was facing the fire. He was tall, pale and gaunt, and his dark eyes teemed with sadness and fatigue. He shoved his bony left hand into the pocket of his trousers as he wiped the fatigue from his eyes with the other.

"Euguene, darling! I thought you were in your study!" Mrs. Bolten said, walking toward her husband. She hooked her arm in the crook of his and led him to a sofa. "You do not need to be sitting so close to the fire, dear. It is much too hot. Come! Why don't you meet Richard's pretty, little friend?"

He sized Agrippina up, who had yet to say a word since she arrived. He removed his arm from his wife's grip and stepped toward Agrippina to get a better look.

Richard gently put an arm on his uncle's back. "Uncle, this is Miss Agrippina Greystone. She is here to help with our problem."

Mr. Bolten looked sharply at his nephew before turning his gaze back to Agrippina, his brows creased. "This is the help you have brought back with you?" He shook his head. "You told me you were going to bring back a doctor.

Someone who had dealt with something like this before."
He continued to shake his head, rubbing his hand across his
mouth. "No, she is much too young to have any experience
in this sort of thing."

"You are right, Mr. Bolten," Agrippina replied, finally saying something. "I am rather young, and I have not investigated allegations of witches, but I have recently investigated and solved the murders of five young women who
were believed to be killed by a werewolf. Well, a woman in
that incident was accused of being a witch, but my uncle
and I had her exonerated."

Mrs. Bolten let out a small gasp. "A werewolf?"

Agrippina nodded. "It was all smalltown superstitions,
of course. There was no werewolf. The murderer was just
another unassuming person. She killed nine people in all.
The five young women and then four more to help cover up
her crime."

"A woman?" Mr. Bolten said incredulously. "A woman was
the murderer, and she was not a witch?"

Agrippina wondered for a moment as to whether she
should divulge that the murderer claimed to have slept with
the devil to gain supernatural powers but thought better
of it.

She shook her head. "No, sir, she was just a sick and
depraved person like any other murderer."

He nodded and moved to a sofa to sit down.

There was a brief silence as Mr. Bolten buried his face in
one of his hands, his other one tapping against an end table.

"Gracious me!" Mrs. Bolten said in a flurry of anxiety.
"I have forgotten my manners again. You both must be
exhausted from your long journey. I shall have supper prepared and tea brought in while we wait! Janet!" she said to
the maid who was still awkwardly standing by the door. "Do

show Miss Greystone to a room so she might freshen up. Perhaps the one in the east wing corner overlooking the cherry trees." She turned back to Agrippina with a smile. "They are in bloom now. Quite beautiful."

Agrippina took the hint and allowed herself to be ushered out of the parlor.

6

AGRIPPINA THANKED THE MAID WHO RUSHED OUT OF HER
room to bring a pitcher of water and a towel so she could
freshen up.

As she waited, she walked to the window and admired
the white blossoms of the wild cherries seeming to glow
as the setting sun glittered through their branches. They
appeared to shimmer even more as the wind blew through
them, causing a rippling effect among the leaves.

Janet appeared a few minutes later with a couple of footmen who brought in Agrippina's trunk and carpet bag. She
then poured the water in the basin for Agrippina and then
began to open her trunk to help her unpack.

"I would much prefer if you did not," Agrippina told her
gently. "I am a strange creature and always pack and unpack
my own things."

"'Tis no trouble, miss," Janet said quietly. "'Tis part of my
job."

"Well, I will not tell anyone you did not do it, if you do not
tell anyone that I did."

Janet curtseyed. "Yes, miss. Would you need 'elp gettin'

dressed?"

Agrippina opened her mouth to say 'no' but thought better of it. "Yes, please. The blue dress should be fine."

Janet pulled the dress out of the trunk and laid it gently over the dressing screen. Agrippina slipped behind the screen and undid her dress, stepping out of it as it fell to the floor. She picked it up and draped it over the screen before taking the blue dress Janet laid out for her.

"How long have you been working here, Janet?" she asked in a casual tone.

"Oh, two years or so. My uncle is the butler. 'E's the one who got me the position."

Agrippina nodded as she slipped her fresh dress on. "That was very kind of your uncle."

"'Tis Mr. Bolten who's kind," Janet offered. "'E's the one who insisted I learned me le'ers."

Agrippina took a few steps backward so Janet could button up her dress. "That is very kind of him. Has he gotten you a tutor?"

Janet shook her head. "Well, yes, and no. When I first signed on, there were a woman who came to taught me to read. But that was only for a few months. After that, I was encouraged to read on me own. Mr. Bolten allows me use of the library when I'm not workin', o' course."

"And what do you read, Janet?"

"Poetry." Agrippina could hear the smile in her voice. "I can never remember them well enough tuh recite from memory, but I do like how they sound when I read them. It does make me heart swell sometimes."

Agrippina nodded. "Poetry does have that effect on us. It is what it was written for, to appeal to our emotions."

Janet fastened the last button. "There, miss."

Agrippina smoothed out her dress and thanked her.

"Should you like a touch up on your hair?"

She looked at herself in the mirror and shook her head. "This will suffice. Thank you for your help, Janet."

Janet curtseyed. "If ya should need anythin', miss, just pull the call bell." She opened the door to leave and was startled to see Richard poised to knock. "Master Maddox, I beg yer pardon, sir."

"It's alright, Janet," he said gently. "I have only come to escort Miss Greystone back downstairs."

"Is it time for supper already?" Agrippina asked.

He shook his head. "Soon, to be sure, but I came to tell you tea is ready." He held out his arm, indicating the way.

She followed him out into the hallway and fell in line with him. "Your aunt must think I am going to get in the way."

He furrowed his brows. "What makes you believe that?"

"She gave me the bedroom farthest from everyone else."

"Perhaps she just wishes to make sure you have privacy."

She lifted her brows at him. "Well, you know your aunt better than I would."

He let out a small laugh and nodded. "It appears you understand her quite well yourself."

"She seems to think all of this will pass on its own. Or that nothing is truly wrong in the first place."

Richard sighed. "She is not an easy nut to crack. She believes every issue should be kept within the family. Bringing an outsider would be risking someone realizing we are not perfect after all."

"An imperfect family." She shook her head. "What a shame."

"Is that your attempt at a joke?" he asked, half laughing.

She smiled, lightly. "I never joke, Mr. Maddox."

He laughed again as he opened the door to the parlor. His aunt barely registered their entrance, sitting at a small table with the tea fixings on it and sipping from a cup. His uncle appeared to be in the same place he was when she went upstairs to change.

"How do you prefer your tea, Miss Greystone?" Mrs. Bolten asked, barely looking up from her own cup.

"A splash of cream, please," she replied approaching the table.

She thanked her, taking the proffered cup and moving toward a sofa facing the uncle. She blew on the steaming liquid before sipping carefully. She then placed the cup on the end table by the sofa and folded her hands in her lap.

"Should we start with what you believe is going on?" Agrippina asked.

Mrs. Bolten dropped her spoon in agitation causing a clatter of noise in the wake of silence Agrippina's question created. "Dear heavens!" she exclaimed. "You certainly know how to ease yourself into conversation." She shook her head. "This is not something I think we should be discussing."

"It is exactly what we should be discussing," Richard broke in. "I understand you would rather sweep the whole subject under the rug, Aunt Lucy, but this cannot be ignored. If it is too delicate a subject, perhaps you should leave."

His aunt gaped at him for a moment before finding momentary solace in her tea.

"Uncle?" Richard said gently. "I brought her to help."

Mr. Bolten pressed the back of his hand to his lips as he drummed the fingers of his other hand on the side table. He then stood, quite abruptly, from his seat and walked to the window, letting out a heavy sigh.

His aunt huffed into her tea. "Richard, honestly." She took a sip of her tea before placing it soundlessly back onto the saucer. "There is nothing to 'help' with. Must we throw ourselves into a frenzy or hysterics because the little white mice are about?" She let out a short, dry laugh.

Agrippina tilted her head in thought. "The little white mice are about?" she repeated thoughtfully. "I have never heard such an expression."

Mrs. Bolten waved her hand elegantly. "Oh, it is just something we say around here. Means we have had a bit of bad luck."

"That is not the history of the expression," Mr. Bolten mumbled from the window.

Mrs. Bolten laughed haughtily. "Oh, what does the history of the expression matter if it still fits the situation?"

"White mice are often used as familiars for witches," Richard explained. "Animals they use to do their bidding. Cats, crows, bats, dogs—you get the idea. White mice are," he hesitated, "different. More special somehow. Reserved for the strongest of witches."

"So, when you see them, bad things are afoot?" Agrippina suggested.

Richard nodded. "Precisely."

"Have you seen any then?" Agrippina looked from one to the other.

Richard shifted where he stood. "There were a few white mice found on the two farms where the trouble began, I believe."

"Coincidence, I am sure," Mrs. Bolten said, burying her face once again into her cup.

"I would often agree with such a conclusion," Agrippina began. "Mice on a farm is not unusual. But when you mean white mice, do you mean albino?"

Richard shook his head and shrugged. "White fur and red eyes."

Agrippina opened her mouth to speak, but instead, smiled and picked up her teacup. She took a few sips before setting it back down. "Mr. Bolten, might you be able to elaborate on the experiences you have been having?"

Mr. Bolten continued to stare out the window, an arm resting on the frame while his other hand rested in his pocket.

"I have heard what you have experienced from another person's perspective. I would like to hear it from you."

He shook his head. "How are we sure she can help?" he asked no one in particular. "Telling her what I have seen and how I feel will not release me from the curse."

Mrs. Bolten stood up, shooting from her chair with such force, she nearly knocked the tea table over. "That is enough for today, I believe. My husband is tired."

"Aunt Lucy, you cannot—"

"This is not your house yet, Richard," she said in a warning tone. "It is still your uncle's and mine. I will be damned if you order me around it."

Richard seemed struck by his aunt's harsh words and tone but relented with a silent bow.

"Enjoy your supper," she said, gently putting an arm through her husband's, her tone civil but forced. "Perhaps we might continue tomorrow after we have all rested." Mrs. Bolten ushered her husband out of the room who willingly ambled alongside her.

Richard shook his head. "My uncle never used to look so weak and frail. These past few months have really made him into a shadow of who he once was."

Agrippina took another sip from her tea.

"I must apologize for my family. I understand how strange this all seems."

She stared into her teacup for a moment. "I am sure all families have their little nuances. I know my uncle was often called strange for not ever having sent me away to school or hiring a governess." Her eyes glowed with warmth as she talked about her uncle. "He took on my education

40

by himself. Tutored me with the other boys he was hired to teach."

"He is lucky you are so bright. You must have been his star pupil."

She smiled. "I believe it is I who was lucky. He raised me after my parents died, having buried his own wife and child not long before. We were each other's saving grace."

"Your uncle is a good man."

She nodded suddenly feeling tired. "I do not wish to be rude, but I think I will follow your aunt's example and go to bed."

"Are you not hungry for supper?"

She shook her head. "No." She stood. "I will try and talk to your uncle again tomorrow. Good night, Mr. Maddox."

He nodded and bowed. "Good night, Miss Greystone."

Agrippina made it to her room, the last glows of the sun casting shadows in the pink and orange rays that peeked through the cherry trees. A candelabra was burning on the vanity, and she used its light to unpack the few things she brought.

After siphoning through her clothes, she stopped, not remembering having packed what was resting in between two of her dresses. She picked it up, holding it in the light and let out a small laugh through her nose. It was a circular stone with a hole in the middle on a thin leather strap.

An adder stone. A talisman against witchcraft.

Bertie, the woman she had saved had hung this on her door while she was investigating the murders in Blindburn. She had left it when she returned home to Cambridge, but Bertie begged Mr. Mackland to send it to her on her behalf.

Her lips spread into a small smile. Her uncle must have slipped it in her luggage.

On top of warding off witchcraft, the adder stone was

supposed to see through a witch's disguise, revealing its true form.

She looked down at the stone, no bigger than a walnut. A strange compulsion took her to the window where she lifted the stone to her eye and peered through. She scanned the landscape of the orchard, seeing the trees swaying in the wind.

She laughed at herself as she moved from tree to tree, looking through the stone. When she got to the last row, she gasped. A dark figure stood between two trees and appeared to be staring up at her.

She removed the stone from her eye to get a better look, her heart pounding, a scream swelling in her throat as she reached for the service bell—but nothing was there. She blinked at the same spot she thought she had seen something, and it was empty. Nothing but the breeze running through the branches of the tree.

She let out the breath of relief she didn't realize she was holding, and shook her head. She then finished unpacking, dressed for bed, and placed the adder stone on the bedside table before blowing out the candles.

7

AGRIPPINA FOUND HERSELF ALONE IN THE BREAKFAST PARLOR
the next morning. Starving after skipping supper and the
long journey the day before, she wasted no time in eating
whatever they had to serve.

After a second plate, and still no one to join her, she took
the opportunity to look around the grounds. She began, of
course, with the cherry trees to explain away that strange
shape she saw the night before.

The grounds were beautifully kept with several perfectly
manicured rose bushes waiting to bloom and rhododen-
dron bushes in neat rows around a paved patio with a pond
in the middle. Morning glory blooms glittered with dew as
they weaved their way around the butterfly bushes planted
around the pond. A gardener, busy hacking away at the
beautiful pest tilted his hat in her direction.

Birds twittered about the grass and bees buzzed from the
early blooms as she passed through. She paused a moment
when the trees came into sight, her heart thumping wildly
as she remembered the fear that had shot through her the
night before.

There had to be an explanation, however, and she was going to find it. She made her way to the last row of trees and stood at its opening. She stood for a moment trying to remember how far down she imagined the figure to be.

She turned to the house and found her bedroom window, estimating the distance. A couple trees down, perhaps.

She made her way down the row, examining the ground and trees, when she came to a low hanging branch. It was partially hidden by the tree trunk it was connected to, but as the wind blew, it reached out into the row, making it visible from her window. And, hanging from that branch was a black shawl.

Agrippina smirked, reprimanding herself for being so frightened in the first place. A tree branch with a shawl dangling from it. She gently detached the shawl from the clutches of the branch and studied it.

It was a nice shawl of decent quality. Perhaps not fancy enough for the women of Bolten House to wear, but a little too extravagant for a servant to own. She rubbed the material of the shawl between her fingers as she examined it, finding a small tear.

Perhaps this is where it had caught onto the branch as the wearer—

Agrippina felt the fabric again. It was sturdy fabric; one that might not tear easily. She glanced back at the branch, noticing on closer inspection that it was broken at the base of the tree.

Someone had been running through the trees where their shawl was snagged by the branch. The branch bent but did not fully break, ripping the shawl as it was pulled from the wearer.

Agrippina peered in the direction the person—a woman from the shawl—was running from. Who or what was she running from?

"Miss Greystone, I presume?"

Agrippina whirled around, half startled out of her reverie to see an older man about her height, watching her from just outside the trees. His stern, dark eyes appeared emotionless as he stood there, proud and stiff.

She observed his livery and assumed he was a higher ranking servant. "Yes, I am."

He bowed. "Forgive me if I startled you. I am the butler here at Bolten House. Frank Arter. I observed you from the kitchen window and thought I should introduce myself as I was unable to yesterday evening."

Agrippina made her way back out of the rows of trees.

"Is there anything I can help you with?" he asked in a bland tone.

"Yes," she said holding up the shawl. "Does this look familiar to you?"

He glanced at the shawl for half a second. "No, miss, I am afraid it looks like every shawl I have ever seen."

"Every shawl?" she questioned, skeptical. "Every shawl you have ever seen is black cashmere with a lace trim?"

His eyes flashed back over the shawl, the pallor of his skin tinting a subtle red on further inspection. "I wouldn't know a cashmere shawl from a woolen one, miss."

"Hm." Agrippina studied the tear in the fabric once more.

"Is there anything else I can help you with?" Mr. Arter asked in a terse tone.

"Is the family awake yet?"

He pursed his lips. "Master Bolten is in his library, but he asked not to be disturbed."

If Agrippina had not grown up with the borderline impertinence that her maid Abigail exuded on almost a daily basis, she would have been offended by the unwelcoming attitude the Bolten's butler displayed. Undeterred, however, she flashed a brief smile.

"Is there coffee, Mr. Arter? Do have some made for me, would you?" She gave a singular nod and made her way back to the house, the cashmere shawl still clutched in her hands.

She paused for a moment as she studied it. There in the bottom corner were the initials C.P.M in white lettering. The stitching was crude and was not made by the same hand that made the shawl.

"C P M," she whispered to herself as she walked into the parlor.

"Who is that?" Richard asked as he came up behind her.

Agrippina raised a brow, looking over her shoulder at him. "Finally awake, are we? I thought you would sleep the morning away."

Richard frowned as he pulled out his pocket watch and flopped down on a sofa. "Sleep it away? It is barely half past seven."

"Most people are up and functioning at this time."

"Who are most people?"

"Servants, workers, people with half a brain and a shard of ambition."

Richard laughed. "Thank God I am neither of those things." He nodded his head, indicating the shawl in her hand. "What are you intently studying?"

She walked over and handed it to him. "Does this look familiar to you?"

He observed it, shaking his head. "No." He frowned. "Wait a minute. These initials, they are the same as my sister's. Cecelia Patricia Maddox." He pursed his lips together. "But I do not believe this belongs to her. She would never wear something lacking in color like this."

He tossed it back to her.

46

"Hmm," she mused while looking it over again.

"Where did you find it?"

She hesitated a moment, not wanting to tell him how she came about investigating the cherry trees, but decided it was best to be truthful.

Richard's face darkened when she told him. "Then there was someone outside in the orchard last night."

Agrippina shook her head. "By the look of the branch, the break was not recent. The shawl might have been there for at least a week." She fingered the initials. "Where is your sister, might I ask?"

He raised a questioning brow. "She is in Colchester, visiting her fiancé's family. They are to be married in a few months. She and," he shook his head, "Henry Randolph. He seems nice enough, but not who I expected my sister to ever end up with."

"How long has your sister been gone?"

He narrowed his eyes at her. "That is not my sister's shawl, as I said. The initials are pure coincidence. But, to further my point, she has been gone almost a month."

Agrippina nodded, satisfied.

Janet came just then, pushing a cart with coffee.

"Ah! Just what I needed!" Richard said as he walked to the tea table and poured himself a steaming cup.

"Thank you, Janet," Agrippina said as the young woman curtseyed and smiled.

"Is there anythin' else ye be needin'?"

Agrippina shook her head as Richard's mouth was full of biscuit. "That will be all."

Janet curtseyed again and left.

"What time can we have the carriage ready to go to the farms?" she asked as soon as the door was closed.

Richard coughed, half choking on the biscuit he had just

47

taken a bite out of. "Can I not enjoy a cup of coffee first?" He motioned to the table. "Please make yourself a cup. Relax and enjoy the morning for a moment, would you?"

"Perhaps I should see if your uncle would like a cup," she suggested. "Mr. Arter said he was in the library."

"Uncle Eugene is up already?" He took a long sip of coffee followed by another bite of a biscuit. He shook his head. "He is not usually a morning person. That is to say, he prefers his mornings to be spent alone." He waved her over to the table again. "How do you take your coffee, Miss Greystone? I will make you a cup myself."

"The same way I prefer my tea. A splash of cream. A hint of cream really."

He shrugged, allowing a few drops of cream to fall into her cup before handing it to her. "Now, to the order of business. Last night, after you went to rest your pretty little head, I told the staff I wanted the carriage ready no later than eight." He pulled his pocket watch out again. "Which means you have just enough time to finish your coffee before it will be rolling around from the stables."

8

AGRIPPINA TAPPED HER PENCIL ON THE OPEN JOURNAL IN HER lap as she watched the landscape roll by. She let out a sigh as she looked over at Richard who appeared to be dozing on the other side of the carriage.

"I should speak to your uncle soon," Agrippina said, breaking the silence. "He is the main reason I am here, is he not? If he had not been exhibiting strange symptoms like those poor girls, you would not have called for me."

Richard opened one eye to peek at her. "You will," he reassured her. "It is just going to take a little time. He is a bit," he paused for the right word—

"Paranoid?"

"Flighty."

"I think your aunt is keeping him from talking."

He nodded. "You are probably right. As I said before, she does not want it to get out that anything is going on."

"But is your uncle not a majority property owner? Is he not a magistrate? Surely his presence in town will be required at some point. He cannot hide away in his house without someone figuring something is wrong."

"My aunt is a we-will-cross-that-bridge-when-we-get-there sort of person."

She shook her head. "That bridge is going to burn before you are halfway across."

He shrugged. "You are probably correct, but there is not much I can do about it."

The carriage pulled onto a road with rolling green fields on either side. Several cows could be seen grazing as they drove past. Some of them looked up from their chewing, while others did not register them. They stopped in front of a small, two-floor house where a little boy and little girl were being chased by a young woman.

All three of them squealed with laughter, pausing when the carriage pulled up. The little girl ran to the young woman and buried her face in her skirts. The little boy clung to her as well but was too curious to look away.

Agrippina was handed out by the driver, and she smiled over at the trio. Richard sneezed as he stepped down, waving away the dirt that the carriage wheels had kicked up.

The woman curtseyed when she saw him. "Good mornin', Mr. Maddox. I thought it might be you."

He nodded as he sneezed again. "Miss Brown, how are you? We have come to see your aunt and uncle. This is Miss Greystone. She is here to," he hesitated, "investigate Anna's," another pause, "mishap."

She nodded. "Haddy, go find your mother. Allen, fetch your father."

The two young children glanced at the two strangers before running off and obeying their older cousin.

"Can I get either of you something to drink or eat?" Miss Brown asked as she led them inside.

"No, thank you," Agrippina replied.

"You have any of that cider your aunt makes?" Richard

asked.

Miss Brown smiled and nodded. "Yes, she just opened a new casket. Shall I fetch you a glass?"

"Yes, please."

She pointed to a small parlor and invited them to sit down while they waited. "I shall be right back with your drink." She curtseyed and rushed out of the room.

A minute later, a woman, younger than her physical age made her appear, walked down the stairs following the little girl Haddy. The woman pushed back her frazzled hair and smoothed her modest, but clean dress.

"Mr. Maddox," she said, trying to smile. "How are you, sir?"

Richard bowed. "Mrs. Brown. I have brought a friend of mine to help shed more light on what might have been going on with your poor Anna."

A small gasp escaped her lips at the mention of her deceased daughter and her eyes darted in Agrippina's direction. "Are you a witch hunter?"

Agrippina blinked, stuttering slightly as she replied, "N-no. I am here to investigate her death."

Confusion spread over Mrs. Brown's face. "Then you are here for the witch?"

Agrippina cleared her throat. "I do not believe in witches, Mrs. Brown. I believe there is a logical explanation for what happened to your daughter. I am here to find that out."

Mrs. Brown released a small, bitter laugh. "Logical explanation." She shook her head, a sour expression on her face. "What logic could there be to a young girl, healthy and happy one day, and riddled with fear and painful convulsions the next?"

Agrippina pulled out her notebook to where she had written notes on Anna. "Painful convulsions?" she repeated, scribbling it down. "She had those along with her hallucinations?"

Mrs. Brown looked at her incredulously, blinking furiously. "Yes," she finally said after calming down. She took a death breath, shuddering as she released it. "I don't know why else she would be screaming so if she wasn't in pain."

Miss Brown walked in with Richard's cider, a bright smile lighting up her pretty face as she handed it to him. He thanked her and she took a seat across from them, the little girl crawling onto her lap.

"I know this is painful, but could you walk me through the first day you noticed something was wrong?" Agrippina asked, her brows slightly creased in ready contemplation.

Mrs. Brown looked from Richard to Agrippina and then back, visibly uncomfortable.

"It's alright, Mrs. Brown," Richard assured her. He put his cup of cider down and guided her to a chair. "We only want to help."

She nodded as she sat, taking a deep breath as she melted into the chair; it was as if her exhaustion was finally too much for her.

"Shall I fetch you something to drink, Aunt Mary?" Miss Brown asked.

A tired smile spread across the woman's face as she shook her head. "No, thank you, Penny. I will manage." She took another deep breath before turning her attention to Agrippina. "It began on a Saturday the last of the month of July. I remember because Mr. Bolten came to collect rent."

Agrippina stiffened at this last bit of information, casting a fleeting glance at Richard.

"There was nothing special about the visit," she continued. He brought us his usual little gifts for the children. Toys for the little ones, a bonnet for Anna. He had recently returned from London and had brought me some very nice tea."

Richard nodded, urging her on.

A flash of a smile brightened her face for a short second. "Anna was so happy to receive the bonnet. It was so pretty and went so well with the dress she had been wearing that day she put it on immediately, deciding to take a walk down the lane." She shook her head, tears beginning to well up in her eyes. "I should have kept her in. I should have insisted." She buried her face in her hands and let out a shrill sob.

Richard pulled out a handkerchief, putting a gentle, comforting hand on her back. "I know this is difficult," he said, putting the handkerchief in her hand, "but in order for Miss Greystone to figure out what might have happened, she needs to know the details."

Mrs. Brown nodded, her face buried in the handkerchief. She sniffed and raised her head, dabbing at her eyes. "Forgive me," she croaked, clearing her throat. "She was gone for a long time. At first, I thought she might have walked to the Hammertons'. It is about a mile down the road, and she was on friendly terms with their daughter." She shook her head. "But when it began to get dark, and she still hadn't returned, I began to get worried." She rubbed her forearms as she recalled that day. "I sent John, my husband, over on a horse. When he arrived, they said they never saw Anna." Her voice began to break.

"Mamma?" the little girl Haddy squeaked from Miss Brown's lap, her voice unsure.

Mrs. Brown forced a smile for her daughter. "I'm alright, my love." She nodded, clearing her throat again. "Mr. Hammerton, bless him, got on his horse to help John search for her. They found her a few hours later, hiding under a bush by the road. She was—" she paused and looked over at her niece. "Penny, would you mind taking Haddy outside to play, please?"

Penny looked like she wanted to object, but she stood, the little girl scooped up in her arms, and did as she was bid.

Mrs. Brown waited until she heard the front door close before continuing. "Anna was curled up in a ball, crying, her dress torn and scratches all over her. At first, all she did was scream and cry, her arms lashing out at something that wasn't there, or something only she could see."

"How long did this episode last?" Agrippina asked as she scratched down notes.

Mrs. Brown shook her head. "She wasn't lucid until the following evening. At first, she wouldn't tell us what had happened. She was too terrified. We sent for the local vicar and he was able to coax it out of her." She began to wring her hands in agitation. "She said she had been walking when a woman walked out from the trees. A woman all in black. She couldn't see her face because it was hidden behind a lace veil, but she was crying." She sniffed and paused for a moment. "My dear girl said she asked the woman if she needed help. But when she got close enough, the woman attacked her, and blew some sort of powder into her face."

"A powder?" Agrippina repeated, pausing in her notes. "Was your daughter able to describe this powder?"

Mrs. Brown blinked at her incredulously. "I don't believe it was something my daughter thought was important at the time," she replied in a cold tone.

Agrippina ignored her harshness and pressed on. "Perhaps she did not think it important, but can you recall her mentioning anything about the powder? Smell, taste, color?"

Mrs. Brown shook her head. "No, but she remembered the woman whispering to her." She let out a shaky breath and closed her eyes to compose herself. "Whispering that the devil would come for her."

"Was there anything else she would say?"

Mrs. Brown gently rubbed her lips. "She would talk about hearing the mice within the walls. Saying the white mice had come for her."

Agrippina looked up, intrigued. "Did you see any of these mice?" she asked, leaning in a little.

She shook her head, sniffing. "No, but Anna swore she could."

Agrippina nodded as she thought. "Did she have these fits of hysteria or hallucinations every day? Or were there breaks in between?"

"Every other day, perhaps. And every time they began, she was outside taking a walk." She furrowed her brows. "I remember walking outside with her and she—she just—" she pressed a hand to her mouth and shook her head. "The scream that escaped her lips, I shall hear until my dying day."

Agrippina looked up from her notebook, glancing over at Richard who was busy staring at the floor. "This next question might be difficult, but could you tell me about her last day? What led up to her death?"

A tear rolled down Mrs. Brown's cheek and she averted her gaze to her lap. "She had been getting worse, the drafts and remedies the doctor made for her only increased her suffering." She licked her lips and rubbed them together. "Then one morning, she was just gone."

"How many days had she been convulsing before she—" Agrippina checked herself, "went missing?"

"Just a few days."

"Do you know what kind of drafts or remedies she was given?"

Mrs. Brown shook her head. "No, and I threw them all out months ago. I couldn't bear to look at them anymore." She buried her face in the handkerchief Richard had given her.

"She was such a sweet girl always thinking of others and minding her chores."

"Mary?"

The three of them looked up to see Mr. Brown, a concerned expression on his face.

Mrs. Brown quickly straightened up and wiped her eyes dry. "John," she said with a sniff. "Mr. Maddox brought someone to find out who hurt our Anna."

He gazed suspiciously at Agrippina who stood and curtseyed as Richard introduced her. "Though less important," Agrippina began, "I wish to figure out what happened with your cows as well. To see if the incidents are at all connected."

"Connected?" Mr. Brown repeated incredulously. "How could they not be?"

Agrippina took a deep breath. "Might you tell me about them?"

"Not much to tell. I realized I was missing a cow, went out to look, and I found her dead. Her throat was cut but there was hardly any blood."

"How long and deep do you suppose the cut to her throat to have been?"

Mrs. Brown put her hand to her own throat, looking uncomfortable.

"This is a bit inappropriate with a lady present, is it not, Mr. Maddox?" Mr. Brown asked, turning to him.

"Am I not a lady?" Agrippina cut in.

Richard flashed her a look. "She would not ask if she did not think it necessary to know, Mr. Brown."

"It is alright, John," his wife said, smiling weakly. "Tell her what she needs to know."

He nodded. "The cut was only along the main vein in the neck. I know some rumors said the head was removed but it wasn't. The cut was only as long as my finger, perhaps," he held up his pointer finger to exhibit, "and only deep enough to open the vein. Same with the others."

"And you found nothing unusual around the cows?" she pressed. "No markings in the grass? Footprints? Tracks of any sort?"

He shook his head. "I don't know. I was so confused by the dead cow; I didn't think to look. The second cow we didn't find for a couple days, and it had rained heavily the night before we found him. The other two," he shook his head, "same as the first. Each of them dyin' only days apart from each other."

Agrippina tapped at her notebook with her pencil. "Was there anything remarkable about the cows' bodies? Any markings or discoloration? Anything you could hear, see, smell?"

He shrugged. "There was some foam around the first cow's mouth, maybe." He held up a finger, pausing. "There was a strange smell too. Almost something bitter. Like, bitter almonds, or marzipan maybe." He shook his head. "Other than that, there's not much to tell."

"Bitter almonds?" Agrippina repeated, scribbling it down into her notebook.

Mr. Brown nodded again. "I know that makes little sense, but it was the only thing I could think to describe it."

"That is very specific. Thank you." She looked from the husband to the wife and back again. "Might you be able to tell me how long it was from the first cow dying mysteriously to your daughter seeing this woman in black and then your daughter passing away?"

The Browns exchanged glances for a moment.

Mr. Brown cleared his throat. "A week from the first dyin' to the start of Anna's fits perhaps. The fourth cow died the day before, I believe. And then, another week and a half until she--" His voice broke, and he wiped his mouth. "I apologize."

"There is no need. Thank you for your time." She nodded and stood. "I apologize for any distress my questions may have caused you and I am sorry for your loss."

Mr. Brown showed them to the door nodding a farewell as they walked by.

Agrippina paused a moment and turned around. "Did you find any white mice during the time all of this was going on?"

Mr. Brown half shrugged and nodded, looking down at the ground for a moment. "There was a dead one next to each of my cows after I found them." He shook his head. "But I never saw them once Anna began her fits."

"Hm." Agrippina nodded and thanked him again.

Richard handed her into the carriage and tipped his hat to the Browns before following in behind her. The carriage let out a small groan as it rolled into motion, the modest farmhouse soon behind them.

# 9

"WHEN WERE YOU GOING TO TELL ME THAT YOUR UNCLE owned the farmland the Browns live on?" Agrippina asked as she stared down at her notes.

Richard stammered. "I did not think it all very relevant."

She looked up at him sharply. "Does he own the farmland where the wheat field caught fire as well?"

Richard's mouth hung open.

"And the silk merchant?" she continued staring at him. "Does he own the silk the merchant was selling?"

Richard cleared his throat. "Yes."

"Why did you not tell me?"

"As I said, I did not think—"

"I might tease you on your lack of judgment and arrogance, but I know you are more intelligent than you sometimes care to reveal, Mr. Maddox. I can see through your façade of wanton behavior and lackadaisical approach to academics. You may choose the image of lower intelligence to serve some strange purpose of 'fitting' in, but do not dare insult mine by lying to me."

Richard quickly closed his mouth.

"If you truly think that I am going to believe that you thought it was of no importance that your uncle stands to lose a great deal of money as a result of these mishaps, then I do not know why you would ask for my help. If you think me that stupid, why would you waste my time and yours and everyone else's who I am going to speak to?"

Richard remained silent.

"This is not a game, Mr. Maddox! A young woman has died. I might not be the most empathetic person in the world, but I can recognize agony when I see it, and that mother breathes it every day."

Richard nodded. "You are right. I knew it was important." He took a deep breath and let out slowly. "I thought, if my uncle was the only one affected, or who stood to lose from this, you would not come. I thought you hated me, and would not come if you knew it was only my family that was being targeted."

"You truly do not know me well, Mr. Maddox," she stated plainly.

Richard's face brightened for a moment.

"I do not have to like someone to help them."

His expression fell and he frowned slightly.

"It would not be very Christian of me now, would it?"

"Hm."

A tiny laugh escaped Agrippina's mouth and she quickly pressed a hand to her mouth and coughed to suppress it.

Richard heard it, however, and shot her a suspicious look. "Did I just hear you laugh?"

Agrippina cleared her throat. "Forgive me. The expression on your face was so forlorn and unbecoming."

He stared at her for a moment, his tongue pressed against the inside of his cheek. "You do not have many female friends, do you?"

She tilted her head as she thought, then shook it. "No. I befriended a governess that taught the children across the street from us, but she married not too long ago. But as far as ladies of my own rank, or age—" She stopped herself. "I understand I am not an easy person to get along with, Mr. Maddox. I admire intelligence over most things—all things really—and it is difficult to find things in common with other women who have grown up learning how to be a wife and mother. I do not blame them, nor do I demean their intelligence, for a lot of them are well spoken and bright. However, while they would gossip and pour over their love of the most handsome of men that season, I was talking politics, or the new scientific studies with their fathers."

Richard threw his head back and laughed. "Never has a scene sounded so much like you as that."

A simple smile spread across her lips. "I really only had one friend during my childhood. A student my uncle tutored for several years and who I learned alongside of. We lost touch when he was sent to Oxford to complete his education."

"Why did your uncle not send you away to school?"

She shook her head. "I did not wish to go, and he knew I would have been miserable. My Uncle Henry was quite furious when he found out. The daughter of an earl should be properly educated, he said, but I thought I was being properly educated, and I do not regret it now."

Richard shook his head, confused. "I'm sorry, but did you say, 'daughter of an earl,' just now?"

"Oh, did you not know?"

He huffed. "No, I think that piece of information would have stuck with me."

"My father was the ninth earl of Ipswich. Uncle Alfred should have been the tenth, but he did not want it. He passed the title to his younger half-brother Henry on the condition

that Uncle Alfred raise me and that I retain my inheritance."
She shrugged. "Uncle Henry was quick to agree."

He shook his head as he looked at her more closely.
"You are the daughter of an earl, and yet, you dress so," he
scratched the back of his head, trying to think of the word,
"out of rank. I would never have guessed."

"Yes, poor Abigail has been trying to get me into finer
clothes since I was a little girl. She was ecstatic when you
invited me to the gathering at the Halls and I was finally able
to wear that elegant dress Uncle Henry had bought for me."

He chuckled. "That was a great night. I especially enjoyed
all the money you won me at billiards. You are a rather sur-
prising person, Miss Greystone. Despite not having been
sent to some school for girls, you will make someone a fine
catch." He smiled devilishly. "Perhaps Professor Hartley."

She scowled at him, making him laugh harder.

"I am joking!" he exclaimed through his laughter. "Though
Professor Hartley is a very smart man, I would hate for you
to throw your life away on a lush such as he is."

"And a man more than twice my age," she concluded.

His smile never left his face. "You need to learn how
to find a little more joy in your life other than your books
and studies."

She blushed as the thought of Mr. Mackland came to
mind and she quickly averted her gaze to avoid notice.

It was too late, however, as Richard had already seen it.
"Miss Greystone, do you have a lover?"

Her blush deepened. "How far away is this river where
Anna Brown was found?" she asked, avoiding answering.
"Perhaps we should be going to the closest point of the
river from her house. There is no way she walked this far in
the middle of the night."

"Maybe she didn't walk," Richard said. "What if she was

carried? Or transported?"

Agrippina considered his statement for a moment. "Who was the magistrate that attended to her? Was a doctor called to examine her?"

Richard's mouth hung open as if in midsentence, a hand poised in the air. He let it drop after a brief pause and shook his head. "I am not sure. I was away in London when all of this happened. I do not know a lot of the particulars, but I can find out."

They arrived at the spot where Anna Brown was found a few minutes later. Agrippina stood at the edge of the river on the grass, looking upstream as the water flowed. The water did not seem to be very deep, nor did it appear to be turbulent. She turned and looked downstream. The town of Halstead was just visible from where she stood.

"Is the water usually this low and had it been raining before she went missing?" she asked looking back down at the water.

"I cannot recall about the rain, but it is not a very deep river in these parts," Richard replied examining the river himself.

She studied the river a few more minutes, noting the low hanging trees on one side of the bank and the three-foot drop to the water below. "I think you are right."

Richard turned to her in surprise. "I beg your pardon? Did you—did you just say I was right?"

She cleared her throat. "I think there is a strong possibility that your theory of her having been transported here might be correct."

He clapped his hands together in glee. "Beautiful." He sighed, smiling. "How much did that hurt to say?"

She disregarded his question, a raised brow her only reply. "Shall we return?" she asked, turning to make her way back to the carriage. "I am rather famished."

After a late lunch, Richard went to his room to write a letter to Dr. Hansby, the main doctor in Halstead who most likely examined Anna Brown after she was found. Agrippina wrote her own letter to her uncle, and another to Mr. Mackland.

She blushed again as she thought of him, her heart simultaneously slowing and increasing in beats per minute. She certainly admired him and esteemed him above all other men of her acquaintance, but could she call him a lover?

She hesitated beginning her letter to him, another flutter of emotions confusing her. She took a deep breath after deep contemplation and wrote a few short lines.

*Mr. Mackland,*

*As we have been corresponding these several months, I wish to make a small request. I would very much like it if you addressed me in your future letters as Agrippina, or even Aggy if you would prefer. And, in return might I call you James?*

*Yours*

*— A.G.*

She sealed the letter and made her way back downstairs, placing her letters on the tray to be posted. She moved toward the parlor when she heard a noise coming from one of the back rooms. A crash was heard behind one of the closed doors followed by a man's scream.

"She is here!" Mr. Bolten cried out. "She is here! She has come for me!"

Agrippina ran to the screaming. She tried opening the door where it was coming from but something was barring her entrance. She pushed hard, but whatever was in front of the door was heavy and wouldn't budge.

The screaming continued, followed by the sound of breaking glass and things falling to the floor. She tried the door again, throwing her weight into it, but it barely moved.

"Get away! Get away from me!"

"You will pay for your sins!" came the growling whisper.

Agrippina's breath caught in her throat and her skin prickled.

"No! No, please! I have done nothing!"

Mr. Bolten screamed again followed by the sound of cackling before a final 'thud,' then silence.

"Mr. Bolten?" Agrippina asked tentatively at first, then louder. "Mr. Bolten?"

Richard came out of nowhere yelling for his uncle as he took over pushing against the door. He yelled in frustration when the door could not be moved. He ran his hands through his hair thinking.

"The window!"

He ran into an adjacent room and Agrippina watched as he threw open the window and crawled out. She returned to the door to listen, Mr. Bolten's cries mere whimpers.

She looked through the crack in the door and saw books strewn across the floor, a shelf perhaps, blocking the entrance, and—she gasped—two feet on the ground. Had Mr. Bolten fainted?

"What is happening?" Mrs. Bolten asked as she came up beside her, eyes wide with confused concern.

Agrippina shook her head. "I heard Mr. Bolten screaming. I tried the door, but something is blocking it. Mr. Maddox is trying the window."

"Eugene?" Mrs. Bolten called out, hitting the door with her hand. "Eugene, are you alright? Answer me!"

Richard's face appeared in the crack of the door. "A bookshelf fell in front of the door," he said. "Uncle Eugene is breathing but appears to be unconscious. Send for the doctor and bring your smelling salts."

Mrs. Bolten pressed a hand to her mouth. "Mr. Arter!" she yelled as she ran off to find the butler.

Richard grunted as he pulled the bookshelf from the door, allowing Agrippina entrance. She gasped as she fully saw the chaos of the scene. She stepped over books thrown about the room; her feet crunched on broken glass from a decanter, the smell of port permeating the air.

She knelt by Mr. Bolten who was lying motionless on the floor. She placed a hand on his chest, feeling it rise and fall. She then gently lifted one of his eyelids to find his pupil dilated. She just as gently moved his head from one side, checking for any marks or cuts, before observing the other side.

"There are no substantial injuries. He has a few scratches on his face and neck, but I do not see any blood." She stood and turned to Richard who appeared pale. "Was he the only one in the room when you came in?"

He nodded absently.

"You did not see anyone climbing out the window or fleeing the scene?"

He finally met her gaze, his eyes intense. "No, why?"

She pointed to the door. "Is that the only way into this room?"

"Yes, but again, why?"

She shook her head. "I do not know. I—I thought—" She shook her head. "I thought I heard someone else in here with him. "It was only a whisper but your uncle reacted to it." She cleared her throat. "It said, 'you will pay for your sins,' or something of that kind."

Richard's face grew more pale and he staggered backward.

"Mr. Maddox!" she called out, taking him by the arm. "You need to sit down at once!" She guided him to a chair.

He shook his head but dutifully obeyed, sitting.

"Why did that phrase shake you so much?"

He looked up at her, a distant look on his face. "You heard a woman?"

Agrippina shook her head. "I am not sure. The voice was too low and unclear. I could have heard a maid or your aunt in another room. There is obviously no one else in here."

He shook his head again. "Not with that phrase. The servants do not know the importance of it and my aunt would never."

There was a brief pause.

"I think it is time you tell me about your family curse."

"There is no curse!" Mrs. Bolten proclaimed as she entered, her expression hard. "I will not let this family lose themselves to this ridiculous notion of witches and curses." She gasped when she saw her husband. She knelt by him and cradled his head, pulling out her smelling salts.

Richard stood from his seat and knelt by his aunt. Mrs.

Bolten opened the bottle of smelling salts and waved it in front of her husband's nose who jerked his head away in reaction. He groaned after another inhale, his eyes fluttering open.

"Eugene!" Mrs. Bolten cried, stroking his hair.

"Lucy? Lucy, is that you?" he moaned taking her hand and pressing it against his cheek. "Do not let her get me. Do not let her win."

"She will not, my love. She will not." Mrs. Bolten motioned with her head to Richard who took his uncle's other hand.

"Come, uncle," he said softly. "Let us get you to bed. The doctor will be here soon." He grunted as he helped his uncle back onto his feet.

"Lucy always wanted children," Mr. Bolten said to no one in particular as they left the room. "But I am glad we have none for the curse will finally end with me."

Agrippina looked over at Mrs. Bolten who straightened, still in her kneeling position, her expression stoic. She could see that Mr. Bolten's comment did not sit well with his wife. She recovered, however, and stood, brushing off her dress and putting on a soft smile.

"I think I shall have some tea. Would you not join me, Miss Greystone?"

Agrippina admired the woman's composure, nodding. "Yes. I would like to look around for a few minutes if you do not mind."

Mrs. Bolten gave her a silent, singular nod and walked out of the room.

Agrippina heard her soft footsteps receding down the hall. She waited until she could no longer hear them before slowly spinning around the room. The large oak desk by the window—papers strewn across it with a glass of possibly port on top—told her it was most likely Mr. Bolten's office.

She picked up the glass and sniffed it tentatively. Her nose wrinkled as the smell of alcohol invaded it. It smelled like port spiced with licorice. She put the glass down and continued her observations.

The bookshelf that had fallen in front of the door was the only one in the room and held journals of business, law, and almanacs. On the other side of the room was a globe and a table that held a few decanters of spirits and a cigar box, a tapestry hanging from the wall above it. A couple of chairs lined the fourth wall, a small table between them.

Agrippina sighed as she moved around the room. There was something strange about it. For a house as large as this one, the study was unusually small. Her uncle's house—which was nowhere near as large as Bolten House—boasted a larger study than this one.

A cool breeze floated in through the still-open window and Agrippina shivered. She moved to shut it as the papers on Mr. Bolten's desk began to flutter to the floor. There was another movement on the floor that caught her attention as she closed it.

She bent over, reaching under the desk and pulling out a black ribbon. It appeared to be well worn as the ends were tattered and beginning to unravel. A black shawl, a black ribbon, a woman in black.

Agrippina spun around, looking about the room. There had been someone else in the room with Mr. Bolten. She was sure of it. She moved back to the window and peered out, wondering if there was somewhere to hide, if someone climbed out of the window and hid without Richard seeing them.

The sound of a creaking floorboard behind her caused her to pause, her skin prickling. Unexplainedly, she felt the sensation of being watched. She could feel eyes observing her, roaming over her.

Fear began to creep into her brain and her heart raced when she heard the creaking again. Slowly she whipped around, expecting, hoping to see Richard standing there watching her, but she was alone.

## 11

UNEASINESS COURSED THROUGH AGRIPPINA AS SHE RUSHED out of the room. She quickly stepped over the scattered books and slid through the door. She didn't make it more than five steps when she ran into something solid.

She let out a startled gasp as she fell back onto her rear. She groaned in pain and shame as she looked up at the butler who was staring down at her curiously. He held his hand out, however, and helped her up.

"Forgive me, Miss Greystone," he said with a bow.

"No, forgive me, Mr. Arter," Agrippina replied, straightening her dress. "It was I who was being careless."

He bowed again in response. "Mrs. Bolten wished for me to tell you tea was ready in the music room."

"Oh." She nodded, still breathless and feeling silly. "Thank you. Where exactly is the music room?"

He pointed down the hallway opposite from the study where she had just come. "The last door on the right."

She thanked him again and moved in the direction he indicated, pressing a hand to her forehead. She had never felt so ridiculous in her life. Scared because she heard a noise? A creaking floorboard? The house was old; it was bound to make noises all on its own.

The sound of soft tinkering on piano keys drifted down the hall the closer she got to the music room. It was not an actual song, but the mindless pressing of keys just to hear the sound it produced.

Agrippina paused at the door for a moment, taking a deep breath before she entered. Mrs. Bolten sat at the piano, her hands moving listlessly over the keys as she looked out the window into the orchard.

She cleared her throat after a few seconds. "Are you doing alright?"

"In what way?" Mrs. Bolten didn't look away from the window.

Agrippina was not sure how to respond.

"Am I alright after witnessing the unconscious body of my husband on the ground? Or am I alright after hearing my husband say he was glad I have not been able to bear him children?"

"The latter is really none of my business."

Mrs. Bolten laughed bitterly through her nose, shaking her head. "None of this is really your business." She let out a shrill sigh. "And yet you are here. In the hopes of seducing poor Richard into a marriage proposal no doubt."

Agrippina frowned. "No doubt?" She shook her head. "I have no intentions of marrying your nephew."

Mrs. Bolten finally looked over her shoulder at her, sizing her up like she had when she first arrived. "You are telling me a woman of your age is not trying to whittle her way into the good graces of a young man set to inherit this estate and an income of seven thousand a year?" She shook her head. "It is difficult to believe."

Agrippina frowned. "There is more to life than marriage

and money. I might not be married or engaged, but a fortune seeker I most certainly am not."

Mrs. Bolten looked at her curiously but did not reply. She simply went back to molesting the piano keys with no specific song in mind. "And so you are here then, to solve our little mystery."

"Something you clearly choose not to believe in," Agrippina replied tersely.

"I must seem rather cold, and, perhaps, a little unfeeling to you, Miss Greystone," Lucy said tapping at a piano key without fully pushing it down.

Agrippina shook her head. "No, ma'am. You seem level-headed and practical."

Lucy smiled, turning on the piano seat, finally facing her. "Level-headed and practical. I do not believe I ever have received a better compliment. When I was young and inexperienced, I thought being called beautiful was all one could hope for. Now, being long past my youth, I know beauty is fleeting. There is no mystery to it. Skin will wrinkle and loosen, eyes will lose their shine, and hair will turn gray. But the mind will continue to sharpen through the years if you keep it well tuned." Her smile deepened. "You, I am sure, will have no problem fine tuning your mind through the years. You are quiet, but very observant, and your eyes are full of intelligence."

Agrippina's mouth twitched into a small smile. "Thank you."

Lucy Bolten nodded, turning back to her piano. "Do you play?" she asked as she began a tune, Mozart's Sonata number one in C Major. "I believe music to be one of the tools to keep the mind sharp."

Agrippina nodded. "I do play. Perhaps not as well as I once did; I rarely practice anymore."

Mrs. Bolten looked over at her, her fingers still striking the keys with perfection. "My piano is yours while you are here. I find it helps soothe my nerves and collect my thoughts. Perhaps it shall help you too." She abruptly stopped and sighed. "I am the worst of hostesses. I have forgotten about your tea." She stood from the piano and moved to the cart where the tea things were placed. "A splash of cream," she said as she prepared Agrippina's cup.

Agrippina finally took a seat near the piano thanking Mrs. Bolten as she handed her the cup. "Might I ask you for your version of the family curse?"

Mrs. Bolten laughed, a short trill that floated from her mouth. "I do admire your bluntness. There is no 'beating around the bush' with you. If you were anyone else, you would try to flatter me or think of any other topic in the world before coming to what you truly wanted to talk about."

Agrippina watched her over the brim of her teacup.

Finally, Mrs. Bolten nodded. "Yes, I think I would like to talk to you about the family curse." She sat back down at the piano bench and sighed. "It seemed silly when I first heard of it, but the belief of it is rooted so deep within Eugene," she shook her head, "you would have to be level-headed and practical just to keep your sanity."

She brushed her hand over the keys as if she wanted to play but refrained.

"He told me the day before we were supposed to wed," she continued almost laughing. "I can still see his desperate face as he relayed his family's history." That time, she did strike a key, holding it down so the sound continued to echo through the room. "At first, I thought he was telling me because he wanted me to call the wedding off. I thought at first, he did not love me and was respectfully giving me a way out." She shook her head. "But in his mind, he told me

74

before we wed because he loved me." She looked over at Agrippina. "You do understand?"

Agrippina creased her brows and blinked.

"Back in 1572 the Boltens were of no consequence. They owned very little property. A farm that could barely grow grass for its livestock, much less wheat or barley. They were poor farmers scraping by. Then one day a neighboring farmer complained that a few of his cows were acting strange and he thought them bewitched." She shook her head. "I am not sure as to how a bewitched cow acts, but it was suspicious enough for the farmer to suspect witchcraft." She shot an amused smile at Agrippina. "We can be such ridiculous creatures, can we not?"

Agrippina nodded in agreement.

"A month or so later, a different farmer found one of his cows acting strangely and came to the same conclusion. It must be witchcraft!" Her tone was mocking and haughty. "The town began to panic. Four bewitched cows? Well, that is unforgiveable. But it was not until the wife of a successful yeoman became ill that the officials took everyone's concerns seriously."

"They attributed her illness to witchcraft as well, I imagine?" Agrippina asked, taking a sip from her tea.

Mrs. Bolten released a short laugh. "Naturally. The town wanted the issue dealt with, they wanted the witch brought to justice, but no one knew who the witch was." She paused a moment to lightly drum a key. "The yeoman offered an award of fifteen pounds to anyone who could identify the witch responsible, an opportunity that Geoffrey Bolten—Eugene's several times great-grandfather—took full advantage of."

She stood from the piano and moved to the window that faced the cherry trees.

"Geoffrey was a widower with three young children. He had hired a poor spinster—Agnes Steadman—that, for room and board, took care of the house and children while he worked on the farm. But people become lonely and what started as a professional relationship soon grew," she paused looking over her shoulder, "intimate."

Agrippina nodded, understanding what she meant.

"Everything was going better for Geoffrey. His crops were producing a yield, his livestock was healthy, his children were well taken care of. But then Agnes came to him one day claiming to be with child. He did not believe her at first. A woman at the advanced age of forty-five with child? It did not seem possible. She insisted it was true, however, and that he needed to marry her to save her and the child's honor. The yeoman's reward came just in time for Geoffrey. Instead of marrying poor Agnes, he accused her of being the witch. He further claimed she seduced him and put spells on the other farmers' livestock so that his would thrive."

"How awful!" Agrippina proclaimed, her mouth gaping in horror.

Mrs. Bolten nodded, moving to the tea cart to pour herself a fresh cup. "She was hanged a few months later for her perceived crimes. While she was on the scaffold, she saw Geoffrey Bolten in his new clothes and a hatred must have burned through her because in front of everyone in town who came to watch her die, she cursed the Bolten family. She said she would allow him to profit and grow from his blood money, but no one born of the Bolten name would live past the age of forty-five.

"Geoffrey invested his money in the silk trade, increasing his profits several times over. He was able to buy this land and begin building Bolten house. He leased out his old farm for more profits, accumulated more land over time and then, one day, fifteen years after Agnes was executed, he was found dead," she took a sip of tea, "at the age of forty-five."

Agrippina shook her head. "What happened to Agnes's child?"

Mrs. Bolten absent-mindedly rubbed her belly.    "She miscarried while in jail awaiting trial." She took a deep breath and let it out slowly. "It was just another sign that she was evil. For if God approved of the child, surely he would have allowed it to live."

Agrippina recognized the sore subject she had touched on and steered away from it. "Is this story just family lore? How do we know Geoffrey and Agnes had an affair? Or that she ever spit out a curse? Or if she ever existed."

Mrs. Bolten smiled softly. "I admire how unwilling you are to just believe everything you are told. People are too apt to blindly follow." She took another sip of her tea and nodded. "We know this because Geoffrey Bolten wrote in a journal and in his own words, he admitted to the part he played in Agnes's false accusation. He even voiced remorse though it was not until the end of his life he did so." She shook her head. "He enjoyed his growing wealth and power. It was not until he swore he began seeing Agnes that he asked for forgiveness."

Agrippina creased her brows. "He saw her?"

Mrs. Bolten nodded. "The last few months of his life. He claimed, 'The woman in black is forever vigilant, watching, waiting. She says nothing, does not tell me who she is or what she comes here for, but I already know it is her. Agnes, forgive my sins against you.'" She shrugged. "It has been some time since I have read what he wrote, so I am sure I have left out something, but I know you get the idea."

Agrippina nodded. "The woman in black," she said softly

to herself, fingering the black ribbon she found in the study and thinking of the black shawl in her room. "Might I ask how old Mr. Bolten is?"

A weak smile spread across her face, her expression sad. "He will be forty-five next month."

# 12

DR. HANSBY, A THIN OLD MAN WITH WIRY HAIR, FINALLY arrived just before seven that evening. He seemed slightly disgruntled at being called out in the rain but was quickly won over after receiving an invitation for dinner.

He shook his head and tsked as he met everyone in the dining room. "Other than a few scrapes on his face, I cannot see anything wrong with him. A fainting spell will do that to you." He shoveled a chunk of meat into his mouth. "Though I must say," he paused to swallow, "I do not often get called for men who faint. Usually, it is the women." He chuckled softly as if what he said was funny.

"A fainting spell?" Agrippina repeated. "How do you account for the scratches on his face?"

Mrs. Bolten took in a sharp breath. "I appreciate you traveling in this weather to attend my husband," she quickly said, keeping the doctor's attention on her. "He has been under a lot of stress lately with everything that has happened recently."

"Huh," the doctor grunted as he chewed. "He needs more fresh air and tea and honey three times a day. I gave him a

THE CURSE GROWS STRONGER STILL

good letting just now and a little dram to help him sleep, but encourage him to walk the grounds."

She nodded. "Thank you, I shall heed your advice."

"You are the same doctor who examined Anna Brown's body, are you not?" Agrippina asked.

Dr. Hansby paused mid bite and slowly turned to look at her. "I beg your pardon, miss?"

"Miss Greystone's Uncle is a professor at Cambridge," Richard began. "He teaches the History of Medicine, and the Philosophy of Medicine. Though he himself was a medical doctor previously."

Dr. Hansby observed her over the rim of his glasses, his thick brows raised questioningly.

"She is here investigating the strange occurrences that have happened," Richard continued.

"Investigating?" he repeated, almost laughing. "What qualifications do you have to investigate anything?"

Agrippina released a soft sigh and smiled lightly. "Official qualifications? Obviously, I can have none as I am barred from attending university or further schooling since I am a woman. Seeing, however, that my uncle rarely cared for silly restrictions if it hindered the growth of not just an intelligent mind, but anyone with the desire to learn, he taught me, schooled me, encouraged me to read, had me sit in lectures. Yes, it is unconventional since I am a woman, but I never let that stop me before."

The doctor blinked at her, unsure how to reply.

"But if what you really mean to ask is 'what experience do I have,' then that is a different question. One can have all the knowledge in the world, but if that knowledge is not put to use, then it is useless."

He scoffed. "You are quite opinionated."

"I do not disagree."

"Huh." He sniffed, still looking at her in curious disdain. "Do you have experience then?"

"Miss Greystone solved five murders—"

"Nine," she gently corrected. "It started as five, but, unfortunately, I was not able to stop the murderer until four more lost their lives."

"Nine murders last year up in Blindburn," Richard said grinning at the bewildered expression on the doctor's face. "The king sent her and her uncle to investigate. Several women were found mauled to death and the townspeople thought they had a werewolf. She found the true killer."

"The king did not personally ask for us," Agrippina clarified. "He asked an advisor of his to find someone. A friend of mine whose father is on good terms with the advisor asked us to go. But, the king did personally reward me with a thousand pounds. I sent it to Blindburn to help the families of victims recover."

The doctor gaped at her. "You gave a thousand pounds of the king's money away?"

She blinked at him. "It was no longer his money if he gave it to me. Besides, he wanted to give me a silly diamond necklace, but the money was much more practical."

Richard pressed a hand over his mouth to stifle a laugh.

Mrs. Bolten stared at her wide-eyed. "You refused a diamond necklace from the king?"

"I did not refuse it," Agrippina said with a shrug. "He gave me the option of the money or the necklace, but I could tell he wished I would take the necklace. 'A pretty piece of jewelry for a pretty lady,' I believe is what he said."

"You refused a gift from the king?" Richard asked, trying hard not to laugh.

"I did not refuse!" Agrippina corrected in defense of herself. "I chose the more viable option. The necklace was far too grand for me. When would I have worn it? To one of my uncle's lectures? A bit pretentious if you ask me."

"Extraordinary," the doctor mumbled still staring at her.

"Thank you. Now, back to my question, Dr. Hansby," she said looking at him. "Were you not the doctor who examined Anna Brown after she was found?"

He took a sip of his wine, nodding. "I was."

She opened her mouth to ask another question but stopped, looking over at Mrs. Bolten. "Forgive me, ma'am. There might be a few answers to questions you might not approve."

"If the subject is too delicate, aunt," Richard began, "we can talk to Dr. Hansby after dinner."

Mrs. Bolten's face dropped. "Delicate?" she repeated, offended. "That is the second time you have referred to me as delicate in the past two days. Do you think I am delicate, Richard? Have I ever given you that impression before?"

Richard stammered a moment. "Well, no, but I thought— it is just that—" He shook his head clearing this throat. "I apologize."

She gave a single, curt nod. "Proceed, Miss Greystone."

"Were there any apparent injuries to her?" Agrippina continued without hesitation.

The doctor puckered his lips as he thought back. "She had a few scrapes and scratches, if I recall. But nothing substantial."

"No broken bones or bruising?"

He let out a breath. "That, I could not say. There was some discoloration and decay. She had been dead for a number of days in the late summer, floating in the water."

"Was there fluid in her lungs?"

There was a heavy silence as the doctor looked from one person in the room to another.

"Are you asking if I performed an autopsy on her?" he asked almost in a whisper. "That is—that would have been—" he shook his head. "She was a young woman from a respectable family, not a criminal to be used for scientific exploration."

Agrippina lifted a brow at him. "We are not going to tell the family, but I need to know if she had fluid in her lungs."

He took a deep breath through his nose and let it out slowly. He then took a long sip of wine before answering. "No. I did not find any fluid in her lungs."

Agrippina pressed a hand to her mouth as she sat further back into her seat, thinking.

Mrs. Bolten shook her head. "What does that mean?"

"Anna Brown did not drown," Agrippina replied in a low voice. "She was dead before she hit the water." She scowled at the doctor. "You know this means she could have been murdered? And you said nothing."

Dr. Hansby shook his head vehemently. "No," he said holding up a finger. "It means she was dead before she hit the water. She could have died while walking along the river and fell in."

"The river is more than three miles from her house," Agrippina pointed out. "Do you really believe she walked or ran all the way from her house in the middle of the night and then died as she fell into the river?"

The doctor shrugged as he cut his food. "Stranger things have happened, Miss Greystone. The girl was disturbed."

Agrippina was not satisfied but did not want to risk angering him. "Were the scratches pre- or postmortem?"

Dr. Hansby waited until he was done chewing before answering, using that time to consider his answer. "Postmortem from what I could tell. As I said, decay had already started settling in. The poor girl was bloated and stuck in the branches of a fallen tree." He wiped his mouth with his napkin. "And before you ask, no, I do not know where along the river she fell in."

"Or was put in," Agrippina added.

"There is no evidence to suggest she was placed in the river."

"And from what I can tell by your answers, there is no evidence to rule it out."

The doctor smiled. "It is a shame you cannot receive any proper qualifications or traditional education, Miss Greystone. You are quite inquisitive. You are lucky to have had an uncle who fostered your inquisitiveness."

Agrippina felt his compliment and smiled, thanking him. She had a few more questions burning to be asked, but the sensitive subject she was about to breach would have to wait until she could speak to him alone.


AFTER DINNER THE DOCTOR ENJOYED A CIGAR AND WHISKEY with Richard while Agrippina waited in the parlor alone, Mrs. Bolten having gone upstairs to check on her husband. She paced by the door so she could hear them as they walked by, going over her notes.

An hour passed before she heard the laugh of Dr. Hansby echo in the main hallway. She closed her notebook and left the room catching him as he was taking his hat from the footman.

"Ah, Miss Greystone, I was hoping I would see you before I left. I shall find my journal with the notes about that poor silk merchant. I will have it sent over to you once I find it."

"It is very much appreciated."

He put his hat on his head and bowed. "It was quite the pleasure meeting you."

84

She nodded. "Yes, I thank you for indulging me. I do, however, have a few more questions of a," she cleared her throat, "sensitive nature. Might I follow you outside?"

"Of course!" He waved her along.

"Are you of the opinion Miss Brown did not meet with foul play because you performed an autopsy on a young girl without her family's permission?" she asked as they stepped out into the drive.

Even in the dim glow of the lanterns, Agrippina could see the doctor blanch in anger. "How dare you?"

She quickly shook her head. "It is not my intention to sully anyone's name or spread solacious gossip. I do not ask so to judge. I want to know your true opinion."

Dr. Hansby shifted from one foot to the other and shook his head. "I—I do not think—"

"You do not have to answer me right now," Agrippina told him. "Go home and consult your notes. Revisit them and see if your opinion has changed."

The doctor wiped his mouth as he nodded. He turned toward his waiting carriage when Agrippina stopped him again.

"I do have one final question."

Dr. Hansby let out a heavy sigh. "What else could you possibly wish to know?"

"Was Miss Brown still a virgin?"

# 13

AGRIPPINA SAT UP IN HER BED STARING AT THE GLOW OF moonlight flooding in through the window as she replayed the doctor's answer in her mind over and over again.

*Was Miss Brown still a virgin?*

The doctor hesitated but did not appear surprised by her having asked. He let out a long sigh matching his last one. "What would make you think to ask that question?"

"Most young women do not just sneak out of their house in the middle of the night to take long walks in the moonlight by themselves."

"The girl had been out of her mind for weeks."

Agrippina had looked at him, waiting for his answer.

The doctor had huffed. "I was hoping you would fail to ask me this, but at the same time, I expected it. I do not know why I am telling you this, but know, that if you repeat any of this to anyone, I will deny having told you."

"You have my word," Agrippina had reassured him.

"Not only was she not a virgin, but she was with child."

Agrippina gently tapped the back of her head against the headboard as she thought. Anna Brown appeared to have had a secret lover—or something more nefarious happened to the poor girl.

She sighed, her grip tightening on the adder stone as she continued to focus on the light coming through the window. Whatever was happening in Halstead went far deeper than the Bolten Family curse.

She let out a small laugh. Family curse. She shook her head. The story of Geoffrey Bolten could be seen as compelling when compared to the events the current Mr. Bolten was going through. But what if Geoffrey Bolten's experience was based on his guilt? He was losing his mind and saw visions of a woman in black and associated it with Agnes Steadman, the woman he sent to hang for crimes she didn't commit.

The guilt was a disease that wore away at his mind. Did he see her because she truly haunted him or was his mind playing tricks on him? As for Mr. Bolten, the fear of his family's curse is so engrained within him, the story of his several times great-grandfather so well known that it has influenced his mind to see what the late Mr. Bolten saw.

She shook her head. Then who did she hear in the study with him? Whose ribbon did she find under the desk? Whose shawl did she collect from the orchard? C. P. M. certainly does not stand for Agnes Steadman.

She looked down at the adder stone and picking it up, she once again looked through its hole, scanning the bedroom. She went from one side of the room to the next, over each corner thinking how silly she felt.

She moved across the far corner of the room and stopped, the room suddenly growing very cold and her skin prickling hot with fear. She heard a shuffling noise, and her heart skipped a beat, her breath caught in her throat. She slowly scanned back to the corner and froze in horror.

The woman in black emerged from the darkness rushing toward Agrippina with her arms outstretched, and her mouth open wide in an endless scream.

AGRIPPINA JOLTED AWAKE, GASPING FOR AIR AND FIGHTING off no one, the sounds of piano keys all being pressed at once rang through her ears. She pressed her hand to her chest as she tried to catch her breath, trying to tell herself it was just a dream.

She sat for a moment, her ears buzzing, the sound of piano still drifting from the music room right below her. What was Mrs. Bolten doing playing the piano so early in the morning? Could it be morning already? She felt as if she had just drifted off to sleep.

She swung her feet out of the bed and took another calming breath before standing, squinting at the sunlight that shone through a crack in the curtains.

She shuffled to the water basin and splashed the cool water on her face, holding her hands over her eyes for a few seconds before standing and grabbing a towel to dry off. She then moved to the window and pushed the curtain aside to flood the room with light. Movement down below caught her eye and she paused to look out.

Janet was by the cherry trees with a young man, the pair in what appeared to be a heated discussion. Agrippina watched as Janet threw her hands in the air as she spoke before pointing an accusing finger at him.

The young man, whose face she couldn't see, shook his head and raised his arms in defense, moving his arms wildly as he spoke, pointing at the house, at the trees, before shrugging. Mr. Arter showed up just then and began to seemingly scold them both. He pointed a sharp finger at the young man before shooing him away and turning his attention to Janet. He put a hand on her shoulder and bent over to talk to her, her head nodding.

Janet wiped at her eyes and made her way back to the house while Mr. Arter stood there scowling. He sharply looked up at Agrippina's window and she quickly moved out of the way gasping in surprise.

Her cheeks flushed with embarrassment as she realized she had been caught spying on the staff. She quickly shook it off and began dressing herself for the day. She then pinned up her hair and moved toward the door when she stopped.

The adder stone lay on top of the bedside stand. She stared at it a moment before picking it up and placing it over her head. She tucked it neatly in her dress as she grabbed the door handle and gasped, startled by the appearance of a maid on the other side of the door.

"Forgive me, miss!" The maid bowed her head allowing dark tresses to fall from her cap. "I've only come tuh see if ye needed anythin'."

Agrippina swallowed, smiling slightly as she pressed a hand to her chest. "It is quite alright."

She took a deep breath, standing taller, noticing in the dim light of the hall the strangeness of the maid's uniform. It was different than Janet's and the other maids she had seen about the house. The sleeves and pattern looked outdated even to Agrippina's untrained eye, and the cap she wore barely covered the dark tresses that cascaded from it.

"Forgive my silliness at being startled," Agrippina said after her brief observation. "But Janet has been very attentive to my needs."

"I'll be sprucin' up yer room then." The maid curtsied. "Breakfast is warm and waitin', miss."

"What is your name in case I need to ask you questions?"

The maid blinked at her a little confused. "Questions, miss? No one ever feels the need to ask me those. Been told I've not been hired fer my opinion."

"Yes, well, while I am here, everyone's opinion and experiences must be taken into account."

She smiled, lighting up her pretty face. "My name's Catherine, miss. But everyone calls me Kitty, so Kitty will be just fine."

Agrippina nodded slightly. "Thank you, Kitty."

The maid curtseyed, though sloppily, smiling sweetly.

Agrippina left her to her tidying and moved down the hallway to the stairs when a cold chill rushed over her. She paused, the remnants of her dream still making her uneasy. She turned slowly, looking over her shoulder, but it was only the maid slipping into her room.

She shook off her paranoia and made her way to the breakfast table where Mrs. Bolten greeted her.

"Is your husband any better?" she asked as a plate of food was set before her.

Mrs. Bolten nodded. "He appeared to sleep soundly last night. I have arranged for the phaeton to be brought around. A good ride around the property would do him well. Then a turn or two around the garden."

Agrippina nodded. "Do you think he shall be up to talking to me today?"

Mrs. Bolten cleared her throat as she wiped her mouth with a napkin. "I am not sure. His state of mind is so delicate that a mere mention of the subject could set him over the edge."

She smiled briefly. "Of course. I shall question him only at your discretion and if, at any time you think I am going too far, you can stop me."

Mrs. Bolten yawned into her teacup. Only then did

Agrippina see how tired the woman actually was. Her hair had a few strands out of place and her dress appeared to have been put on in a hurry and without aid. She smiled despite her fatigue, her skin still seeming to glow.

"Thank you," Mrs. Bolten told her in a soft tone. "I know you wish to have as much access to information as possible, but I cannot allow certain things at the cost of my husband's wellbeing."

Agrippina shook her head. "I would never expect or wish it. Today, Mr. Maddox and I are headed to the farm where the second incident took place. I should be able to question the young girl involved."

"I appreciate your dedication to helping my family," Mrs. Bolten said. "Are you sure you do not wish to marry my nephew?"

Agrippina blinked at her, her fork poised in midair.

Mrs. Bolten laughed gently. "I do not mean to put you on the spot. My nephew just lacks direction, and I believe a woman such as you could gently steer him toward the correct path."

"Thank you. I realize you voicing the wish of me uniting with your nephew is the best of compliments. However, as much as I respect Mr. Maddox, we will truly only ever be friends."

She shrugged, taking another sip. "I had to try. I wish to see him settled in the next year or two. Though you are certainly not conventional wife material, I think you would make him a fine match." She stood from the table looking a little pale. She smiled, however. "Please, eat your fill. I have a few matters I need to attend to." She nodded to her and then glided out of the room in a graceful, if not hurried, manner.

Richard entered not long after his aunt had left, yawning. "I hope you slept better than I did," he said, biting into a sausage. "I feel as if I have not slept this entire year." He yawned again as he poured himself some tea. He took a sip and cringed. "This tea is not nearly hot enough." He sent for a fresh pot before piling several servings of meat and potatoes on his plate.

"I slept fine," Agrippina replied watching in mild disgust at the amount of food Richard put on his plate. "I woke up feeling as if I only slept a few minutes, but now that I've put some food in my stomach, I feel more energized."

He nodded, perhaps not completely listening. "So, we are headed to the Rupert farm today." He grabbed a piece of toast and began buttering it. "I do wonder what we will discover."

"How old is the daughter at this farm?"

Richard nodded as he chewed. "I believe she is the same age as Anna Brown."

"Have you ever spoken to the Ruperts?"

Again he nodded, wiping his mouth with a napkin. "Yes, I see them every month to collect rent. I never questioned them as you did with the Browns, though. I only know what I have been told."

A chill ran over her as the memory of her dream popped into her head. She poured herself a cup of tea when the new pot came and splashed some cream into it, taking a sip.

"Do you have any theories yet?" Richard asked after a moment regarding her over his toast.

She pursed her lips and shook her head. "There is so much more information to consider. I do not want to make a conclusion that could further taint the way I perceive my investigation."

He paused mid-bite to stare at her. "You are a very unusual person, Miss Greystone."

She smiled slightly. "Perhaps I am my own kind of witch."

He raised his brows, smiling himself. "I would not say that around here. They might try you as one."

"It would be illegal to do so."

A small laugh escaped his mouth. "Yes, I know. But that would not stop people from saying you are one and ruining your spotless reputation. What man would want to marry a known witch?"

She huffed. "If a man did not want to marry me because of a ridiculous rumor that has no factual basis and is superstitious enough to believe it, then he is a man well worth scaring away."

Richard laughed even harder. He took one last bite of his toast, a long sip of his tea and pushed away from the table. "Come, Miss Greystone," he said waving her on. "This farm is a little farther than the last one."

"Might I finish my plate first?" Agrippina replied looking down at her full plate of food.

"No time," Richard told her. "I shall have a basket prepared. You can eat in the carriage."

"That is highly uncivilized of you," she grumbled taking a few more sips of her tea. "Making me eat in a moving carriage. Your aunt, I am sure would be ashamed of you."

"Well, we better leave before she sees us then." He clapped his hands twice. "Chop! Chop! We have a mystery to uncover."

# 14

"W<small>E HEARD FROM THE</small> B<small>ROWNS WE MIGHT BE EXPECTING</small> you," Mrs. Rupert said pouring some tea into a cup.

Agrippina could tell by the color that the tea was weak and by the callouses on Mrs. Rupert's hands that she had taken over several of the household chores. The discolored rectangular spots on the wallpaper told her that a couple of paintings once hung there.

"Would you like some sugar or cream?" Mrs. Rupert asked her.

Agrippina could not ignore the several patches in her dress and realized that what she offered to them was all she had. She politely shook her head. "No, ma'am. I prefer nothing in my tea. Thank you."

Richard looked at her questioningly at first, but taking her lead, replied the same and took the weak tea with a gracious smile.

Mrs. Rupert poured her husband, who was sitting quietly near her, a cup too, but he shook his head. "You drink it, Cassie, dear," he told her gently.

A smile twitched in the corners of her mouth as she sat

obediently and took a sip. "We are very glad someone is taking what has happened so seriously. I know the Browns have yet to recover but they did lose their sweet girl. I still have my Maven."

"Did the two girls know each other?" Agrippina asked, taking a sip of her tea. It was no more than warm, brown water, but she took another sip to be polite.

Mrs. Rupert nodded. "Yes, they did. They were actually quite close, but they had some sort of argument a couple of months before Anna passed. I am not sure what about." She sighed. "I do know she was very upset for several weeks after their disagreement. They were almost joined at the hip at one time." She bowed her head. "She was rather shocked and hurt by Anna's death though, despite the disagreement they might have had."

Agrippina suffered through another sip of tea. "I would like to talk to your daughter, but first, I would like to talk about the fire. Could you walk me through the events leading to it?"

She cleared her throat and nodded again turning to her husband. "Andrew dear." She reached out and squeezed his hand in encouragement.

He took a deep breath and let it out slowly, shaking his head. "It was the first of the month, so Mr. Bolten came to visit us to collect rent."

"Does Mr. Bolten always come in person to collect rent?" Agrippina asked.

They both nodded.

"Oh, yes, he did," Mrs. Rupert replied. "He was a very attentive landlord. Sometimes he brought little things for Maven and myself when he came. Ribbons or books for Maven, teas or marzipan for me. Though the past few months we have not seen him."

"Who has been coming to collect the rent on his behalf?"

"I have," Richard answered beside her. "My aunt did it the first couple of months until I returned, but it has been me the past five months."

Agrippina nodded. "Mr. Rupert, could you continue walking us through the day of the fire?"

He cleared his throat and half shrugged. "It seemed like any other day. We were getting ready for harvest. We were still a few days out but," he ran a hand through his graying, thinning hair. "We were supposed to harvest the day before it happened, but I was recovering from an illness and—"

"I made him forgo it for another day," Mrs. Rupert said looking shamefully into her lap. She shook her head. "It was all my fault. Had I not made you take another day to rest, we would have had most of the fields harvested before the fire started. We wouldn't be in our current state of—"

"I told you to stop blaming yourself, Cassie," Mr. Rupert said gently, taking her hand in his. "You were only doing what you thought you should, taking care of your husband."

"What time did the fire happen?" Agrippina asked, bringing them back to the point at hand.

"I believe it was some time past midnight when one of my hands, a young man who was sleeping in the barn, sounded the alarm." He shook his head. "By then, it was too late. There was nothing we could do to save what had already caught fire. And it spread so quickly, we never would've been able to head it off." He made a face as if he was in pain. "I have three other fields, but that one was my largest. And we lost all of it."

"Who was it you said had alerted you?"

"He was a farmhand I had hired a few weeks previously. A young man less than twenty years of age. What was his name?" He turned to his wife for help.

"Alexander Mosley, I believe," Mrs. Rupert replied. "He was a very nice young man. Very helpful. He was recommended to us by the Browns. He had worked at their farm, but left them before their tragedy."

Agrippina's interest piqued. "Does he no longer work here?" she asked, already knowing the answer.

The husband and wife exchanged embarrassed glances.

"No," Mr. Rupert finally replied. "I, uh, I unfortunately had a fall in revenue due to the tragedy and I had to let a few hands go."

"I am very sorry to hear that, and even more sorry that I have to ask," Agrippina told him, making a note of the worker's name to try and find later.

Mr. Rupert shook his head and smiled softly. "It is a shame that we have had to make a few economies when we had been doing so well, but it is the Browns I pity more than myself. I have lost income, but they have lost their daughter. I would take my situation over theirs any day."

His wife nodded. "Sweet girl as she was."

Agrippina smiled though somberly. "You do not have any enemies, do you? No one you would think would want to ruin you?"

The Ruperts once again exchanged glances, shaking their heads.

"I cannot think of anyone who would ever wish so much harm on my family," the husband said with another shake of his head. "We are God-fearing people, Miss Greystone. We tithe, we pray, we help others who need it. Any other time, we work hard and keep to ourselves."

Agrippina nodded. "And Alexander Mosley did not mention seeing anyone on your property or in the area the night he noticed the fire?"

Mr. Rupert shook his head. "I don't recall ever asking him."

"Oh, but he shouldn't be hard to find," Mrs. Rupert cut in. "The last I heard, he got a position at Bolten House. He is the gardener or grounds keeper, I believe."

Agrippina slowly turned her head to look at Richard who shrugged.

"I have no hand in the hiring of people over there," he whispered.

Agrippina cleared her throat. "Do you recall seeing any white mice after the fire or while your daughter was having her fits?"

The wife blanched and the husband shuddered.

"There were a few found where we believe the fire started," he replied. "Three dead, white mice."

"I would like to see the field where the fire began," Agrippina stated.

Mr. Rupert rubbed his lips together. "I am afraid, I have already had it plowed with new seeds planted. There is nothing left to see."

Agrippina breathed in through her nose, disappointed but understanding. "Of course. It has been several months. I should expect it necessary for you to move on." She offered a small smile. "Might I speak to your daughter now?"

Mrs. Rupert stood with a half curtsey. "I shall go get her." Maven Rupert glided into the room, her dark, raven hair bouncing about her face, highlighting the porcelain features of her skin. Her appearance was sullen even as her eyelashes fluttered above her dark eyes.

"Would you like some tea, dear?" her mother asked lovingly.

Maven shook her head. "No thank you, mamma." She looked up, making eye contact with Agrippina.

"Miss Greystone would like to talk to you for a while, dear," her mother told her. "Please tell her everything you can."

98

Agrippina could see the secrets swimming behind the young woman's eyes, and she felt for her. "Do you think I could talk to Miss Rupert alone?"

The others in the room seemed confused, especially her parents who could never understand what their daughter might not want them to know.

"Please?" Agrippina insisted. "I know this might be difficult for her to recount. I would hate to embarrass your daughter."

Mr. Rupert shook his head. "What could she possibly say to be ashamed about?"

Maven's pale cheeks blushed, and she bowed her head to hide them.

"I am not saying she does," Agrippina replied gently. "I believe she would just be more comfortable if she and I spoke alone."

Mr. Rupert balked again when his daughter stopped him.

"It is alright, pappa," she told him in a soft voice. "I do not mind." She looked at her mother. "Please."

Her mother nodded. "Come now, Andrew. There will be no harm in letting the two young women chat alone." She looped her arm in her husband's and gently tugged him out of the room.

Richard shot Agrippina a questioning look before he followed suit.

Agrippina smiled softly at the young girl. "How are you? I know you had a rough time recently."

Maven smoothed out her skirts. "I am doing better, I suppose."

"You do not see this woman in black anymore, do you?"

Her eyes shot up to hers, wide and in mild panic. She shook her head frantically. "Please do not mention her." She looked down at her hands again. "I might not see her anymore during the day, but every now and then, I see her in my nightmares."

Agrippina once again thought back to her own nightmare the previous night and her skin prickled. "I understand you might not wish to bring her to the forefront of your mind, but I must talk about her. I understand Miss Brown might have been seeing the same woman before she died. The only window I have to look into what she was suffering is you and what you experienced."

Her eyes began to glisten with tears. "Anna was my friend." She shook her head. "I—I don't know how—I don't know why this happened to us. I don't know why she died, and I survived."

Agrippina nodded. "It is difficult to understand what we cannot readily explain. That is why I am here. I came to help clear away the confusion, or bring light to what could have happened."

Maven wiped at her eyes. "What could I know that would possibly help?"

"I would like to begin with before all of this started," Agrippina told her. "Could you tell me why you and Miss Brown had a disagreement?"

Maven blanched before blushing. She quickly averted her eyes. "It all seems ridiculous now," she replied barely above a whisper.

"Was it because of a man?"

Maven's face grew crimson, and she was unsure where to look. She quickly shook her head. "How silly would that have been?"

"Miss Rupert," Agrippina said softly.

Maven looked at her, her eyes telling what her lips did not.

"What was his name?"

Maven shook her head, her dark hair falling over her face. "Please, don't make me do this."

"I will not tell your parents or anyone else. I promise, but I need to know. In order to find out what has been going on here, I need to know."

Maven began to breathe rapidly and wrapped her arms around herself. "How can you promise you will not tell?" She looked up at her with pleading eyes. "You will have to eventually, will you not?"

Agrippina shook her head. "I will find a way around it, but you have to trust me. My wish is not to sully your reputation, or Miss Brown's; it is to find out the truth and stop this from affecting anyone else."

Maven rubbed her lips together for a moment before nodding.

"Was your disagreement with Miss Brown over a man?" Agrippina asked again in a gentle voice.

Maven averted her gaze but nodded.

"What was this man's name?"

"I cannot tell you," she whispered. "I do not want to get him trouble."

Agrippina's blood boiled at this, but she took a calming breath, letting it out slowly. To think this poor girl thought she had to protect a man that would seduce two young girls was illogical to her.

She cleared her throat. "I can understand you do not want to drag someone else's name through the mud, but he could be the key to understanding all of this."

She shook her head.

Agrippina sighed. "Was he the father of Miss Brown's child?"

Maven's eyes snapped up, her mouth open in horror. She gulped in air, blinking. "You know Anna was with child?"

Agrippina nodded. "Is Miss Brown's child connected to all of this?"

Maven coughed, shaking her head. "Stop it."

"Was this man also the father of your child?"

"No, I was never—I was not—" Maven began to hyperventilate. "Please, stop!"

"Who is the woman in black? Were you with child too when she began to visit you?"

Maven shook her head violently, throwing her hands to her face. "Go away! Go away!"

"I need to know," Agrippina said remaining calm despite Maven's growing hysteria.

"Leave me alone! I don't know anything!" Maven screamed as she rocked back and forth. "Go away!"

Her father burst through the door, a look of concerned confusion and panic in his eyes. "What have you done to her?"

Agrippina stood slowly, annoyed at the display before her. "I have done nothing to your daughter. She did not like a few of the questions I asked and is now playacting."

Maven released a high-pitched wail. "Please make her leave, pappa!"

"There is no need," Agrippina said tersely. "I can show myself out. Tell your daughter that when she is done hiding behind this façade, she can talk to me."

"Are you implying my daughter is faking it?" her father yelled, spittle flying from his mouth. "How dare you! Get out!"

"Andrew!" Mrs. Rupert said in alarm. She shifted her gaze from Agrippina to her husband, her eyes wide.

Agrippina curtseyed at Mrs. Rupert as she walked by. "Thank you for your hospitality, ma'am. I apologize for the disturbance." She walked past a gaping Richard who followed closely behind.

"What on earth was that about? What did you do to the poor girl?"

Agrippina climbed into the carriage silently, replaying the scene over and over in her head which was buzzing with anger.

"Are you going to enlighten me as to what just occurred?" Richard asked slowly as the carriage began to pull away.

She turned her angry eyes onto him, and he flinched. "I am beginning to piece together some of the puzzle. I just do not like where or how the pieces lay." She took a deep breath in through her nose and let it out in a huff.

Richard lifted his brows and slowly nodded his head. "Do you care to elaborate?"

"No." She returned her gaze out of the window. "No, I do not. I would like to wait until I have a clearer picture."

Richard continued nodding his head. "Of course."

They rode in silence for several minutes, Agrippina letting the sounds of the carriage dissolve into background noise as she thought.

*What was Maven so terrified of telling her? Who was the man who had impregnated Miss Brown? And had the same man impregnated her too? What does all of this have to do with Mr. Bolten and the Bolten Family Curse?*

Agrippina's tormented thoughts scattered for a moment as they came up to a road sign pointing to the town of Halstead and a new thought popped in her head. She looked over at Richard who was staring out his own window.

"Is there a tea shop in town?"

## 15

"WHY ARE WE HERE AGAIN?" RICHARD ASKED AS THEY PUSHED
through the doors of the tea shop.

"Well, we are not here to buy bricks and mortar," Agrippina
replied walking up to the counter.

A young man greeted her with a smile and a bow. "Good
afternoon, miss. Might I be of some assistance?"

"Yes, I would like a pound of your finest breakfast tea,
and a pound of a nice, spiced afternoon tea."

The shop attendant bowed again. "Right away, miss," he
said as he moved to fulfill her order.

Richard looked surprised. "My word, Miss Greystone. Are
the teas at Bolten House so terrible?"

"They are not for me or for Bolten House," Agrippina
replied as she examined a few more of the teas on display.
She leaned in to smell one. "I wonder if she would appreciate a green tea."

"Who?" Richard asked.

"Mrs. Rupert."

"Why are you sending Mrs. Rupert two pounds of tea?"

Agrippina sighed. "For multiple reasons, Mr. Maddox. One

mainly being that she obviously had cut out tea from her expenses and has been stretching out her reserve. Which is why the tea she served us was so weak."

"I gathered that," Richard grumbled. "But why is it your job to make sure they have tea?"

Agrippina shot him a disapproving look. "You do not see an issue with their growing poverty, do you?"

Richard pouted his lips and shook his head. "It is unfortunate, but I still fail to see your point."

"As owner of the Ruperts' farm, your uncle has the power to decrease their rent or to help them, but by the looks of their lack of furniture and missing paintings on the wall, he has opted not to."

Richard frowned. "My uncle is their landlord, yes, but it is not his duty to lower what they owe him all because they came across some economic hardship. You forget, my uncle lost out when their fields burned too."

She pursed her lips. "Your uncle has other means of income to make up for what he lost. The Ruperts do not."

Richard did not have anything to say in response. He let out a long sigh after a pause and shook his head. "I will be back in a few minutes," he told her a little begrudgingly. "Meet me in the tavern down the street."

She turned just in time to see him rush out the door.

"Is there anything else I can get for you, miss?" the attendant asked, placing two neat bags on the counter.

"This should be it. Could you have it delivered to the Rupert farm?"

"Yes, miss, of course."

"I should like to attach a note to it."

The attendant produced what she needed and waited patiently for her to scribble a few words. She then paid what was owed, thanked the man again and exited the shop.

She stood out front for a few minutes, admiring the quaintness of the river town. She looked around for the tavern, and seeing it, she made her way in its direction. It was a fine spring day and she welcomed the warm sun and chilly breeze as she walked along the river, admiring the flower petals of nearby trees that had fallen into the water.

A cold breeze blew, bringing with it the unsettling feeling that she was being watched. She froze a moment as a prickling sensation raised the hair on the back of her neck and she instinctively reached for the adder stone. Her heart pounded as she slowly scanned the street around her. Men and women of different classes moved about the street, going about their business, but no one was looking in her direction.

She shook her head and frowned as she continued, berating herself for being so ridiculous. She entered the tavern and looked around, not seeing Richard.

"There is a table over here, miss," a young woman said with a smile. She wiped her hands on her apron and gestured toward a seat by the front window.

Agrippina nodded and took the seat offered to her. She stared out the window for a brief moment before she pulled out her notebook and began flipping through her notes.

She was beginning to forget everything about her when she again felt the sensation she was being watched. She looked up from her notebook and out the window. Across the street stood a young man, his dark locks blowing gently in the breeze.

Agrippina tilted her head to try and see if there was anyone out front the man could be looking at, but every time she glanced over at him, she swore he was staring at her through the window.

"What are you looking at so intensely?"

Agrippina almost jumped at the sound of Richard's voice. "Do you see that man across the street?"

Richard sat across from her and followed her line of vision. "Yes."

"Does it appear he is staring at me?"

Richard laughed. "I did not think you the vain type, Miss Greystone."

She frowned and shook her head. "I am being serious. Ever since I stepped foot out of the tea shop, I have felt as if everyone is watching me."

He shrugged. "It is not a very big town. Most people know each other. You are a new, pretty face amongst the old pretty faces. People are bound to stare."

"And that man across the street?"

He shook his head. "Maybe he saw you sashay your way in and is waiting to see you sashay your way out." He smirked and lifted a teasing brow at her.

"Hm." She turned her gaze onto him. "Where did you go, by the way? You left me in quite a hurry."

Richard looked a little ashamed. "I went to the butcher shop to put in an order of meat for the Rupert family."

She smiled. "I am proud of you, Mr. Maddox." She cast another glance in the man's direction, but he was gone.

"Yes, well, I have my moments, I suppose," he replied, shrugging her compliment off. "Let's order something. I am famished."

# 16

THEY ARRIVED BACK AT BOLTEN HOUSE FOR A LATE TEA. Agrippina declined respectfully.

"Thank you, Mrs. Bolten. I have a few letters I wish to write. However, if you could have Mr. Arter bring me your gardener, I would appreciate it."

Mrs. Bolten blinked as she cleared her throat in confusion. "The gardener?"

Agrippina nodded. "I have been told he worked on both the Brown and Rupert farms before both incidents. I believe his name is Alexander Mosley. I have a few questions for him."

"Ah." Mrs. Bolten nodded. "Yes, I will let Mr. Arter know you are looking for him."

Agrippina bobbed her head and excused herself to her room to write a letter to her uncle and Mr. Mackland. James. Her heart fluttered when she allowed herself to think his name.

She pushed open the door to her room to see Janet straightening her things. The maid jumped when she saw Agrippina.

"Oh, miss, you gave me a bit of a fright!" Janet exclaimed.

"I was so wrapped up in what I was doin', I didn't even hear you comin' in."

Agrippina nodded, a burning curiosity arising to ask what she and that young man were talking about earlier that morning.

"I freshened the water in your basin and brought you clean towels."

"Thank you, Janet."

"Any time, miss." Janet hesitated at the door. "Might I ask a question, if you don't think me being rude?"

Agrippina shook her head. "Not at all."

"What is that you're wearing? The stone necklace?"

She let out a small laugh, clutching the stone.

Janet looked a little embarrassed. "I saw it on yer bedside table yesterday, and notice yer wearin' it today."

"This is an adder stone. It is a superstitious relic. People used to believe that it warded off evil. It was also said that if you looked through the hole in the middle, you could see through a witch's disguise."

Janet's eyes grew wide. "Does it work?"

Agrippina shook her head. "I suppose you have to believe in witches to know that."

Janet creased her brows, confused. "You don't believe in witches, miss?"

Agrippina shook her head. "No, not at all."

"Well, how do you explain everythin' that has been happenin' 'round here?"

Agrippina smiled softly. "I cannot explain it yet, but I am not one to jump to conclusions before I have all the necessary information."

Janet shook her head. "But if you don't believe in witches, then why do you have somethin' that protects you from them?"

Agrippina took the adder stone off and examined it a moment. "I did not pack it myself, but believe my uncle packed it for me. Perhaps to get into the mindset needed in order to solve this." She held out the stone to Janet. "Would you like to look at it?" She held it out for Janet to take.

Janet wrung her hands for a moment and tentatively reached out for it, but she stopped before touching it. She shook her head, slowly drawing her hand back. "Your confidence is catching, but I'm not so sure that witches don't exist, miss."

Agrippina looked down at the adder stone. "Perhaps you need this more than I do, then." She offered it to Janet who again shook her head.

"No, miss. *You* need it more. It's the evils we don't know about we need the most protection from." Janet curtseyed. "Good day, miss."

Agrippina watched her leave, considering her words before she remembered why she had come up to her room in the first place. She moved to the writing desk and settled in the chair, pulling out a sheet of paper.

The quill hovered over the page for only a moment before she gathered her thoughts and told her uncle everything that had passed since her last letter. Had it only been since yesterday that she last wrote?

An hour and two full pages later, she was satisfied. She folded the paper and sealed it, scratching on the address when a noise caught her attention. She turned her head slightly to the right hearing the noise again.

Her heart raced as she realized it was coming from *that* corner. The corner where in her dream...

She stood from the desk and looked over at the corner in question. The corner of the room was between the two windows that let in light but was not touched by it, so remained darker than the rest of the room.

She heard the scratching again and moved slowly in its direction. She walked tentatively, each step precise as she came closer. She stopped when she was a few feet away and stared. The scratching noise persisted and a small movement on the ground caught her attention.

She looked down and gasped, taking a step back. There on the ground, scratching at the wall, was a little white mouse. Agrippina looked around her for something to capture it in. Seeing one of her hat boxes, she emptied its contents and coaxed it inside.

The poor creature scurried around for a few minutes trying to escape. Agrippina took one of her handkerchiefs and made it a small bed. As if recognizing her kindness, the mouse curled up under it and calmed down.

She placed the box on the vanity and placed the lid on top, leaving a small crack so as not to suffocate her new ward. She then rang a servant and asked for a small dish and vegetable scraps from the kitchen. The maid appeared confused by her request but did not question her as she scurried away.

Once the maid returned, Agrippina placed the scraps in the box with the small dish filled with water and made a small clicking noise.

"Are you hungry?" she asked the mouse as the handkerchief began to move.

The mouse's pink little nose popped out from underneath it, smelling the food.

"Come on out and eat," Agrippina cooed. "I will not hurt you."

The mouse emerged, cautiously moving toward the food. After smelling it out a little more, it grabbed a piece of potato skin and began chewing.

Agrippina smiled down at it. "There you are, friend. Eat to your little heart's content."

Realizing how late in the day it was, she decided to write James another day. She put the lid back on the box and, taking her letter to her uncle, made her way downstairs. She placed her letter on the tray and entered the parlor.

"Oh, you must be Miss Greystone!" said a young lady with a bright smile and pale, sheen hair. "You certainly are very pretty. Richard did not exaggerate on that point. Though, when he is speaking of pretty women, he rarely does."

Agrippina was so taken aback by the barrage of words being thrown at her that it took her several seconds to realize who this young lady was. "You are Miss Maddox?" she asked slowly. "Richard's younger sister?"

Miss Maddox giggled. "Oh, dear me! I was so excited to finally see you that I completely forgot to introduce myself. It is so nice to have company, you see. Rarely anyone comes to visit us here at dreary old Bolten House. Though I do love it myself."

Agrippina nodded. "Yes, the grounds are very pretty here."

"Yes, yes! Almost as pretty as you! What a beautiful complexion you have. I had hoped by the way Richard spoke of you that he had a fancy for you. However, though I can tell he is fond of you—in a friendly way, of course—I do not detect any symptoms of infatuation. Only respect."

Miss Maddox spoke so quickly and without pause, Agrippina barely took notice of how direct she was. "Thank you," she replied slowly, unsure of what else to say.

"Oh, he also says you are very intelligent, far more than he is. His words, not mine," she continued. "A woman scholar. Just think! I would have liked to have continued my education, but it is not necessary for a woman of my class, or your class, or for any class of woman really."

"I am not a scholar," Agrippina finally cut in. "Though I help the professors with their assignments, I am not officially affiliated with Cambridge."

"That is a shame. Richard said you would make a great professor, or even doctor. I know that is what your uncle is. Richard holds you both in such high regard."

"Cecelia! Good Lord! You shall talk poor Miss Greystone to death!" Richard laughed as he walked through the door.

"I cannot help it, Rick. You know how much I love company. Especially company of my age and sex. It would be so nice to have a sister, you know."

Richard chuckled. "Do not count on it being Miss Greystone. She has her eye set on someone else."

Agrippina blushed, shooting a glare at Richard who smirked.

"Do you have a beau?" Cecelia asked, her excitement rising. She clapped her hands together. "We can talk about our respective ones together. I am engaged, you know, to Henry Randolph. He is the sweetest man and very handsome."

Agrippina gaped at Cecelia's openness.

Richard laughed again. "You are out of luck, I am afraid. Miss Greystone is civil and accommodating, but she is not as open about such things as you are, Cece."

His sister pouted for a moment before shrugging. "That is all well. I cannot expect everyone to talk as I do. I am a little excitable if you could not tell."

Richard kissed his sister on the forehead. "It is good to have you back, Cece," he told her. "It has been a little too quiet as of late."

She giggled again before a serious expression crossed her face. "How has uncle been?"

Richard let out a puff of air, shaking his head. "He might

be worse."

Cecelia looked grim. "I was hoping that was not case. I feel so guilty leaving him these past few weeks, enjoying myself while he withers himself away." She sighed. "That damned family curse!" She blushed and pressed a hand to her mouth. "Forgive me, Miss Greystone! It is very unlady-like of me to use such course language."

Agrippina shook her head. "I am not bothered by it."

Cecelia brightened at this. "We shall get along just fine then, I think."

A servant came in bowing, holding a tray with a parcel on it.

"For Miss Greystone," he said holding the tray out to her.

She thanked him and took it, quickly reading the note. "It is from Dr. Hansby."

"Dr. Hansby?" Cecelia repeated, confused. "What could he be sending you?"

*I give you these two journals knowing you will respect the privacy of the individuals involved. I apologize I could not deliver them myself, but I hope to discuss what you think when you are done.*

*Dr. H*

She opened the parcel and pulled out two journals and a sealed letter from Dr. Hansby labeled "For your eyes only." She quickly tucked the letter into her pocket before the other two noticed.

"Are these his notes on the deaths of Fred Carver and Anna Brown?" Richard asked, reaching out to touch one of the journals.

Agrippina pulled the journals away from him. "I apologize, but Dr. Hansby asks that I not divulge any of the information within these. He has allowed me to go through them and entrusted me with not only his reputation but also the reputation of those involved."

Richard lifted a brow but relented. "I am not happy with his decision, but I guess I shall respect it."

"Oh, good Lord!" Cecelia said softly. "If that is the case, I better not look at them. I cannot be trusted not to tell anyone about it."

"I appreciate your understanding," Agrippina replied. "Do you think I could use the library to go through all of these?"

Richard nodded. "Do you need help finding it?"

She shook her head. "I know where it is." She curtseyed curtly and whipped out of the room, the journals tightly in her grasp.

When she was safe in the library, she shut the door and sat at the window seat to use the dying light of the sun to help her read. First, she pulled out the letter from Dr. Hansby, tearing open the seal to read its contents.

*Miss Greystone,*

*After our conversation last evening, I could not help but revisit my notes and my opinion. Though your theory on Miss Brown having left in the middle of the night to meet her secret lover is compelling in making me believe there is a possibility of foul play, I could not discern from my notes whether there was.*

However, I am not so prideful to think I could have overlooked something or misinterpreted a clue. I await a note from you with your own opinion.

Dr. H

P.S. I have marked my entries accordingly. I ask you stay on the case notes you requested and not let your eyes wander.

Agrippina felt a pang of disappointment. She was hoping his note would have held a little more substance. She shook off that feeling and opened the first journal to where it was marked. It was his notes for Anna Brown. She skimmed through them looking for anything the doctor did not tell her in person.

Ms. Brown, having been caught by a fallen tree in the river, was covered in scrapes and bruises, most likely postmortem. Unsurprisingly, there was debris in her hair and her dress was slightly tattered from the abuse it sustained while in the river.

Her poor body endured the water and elements for at least four days; her skin a sickly grayish purple. There were a few questionable marks about her, but her flesh had

116

*been scavenged upon by crows and possibly a few fish that it was difficult to discern what caused some of her injuries.*

*There is what appears to be a small laceration on the side of her left temple. The wound is not deep and could have occurred from a fall premortem. Though this could have dazed her, I doubt the wound serious enough to have killed her or even knock her unconscious. A fall? Was she struck?*

*Her neck appeared to be bruised, but as her head was stuck between some of the branches of the tree, and her flesh was beginning to peel away from the bone, I could not say for certain what had caused the discoloration.*

Agrippina skimmed through the notes, not finding anything of significance until Dr. Hansby mentioned her belly.

*What at first I thought was a build up of gases caused by the process of decay causing the belly to swell, was, in fact, evidence of the early stages of a pregnancy...Miss Brown was with child. She was not far along, I can imagine, the fetus being very small, no larger than my index finger, but indeed, she was with child.*

Agrippina tapped her finger against her leg as she thought, continuing to read his notes, but when she was done, she found there was nothing of significance in them. Nothing told her how Anna Brown died.

*...lungs clear of water...*

*...other than the laceration to her head, no obvious injuries to her person given the condition of her body...*

*...no signs of a struggle or violence...body too badly decomposed and waterlogged to truly tell cause of death.*

She sighed, staring down into the book, hoping to find something she had missed before, but nothing came to her.

Could it be possible that she died elsewhere and was dumped?

Could it be possible she snuck out of her house, made it to the river, died, and then fell in?

Agrippina shook her head at these theories. She couldn't know for sure without obtaining more information. But who could she talk to that might know more? She closed the notebook, having gained everything she could have from it and picked up the other one that contained the notes from the silk merchant Fred Carver's exam.

*Mr. Carver was a portly man in his fifties.*

*He had a history of gout and a family his-
tory of early deaths due to 'angina pectoris'.
His own father was said to have died with
a hand clutched to his chest.*

*As I do not see anything else to suggest
otherwise, it is my opinion that Mr. Carver,
having found his means of income destroyed
by moths, a sudden burst of fury caused his
heart to give out. His look of surprise and
fear closely matches others who have died
from the same cause.*

The rest of Dr. Hansby's observations of Mr. Carver's body noted no signs of bruising or other injuries to Mr. Carver's person. His death was just an unfortunate circumstance mixed with a possible, preexisting heart condition.

The moths, however, appeared to be of great interest to Dr. Hansby. He recognized them as regular cloth moths and found it strange that a man traveling with fabric to sell would not have carried them in a cedar trunk.

*Surely he must have known cedar would
have repelled the pests. Instead, the trunk
in his possession appeared to have been made
from regular oak.*

Agrippina questioned the carelessness of the merchant as well. Why would he not have traveled with a cedar chest?

She would have to ask Richard to make an inquiry to the warehouse on her behalf.

She sighed and closed the notebook. What could all of this have to do with one another? Were they even related? Whatever happened with Anna Brown and Maven Rupert, there was no doubt in her mind they were connected, but the incident with the silk merchant could be purely coincidental.

The door to the library opened, startling Agrippina. She gasped as she turned to see who had entered. Mr. Bolten, pale and sunken, seemed to be just as surprised to find her there.

"Mr. Bolten," she said, standing to curtsey.

A few, silent seconds passed until recognition flashed through his eyes. "Ah, you are Richard's friend he brought to help with our," he cleared his throat, "situation."

She nodded. "Agrippina Greystone, sir."

His head, which almost appeared too big for his frame, bobbed. "Yes, yes." He waved his hand in a downward motion. "Please, sit."

She dutifully sat back in the window seat. "How are you feeling today?"

He sized her up a moment before venturing further into the library, one arm behind his back as he walked. He moved over to a table and ran his right hand along its surface. "I am feeling better than I did yesterday. I had quite the fall. I apologize if I frightened you."

She shook her head, a little perplexed. "Not at all. The whole scene caused great confusion, but I am not easily frightened."

He smiled at her. "How fortunate."

The smooth tone in his voice caused her to blush uncomfortably. "Would you—would you be open to answering a few questions? I have been here for over two days and have not had the chance to talk to you about what you have experienced."

His expression fell and he turned from her for a moment, sighing. "It would be a waste if you did not talk to me, would it not?" He walked to a table where an empty decanter sat. He cursed lightly before ringing the service bell. "I swear the servants are drinking my port. I cannot seem to keep it anywhere in the house."

Mr. Arter came into the library a few minutes later, bowing. "Sir?" His eyes darkened when he saw Agrippina.

"Bring Miss Greystone and myself a couple of glasses of port, would you?" Mr. Bolten ordered. "And fill this decanter."

"Oh, none for me, I thank you," Agrippina quickly said. "I do not drink."

Both men looked at her with raised brows.

"You do not drink?" Mr. Bolten asked. "You must have port every so often. It is good for one's health."

She shook her head. "I especially do not drink port and the last time I had whiskey, it was laced with a sedative. I will have water, if you please, Mr. Arter."

The butler bowed deeply and hurried out of the room.

"Laced with a sedative?" Mr. Bolten's lip curled into an intrigued smile. "There is obviously a story behind that."

She shrugged. "I was getting too close to catching the killer of those poor girls in Blindburn."

He nodded as he came closer, stopping at the table. "Tell me about the killer," he said, leaning back against the table, his arms crossed over his chest.

"I would rather talk about the young girls who lost their lives. The killer should be forgotten; the victims should not."

He chuckled. "You seem a very interesting young woman, Miss Greystone, with very strong opinions." He shifted his stance so he was leaning toward her. "I admire that." He took a deep breath and pushed off the table, walking to one of the shelves.

"I would like to ask you about your family curse," Agrippina said, watching him search for a book. "Your wife gave me the backstory; however, I would like your take on it as well."

"If my wife informed you of it, then there is not much else to tell." He pulled out a book and held it in the air. "Ah, this is what I was looking for."

"Well, what makes you fear the curse? Or what makes you believe in it so much?"

He handed her the book he pulled from the shelf. "This will tell you more than enough."

Agrippina frowned, confused, but took the proffered book. "The Bolten family Bible?"

He gestured with his hand to open it as he pulled a chair out from the table and sat. "The book begins with my several-times great-grandfather Geoffrey Bolten, born 1542, died 1587, age of forty-five. Frederick Bolten, son of Geoffrey Bolten, born 1565, died 1610, at the age of forty-five. His other two children were daughters and married off so their deaths were not recorded."

Agrippina read as he talked, running her finger down the list of names.

"Geoffrey Bolten, son of Frederick Bolten, born 1591, died 1636 at the age of forty-five." He made a turning motion with his hand. "There are several more deaths, some before the age of forty-five, but never after the age of forty-five. If you look toward the end, a few pages over, you will see the births and deaths of the last few generations."

Agrippina turned the page and found the last several entries.

"Jonathan Bolten, my grandfather, born 1694, died 1739

at the age of forty-five. Henry Bolten, my father, born 1719, died 1764 at the age of forty-five." He took a deep breath and lowered his gaze to his lap. "My brother fought in the American rebellion and died at twenty-one. My sister, Richard's mother, died at thirty-seven of a fever." he cleared his throat. "And I, the first son, was born in 1748. I will be forty-five next month."

Agrippina looked up from the book.

"There is not a death recorded in that book where the person made it past the age of forty-five, Miss Greystone." He shook his head. "Over two hundred years of my family's births and deaths are in that book, and not one of them made it past the age of forty-five." He looked at her intensely. "How could one not believe in some curse?"

She was saved from answering this question by the entrance of the Butler with their drinks. Mr. Bolten took his, taking a long sip before raising the glass in her direction.

"Some things cannot be explained, Miss Greystone. Some things just are."

She looked back down at the book and sighed, not having anything to add.

"Will that be all, sir?" Mr. Arter asked, hovering in the room.

Mr. Bolten looked over at him, surprised. "Are you still in here, Arter?"

Mr. Arter bowed. "I am just making sure you have everything you need, sir."

"You are dismissed," Mr. Bolten replied taking a sip of his port.

"Very good, sir." Mr. Arter cast a lingering glance in Agrippina's direction before he left the room.

"So, you believe you are seeing this woman in black, Agnes Steadman?" Agrippina asked.

Mr. Bolten took another sip and shook his head planting his left hand into his pocket. "I do not wish to talk about this right now. I am sure you must be tired of hearing about it."

Agrippina shook her head. "No, you are mistaken. I wish to hear more about it. In order for me to solve what has been going on, I need to know everything there is to know about it."

Mr. Bolten sucked on his teeth and nodded. "Yes, I do believe this woman in black to be Agnes Steadman, the woman who cursed my family."

Agrippina shook her head. "And you believe her to be haunting you because your ancestor over two hundred years ago falsely accused her of being a witch for which she was hung?"

Mr. Bolten swirled the glass in his hand and tilted his head side to side. "When you put it like that, it does sound a bit ridiculous, does it not?"

"If her revenge was based on this accusation and her spirit is restless because of it, why not have her posthumously exonerated? Publicly denounce Geoffrey Bolten's actions and claim you have evidence she was falsely accused."

Mr. Bolten blinked at her, his glass hovering a few inches from his lips for a moment until he gently put it back on the table. "Your solution sounds so simple and yet obvious." He turned the glass a few times as he considered what she said. "Do you think that could work?"

She half shrugged, half shook her head. "To be honest? No."

Mr. Bolten chuckled and rubbed his forehead. "I guess a witch's curse takes more than a clearing of her name."

"But she was not a witch," Agrippina reminded him. "That is the problem."

"Did she not become a witch once she cursed my

ancestor?" he suggested. "Perhaps her anger was so strong that, after she died, she was able to sell her soul to the devil for the power to haunt my family."

Agrippina closed the Bolten family Bible and placed it on the table. "I would say that is less likely than any other theory I could come up with."

Mr. Bolten sighed and placed a gentle hand on hers.

Agrippina stiffened at the sudden touch.

"Miss Greystone," Mr. Bolten said with a sigh. "I am scared."

She slowly pulled her hand from under his and took a step back. "I can appreciate that, Mr. Bolten. I am trying my best to figure out this mystery."

He nodded, rubbing his hand across his mouth. "I wish there was more I could tell you to help."

Agrippina thought for a moment. "Do you know anyone with the initials CPM?"

He looked at her, slightly confused as he shook his head. "Cecelia, my niece, is the only one who comes to mind. Why?"

"No matter," Agrippina replied. She turned to the window seat and picked up Dr. Hansby's journals when movement caught her eye. She raised her head just as Mr. Bolten let out a guttural yell.

"She's back! She's back!"

Outside the window, in the last light of the sun was the woman in black walking slowly toward them. Mr. Bolten stood beside Agrippina, his breathing short and panicked, his eyes wide and body quaking. The woman stopped several feet away, her face obscured by a veil.

Agrippina, though terrified, leaned in closer to the window trying to see if she could discern any detail about her, but it was too dark, and she was just far enough away.

She moved to open the window when Mr. Bolten put a

hand on her shoulder, pulling her back a little.

"What are you doing?" he asked, his voice stricken, and his eyes dilated with terror.

"I am trying to see who it is," she replied. She reached for the window again, but Mr. Bolten gripped her tightly.

"You cannot let her in! She is coming for me!"

"Mr. Bolten, you are hurting me!" Agrippina cried.

The woman in black swayed almost imperceptibly from side to side, slowly raising a hand, something clutched in her fingers. Mr. Bolten stumbled backward shielding his face.

"Phillip!" came a raspy voice as the woman in black swayed closer.

"No! No!" he cried letting go of Agrippina. He began swatting at something Agrippina couldn't see. His eyes were so dilated, you could barely see the iris.

She gasped when she saw him, his ghastly eyes, and clammy skin more terrifying than the woman outside.

"Phillip!" the woman in black called out again, holding out what she had in her hand. "Your sins!"

"Get her away!" he screamed.

"She is not in here, Mr. Bolten! There is nothing attacking you," Agrippina tried to tell him.

She threw another glance in the woman in black's direction just as she raised her hands toward the sky and screamed. Terror prickled Agrippina's skin as she heard her high-pitched wail. Even muffled by the window, she could hear the woman's anger and pain reflected in that sound.

"Make her stop!" Mr. Bolten cried out as he fell to his knees. "I am sorry! I am sorry for what my ancestor did to you! It is not my fault!"

"Steel yourself, Mr. Bolten!" Agrippina looped her arm under Mr. Bolten's and tried to get him to stand, but he pushed her away and fell to his face.

"Lord, I beg you! Forgive Geoffrey Bolten for his sins against Agnes! Forgive him, forgive me!"

Agrippina looked back out the window, but the woman in black was no longer there. She pressed her forehead against the glass and peered left and right to see if she could see anyone making their escape, but there was nothing but the darkness she left behind.

# 17

A DELIRIOUS MR. BOLTEN WAS TAKEN UP TO HIS ROOM. Agrippina watched as Richard helped him walk while he flinched and continued to swat at something only he could see.

"She's coming for me!" Mr. Bolten yelled as Richard carefully led him up the stairs. "She has come to kill me, the last of the Boltens. The curse! The curse!"

"What happened?" Cecelia asked quietly, pressing a hand to her chest as she watched the terrible scene.

Agrippina cleared her throat. "The woman in black. We saw her outside the library window." She moved to the service bell and rang it. "We must gather a search party and look for her!"

Cecelia gasped. "You *saw* her?" She gaped at Agrippina. "What did she do? Did she cast some spell on my uncle? What happened? Why is he acting like this?"

She shook her head. "I can go over all that later, but right now, we must try and find her!"

"You will not find her," Cecelia said in a low voice. "She always vanishes before we can."

"Does your uncle not keep tracking dogs? Does he not have hounds for hunting?"

She shook her head. "It never really interested him. He said too many things could go wrong hunting. He never wanted to tempt fate."

"So, we are just going to let whoever is trespassing on your uncle's property go?"

Cecelia let out a little laugh. "Well, you cannot catch a ghost, can you?"

Agrippina regarded Cecelia for a moment, considering her comment. "No," she finally replied slowly. "No, I suppose you cannot catch a ghost."

There was a brief silence as they stood at the bottom of the stairs.

"So, she did cast a spell on him?" Cecelia asked shaking her head lightly. "When will this stop?"

Agrippina sighed. "I am going to venture to say that it will stop when I find who is responsible." She paused. "Or until whoever is doing this gets what they want."

"Which is?"

"The death of your uncle."

Cecelia seemed stunned and took a step back. "But who would want to hurt my uncle?"

Agrippina looked over at her. "How well do you know your uncle? Perhaps you can tell me." She glanced around her. "Where is your aunt, by the way?"

Cecelia stammered for a moment, shaking her head. "Uh, she is—I am not sure. She went out for a ride on her horse after tea, but I have not seen her come back."

As if on cue, Mrs. Bolten was at the top of the stairs, fidgeting with her hair. "What has happened?" she asked as she descended. "I saw Richard taking Eugene to his room. He seemed to be raving about the woman in black again."

"Aunt Lucy!" Cecelia seemed relieved, taking her aunt's hand as she reached the bottom of the stairs. "I thought you might have fallen off your horse. It was getting so late, and I had not seen you return from your ride."

Mrs. Bolten nodded slowly. "Oh, yes, well, I did not announce myself when I returned. I went straight up to my room to change."

Cecelia let out a sigh. "I was worried we would have to send out a search party. You know I worry. First uncle, then you? I am not sure what I would do with myself."

"Hush, child. I am well." She looked at Agrippina. "What happened to my husband? Do you know?"

"We were talking in the library when we saw the woman in black outside."

"'We?' Are you telling me that you saw the woman in black too?" Mrs. Bolten asked.

"Yes, she did!" Cecelia cut in. "She even suggested gathering a hunting party to search for her."

"Why would we not?" Mrs. Bolten replied. "If someone is on my property without permission, I want them found and prosecuted."

Mr. Arter came from around the corner, his face a little red. "Did someone ring, ma'am?"

"Mr. Arter! Tell all of the men to search the grounds. There is a trespasser!" Mrs. Bolten ordered.

He nodded. "I have just come from the back, ma'am, with Alex, when we heard the commotion about Mr. Bolten. We have found no one."

"No tracks, or footprints, or anything?" Mrs. Bolten queried a little angrily.

"It was a bit dark, ma'am, and in the fuss, I failed to grab a lantern." He reached into his pocket and pulled something out. "Alex, however, did find this." He handed something to

Mrs. Bolten.

She put her free hand to her mouth as she looked down at the object. After a moment, she closed her eyes and shook her head, balling her fist up and pressing the object to her heart. "How is this possible?"

Agrippina watched Mrs. Bolten's reaction, thinking what she received must have been whatever the woman in black had been holding in her hand.

"What is it, Aunt Lucy?" Cecelia asked, placing a gentle hand on her aunt's arm.

Her aunt shook her head again, unwilling to let go of what Mr. Arter had given her. "It cannot be possible."

Mr. Arter bowed his head. "I know it, ma'am."

Mrs. Bolten's lip trembled. "How?" She looked at Mr. Arter. "Did you check to see if his grave had been disturbed? Did you!?"

Everyone flinched at Mrs. Bolten's outburst.

Mr. Arter shook his head. "No, ma'am. I was going to check in the morning when there was light to better see."

Tears began to run down Mrs. Bolten's face, and a small sob escaped her throat.

"Might I see what it is, Mrs. Bolten?" Agrippina asked calmly, holding out her hand.

She shook her head. "No! It is mine!"

"Oh, Aunt Lucy, you are so pale! Mr. Arter, fetch her a glass of wine." Cecelia looped an arm through her aunt's and gently guided her to the parlor where she could sit. She coaxed her aunt to a chair, and gently stroked her hair. "It will be alright. Do let us see what Mr. Arter has found."

Cecelia tenderly took her aunt's hand and pried it away from her chest. Mrs. Bolten unfolded her hand, revealing a small, tarnished silver spoon. Cecelia picked it up and examined it.

"I do not understand," she innocently said. "It is a baby spoon. Whose is it?"

"Your cousin's, I assume," Agrippina answered when Mrs. Bolten could not.

The confusion only deepened. "But I do not have any Bolten cousins."

"It was fifteen years ago. You were only four when he was born," Mrs. Bolten said in a voice just above a whisper. "You would not remember him." Her lips trembled again, but she kept her composure. "He was my longest and last pregnancy. We thought he would make it where all the others had ended in miscarriage after miscarriage." A smile fluttered across her face as tears flooded her eyes again. "I thought I was finally going to be a mother." She shook her head, freeing a few tears. "But he was born too soon."

She reached out and gently took the spoon back from her niece.

"He only lived for a day, a small moment of my life that has never left me. He breathed his first and his last in my arms." She pressed a hand to her mouth to suppress another sob. "My poor Phillip. That is what I named him. Phillip Henry. He was so small, yet so perfect."

Agrippina's skin prickled at the sound of the child's name. Phillip. It was what the woman in black had been saying.

"Oh, Aunt Lucy! I had no idea!" Cecelia embraced her aunt who crumpled and sobbed.

"I had bought that spoon not long after I felt him moving inside me," Mrs. Bolten said regaining her composure. "I had been so sure he would make it."

"But why would the woman in black have the spoon?" Agrippina asked gently. "Where was it?"

Mrs. Bolten sniffed. "I had it buried with him."

132

# 18

AGRIPPINA WOKE EARLY AND MADE SURE HER LITTLE MOUSE was fed before meeting the butler downstairs. Mr. Arter was impatiently tapping his foot on the floor by the time she arrived. They shot each other less than welcoming glances.

"Good morning, Miss Greystone," he said in a terse tone.

"Good morning, Mr. Arter. I appreciate you waiting for me."

He nodded curtly before opening the front door for her and briskly following her out. The early spring morning was crisp with a slight chill to the air, but it cleared Agrippina's mind from the oppressive atmosphere she felt inside the house.

"How long have you been working for the Bolten family, Mr. Arter?" she asked as they walked to the eastern part of the property toward a little knoll a quarter of a mile away.

"I obtained my position when Mrs. Bolten married Mr. Bolten."

She glanced over at him. "You worked for Mrs. Bolten's family before she married?"

Another curt nod. "She was Miss Lowry back then and I

was only a footman."

Agrippina thought for a moment. "So you have known Mrs. Bolten for..."

"Thirty years. I have been butler here for twenty."

"And what do you think of the family curse?"

He shot her a cold look. "It's hard to say. It is easy to say something is going on, but whether it has anything to do with a witch or her ghost, I am not the one to tell you."

"Do you believe in witches or ghosts?"

He cleared his throat. "I was rather skeptical beforehand, but I have more of an open mind given recent events."

Agrippina thought for a few moments. "Do you know anyone who might want to hurt Mr. Bolten?"

He glanced at her sideways but did not immediately answer.

"He seems to be the target for all of this. His farms, his silk, his house. Is it not obvious someone has it out for him?"

"Nothing is obvious, miss. If you live long enough to understand that."

His words sounded ominous, but his tone wasn't threatening.

"You still have not answered my question." she pressed. "Do you know anyone who might want to hurt Mr. Bolten? Someone who would benefit from his death, and knows intimate knowledge about the Bolten Family curse?"

"That was more like three questions, miss."

"Well?"

"If you take wanting to hurt Mr. Bolten out, then the main person who fits the rest of those questions is Master Richard, but all of this started while he was away. He was gone for a good portion of it actually."

"Richard is quite far from being on my suspect list," Agrippina told him. "He is a good man and holds himself intelligently, but he lacks cunning. Even with all his charm and good looks, he lacks mystery. And even with his ease of manners and ability to turn anything into a joke, he is wanting in the ability to deceive."

Mr. Arter raised a questioning brow at her. "You seem to understand Master Richard's character quite well."

Agrippina caught his meaning. "It has nothing to do with any sort of attachment between us. I have known Mr. Maddox for a few years now. He is a flirt and a tease, but harmless. And as unlikely as I would have thought this last year, we have become rather good friends."

"The basis of any good romance starts with friendship."

"Are you talking from experience?"

Mr. Arter cleared his throat. "I have been a little remiss to your needs as a guest since you arrived. Has my staff been treating you with respect?"

"I am not blind to your distractions, Mr. Arter," Agrippina told him. "I know you are avoiding answering my questions."

He laughed through his nose. "You are not a silly girl, and it is obvious that you are very intelligent."

"Nor do I not need compliments.."

His expression turned grim. "Mr. Bolten is a complex person, miss," he finally told her. "He has a great mind for business, but," he hesitated, taking in a deep breath and letting it out in a rush of wind, "he is damaged."

Agrippina waited for him to continue when he stopped walking and turned to her, making her halt abruptly.

"There is a curse connected with this family, but it is not what you might think." He rolled his shoulders and straightened his jacket.

For a moment Agrippina thought he was going to say something else, but he just looked at her intensely, his eyes a little sad.

135

As abruptly as he had stopped walking, he resumed on their course. "I know of no one that would want to harm Master Bolten. He has always been respectful in his business dealings and is a dutiful landlord."

"Hm." She let a brief silence hang between them. "And what of Alex Mosely?"

Mr. Arter stiffened for a second. "What of him?"

"He is of the Bolten's employ, is he not?"

He nodded slowly. "He is the gardener, yes."

"I would like to question him about his time working at the Browns' and Ruperts' farms."

Mr. Arter shook his head. "I am afraid he will not be of much help. Poor Alex is very simple minded and upsets easily. He does not do well with strangers."

"I could question him in your presence if that would put him at ease."

"Yes, but I do not think it would do much good. He was not there at either place for very long."

Agrippina, extremely dissatisfied with his answer, opened her mouth to press him further, but he interrupted her.

"I will answer no more questions, Miss Greystone. There is no point in asking what I can only speculate."

She knew he was not being truthful, but understood that if she angered him, she would ruin her chance of being able to ask him at a later time. So, against her better judgment, she let it go.

Finally, they crested the knoll where the family cemetery was located. Over two hundred years, and an unknown number of generations rested before them. Several intricate headstones marked the graves of past family patriarchs, while plain, smaller ones marked those of wives or children.

"It is over here," Mr. Arter directed her, indicating with a nod of his head toward a large willow that hung over some of the stones.

Agrippina followed him, pulling her skirts tighter against her legs so as not to snag them on the closely-lined grave markers. She marveled at how well the cemetery was kept. There was no overgrown vegetation, the grass was neatly trimmed, and not a speck of lichen or moss touched the headstones.

Mr. Arter let out a yell of surprise and pressed a hand to his mouth. "Oh, dear God!" he exclaimed.

"What is it?" Agrippina asked as she came up beside him. Her eyes grew wide, and she let out a small gasp.

There, strewn across the graves of the latest Boltens, was an angel carved in granite that had fallen from the top of its marker. Its cold dead eyes looked up at them, a sullen expression on its weathered face.

Agrippina looked in the direction it had fallen from, but she knew whose grave it was before she could read what was written in stone.

*Geoffrey Bolten.*

# 19

"A FALLEN ANGEL?" RICHARD MUMBLED INTO HIS TEA AND shook his head. "That does not sound like a very good sign."

"Yes, and it appears to have fallen very recently," Agrippina told him.

"How could you tell something like that?" Cecelia asked.

Agrippina turned her attention over to her. "The grass underneath the statue was still green. Had it happened longer ago, the grass would have yellowed."

"Yes, but what of Phillip's grave? Was it—" Mrs. Bolten stopped herself, unable to say it.

"It was undisturbed, ma'am," Mr. Arter told her.

Mrs. Bolten melted into her chair in relief, pressing a hand to her chest.

"Well, if it was undisturbed, then how did the spoon Aunt Lucy had buried with him get out?" Cecelia asked. She looked from one person to the next before settling her gaze on Agrippina.

She cleared her throat. "I have a few possible theories. One, the spoon was removed long enough ago for the grass to grow back. Two, Mrs. Bolten is mistaken and she did not bury the spoon with her child, but locked it away where it was found and taken. Or, three—"

"I was not mistaken!" Mrs. Bolten proclaimed, her face red with anger. "I put that spoon in there myself! Wrapping his tiny little hand around it."

"Aunt Lucy," Richard said calmly, "Miss Greystone is not doubting you per se. She is merely throwing out possibilities. She has to work through all of them to get to the truth."

Mrs. Bolten took a deep breath and bowed her head. "Forgive me. I have been rather upset by all of this."

Agrippina nodded, pushing forward. "Three, it is a replica or identical spoon to the one Mrs. Bolten bought and had buried with her child."

Richard held his hands out, palms up. "Those are three very good possibilities."

"Not the second one," Mrs. Bolten protested. "The other two theories I can agree with, but the second one is wrong."

"I can attest to that as well," Mr. Arter stepped in. "I witnessed Mrs. Bolten putting the spoon in with her son."

"Understood. I will disregard that theory." Agrippina bowed her head slightly.

"Miss Greystone, come eat, will you?" Richard asked, getting up and pulling out the chair next to his. "I am sure you left too early to do so." She thanked him and took him up on his offer.

Mrs. Bolten stood and sighed. "I am in need of an airing." She smiled weakly. "I think I shall go for a carriage ride."

"Would you like some company, aunt?" Cecelia asked timidly. "You do look rather pale."

Mrs. Bolten held out her hand to her niece. "I would always like your company, dear."

Cecelia smiled and followed her aunt out of the room.

"You may go to the kitchen and eat as well, Mr. Arter,"

Richard told him. "Miss Greystone and I will manage without you."

Mr. Arter bowed and silently pushed his way through the door leading through the kitchen. They both waited until the swinging door stopped before talking.

"What is going on, Miss Greystone?" he asked in a hushed voice. "Do you have any idea yet?"

"There is something I am missing," she told him. "Something I have yet to uncover or someone has yet to tell me." She shook her head. "Somone has it out for your uncle. If I can figure out why, then I might be able to figure out who."

He ran his fingers through his hair and huffed.

She took a sip of tea before continuing. "I do not think this is one person alone doing all of this. Whoever they are, they have help." She creased her brows. "That angel did not just fall, Mr. Maddox. It was broken from its stand and caused to fall. And recently. The grass had just been trimmed perhaps a few days ago. So, between then and now, someone, or multiple someones, chiseled away at it."

"You saw chisel marks?"

She nodded. "It did not fall by magic, or because of some curse, but because human hands caused it to."

He took a deep breath and sighed. "How can I help solve this?"

"First, I need you to write to your uncle's warehouse and ask why the merchant, Fred Carver, would travel with an oak box instead of cedar box."

He nodded. "Easy enough."

"Then, I need you to closely monitor everyone's movements in the house."

He frowned at her. "What do you mean?"

"I mean, take note of who comes and goes. Where they go and where they come from, and who they went there with."

He blinked at her. "You want me to ask all that? It is a little invasive."

She shook her head. "I do not want you to ask. I want you to observe. Even the maids, footmen, gardener."

"Mr. Arter?"

"Especially Mr. Arter."

"Even my aunt and sister?"

She nodded slowly. "Yes, even them."

Richard looked like he wanted to be offended, but he shook it off. He pursed his lips together before nodding. "Alright."

"Thank you."

A servant came in carrying a tray with a little bundle of letters for Agrippina. He bowed as he held the tray out to her and waited for her to take them. She thanked him, her cheeks slightly blushed when she saw how many there were.

Richard lifted his brows in surprise. "You have only been here for a few days, and you already get more mail than I do."

"They are from my uncle," she told him.

He smirked at her. "All of them?"

She shot him a glance as she untied the twine keeping the letters together. The top letter was definitely from her uncle, while the other three were forwarded to her by him from Mr. Mackland. Her cheeks flushed when she saw his hand.

"I doubt your uncle solicits that expression from you." Richard chuckled to himself.

Agrippina narrowed her eyes at him. "Fine, there are a few letters from another person whom I greatly admire. He lives rather far away so we exchange letters frequently. That way, it doesn't take a month without us hearing word from one another."

He scrunched his nose. "Oh, Lord. Miss Greystone, I hate to say it, but that is the most girlish thing I have ever heard you say. I am half proud, half nauseated."

Agrippina laughed lightly.

"Well," he began, pushing back from the table and standing. "I shall leave you to your letters. I have been ordered to write one of my own." He bowed before leaving the room.

Agrippina gently fingered the seal on one of Mr. Mackland's letters, but decided to read his last. She put them down on the table beside her and opened the one from her uncle.

*Hello, my dear!*

*I already miss our nightly games of backgammon. Professor Hartley voiced his own disappointment at your going away, but we are not the only ones missing your company and provoking conversation. I am sending several of his letters along with my own.*

*I know I shall soon receive a letter from you voicing your frustrations on this new case. You are brilliant, however, and do not need me to work through them. Do remember to keep an open mind. I am not saying start believing in witches, but I hope you will see that the solution to your problems might not always be so obvious.*

*I know by now you have found the adder stone. I had to laugh when I found it the other day and could not resist putting it among your things. It was given to you once by someone who wished you safe, and is given again in the same hopes.*

*Be vigilant, and open-minded. If a door will not open, sometimes you must break through a wall.*

*Take care my dear.*

*Uncle A*

Agrippina smiled at her uncle's letter. He was always making up his own phrases to help through something she didn't quite understand. He must have known she needed one.

She then took one of Mr. Mackland's letters and opened it.

*Miss Greystone,*

*I have never been a more faithful correspondent than when I began writing to you. I was awful when I was abroad, sending a letter to my family every other month if they were lucky.*

*Karen was better at it than I was. She used to send me letters at least twice a month and update me on everything in Blindburn whether it was just how many days we had gone without rain—which is never too many—or if there was some juicy new gossip being spread around town.*

*I miss her. I had just begun to know my sister again when she was so terribly taken from me. I swear sometimes I feel her presence or hear her tinkering away on her piano. I know you will explain it away as my grief playing upon my imagination, but I like to think she comes to check on me every now and then. To make sure I am not withering away.*

*Do not feel sorry for me though. Even if I am all alone in this house with just my dogs for company, I never really feel alone. Not when I can write to you. My words might take weeks to get to you, but just knowing they are on the way is a relief, and I anxiously wait every morning for a letter from you.*

*I am always thinking of you. I hope you know that.*

*—JM*

Agrippina released a breath she didn't realize she was holding as she read and reread the last line. She felt a rush of heat spread over her cheeks and she looked away from the letter as if Mr. Mackland himself were seeing her through it.

Getting her mild embarrassment under control, she reached for another letter. As she broke its seal, however, someone pushed through the kitchen door interrupting her. She glanced up from the letter and gasped, shocked.

There, coming through the kitchen door was the young man from town. The one who had been staring at her from across the street.

"You!" she yelled in surprise, pushing away from the table. "What are you doing here?"

The young man seemed startled and stumbled backward.

"Who are you?" Agrippina asked moving toward him.

He turned and pushed his way back into the kitchen, the sound of crashing dishes and shouting erupting as he disappeared inside. Agrippina followed him, pushing through the door.

"Stop!" she called out, seeing the man tripping his way out the back door of the kitchen to the outside. She groaned as she zagged her way to the door, kitchen staff casting confused looks.

She huffed when she made it outside, looking left and then right to see if she could tell where he had run to. She chose to go right and ran through the herb garden. As she turned the next corner of the house, she caught sight of him running toward the cherry trees.

"For heaven's sake! Stop running!" Agrippina yelled as she hitched up her dress and continued to give chase. She came to one of the trees and braced herself, trying desperately to catch her breath. Her daily walks around Cambridge were certainly not enough to condition her for this.

She peeked around the tree at the same time the man did further down the row. He let out a yelp as he ducked back.

"Why are you running?" she called out.

"Why are ye chasin' me?" he yelled back.

"Chasing you?" She huffed. "I chased you because you ran!"

He poked his head back out from behind the tree. "No! I ran because ye chased me!" He pointed his finger at her for emphasis.

"What? What did you suppose I would do if I caught you?" she asked, holding out a hand indicating him. "You have at least two stone on me! Did you think I was going to attack you?"

"What are you doing?"

Agrippina gasped and whipped around to see a disapproving Mr. Arter.

"Alex!" he yelled down the row of trees. "Get over here now!"

There was a brief pause, but the young man eventually peeled himself away from his tree and trudged in front of Mr. Arter, his head bowed. Even in this stance, the young man towered over the other. Mr. Arter glared at him for a moment before making a clicking sound with his teeth.

"Why am I hearing about a mess in the kitchen that *you* created? The kitchen staff said you looked like a wild man as you tore through the door."

The young man shifted. "I'm sorry, uncle. I thought she were chasin' me."

Mr. Arter glanced from Agrippina and back to his nephew. "Chasing you? You thought Miss Greystone was chasing you? And that scared you enough to run like a wild animal through the kitchen, breaking several dishes and spilling food all over the floor?"

Alex rubbed his mouth and shook his head. "Sorry uncle."

"Sorry does not restore the mess you made," Mr. Arter told him in a cold tone, "but you will." He pointed in the direction of the house. "I do not want to see your face until every inch of the kitchen has been swept, mopped, and sparkles like the stars in the sky on a clear night. Understood?"

Alex bowed. "Yes, uncle."

"Now go!"

Alex ran back toward the house without another word, leaving Agrippina just as confused as when she first saw him walk through the kitchen door into the breakfast parlor. For a moment, she and Mr. Arter stared at each other.

"Your nephew is Alexander Mosley?"

"Yes," Mr. Arter replied blandly.

"I wonder why you failed to mention that. Is he Janet's brother?"

"They're twins."

"Twins?" Agrippina sounded genuinely intrigued. "Boy and girl twins. Interesting. I have never seen a pair of such twins before!"

He cleared his throat clearly not as amused. "What were you doing chasing my nephew?"

Agrippina held up a finger and shook her head. "He is not recollecting the situation correctly. I stood from my seat to confront him because I saw him staring at me yesterday from across the street while Mr. Maddox and I were in town. I was trying to figure out who he was when he ran."

"And then you chased after him?"

She sighed. "I see what you are trying to imply, but is it not suspicious for him to have run in the first place?"

Mr. Arter answered her with a cold glance. "I told you he was simple, did I not?"

"He seems in control enough of his mental faculties to

handle a few questions. Please tell him I would like to talk to him when he is done taking care of the kitchen."

"You will question him when he is free, but I will not have you detaining him from his duties."

Agrippina narrowed her eyes at him. "Why are you so against me talking with him?" She pushed herself off the tree she was still leaning against, walking closer to him. "What do you not want him to tell me? What are you not telling me?"

Mr. Arter glared at her. "I know nothing worth telling you. I am simply doing my duty and serving the Boltens by keeping their household running smoothly. I do not believe in witches or curses except for the ones we make for ourselves."

She met his gaze. "And what curse have you made, Mr. Arter?" she asked as she brushed by him infuriated by his cold, questioning eyes.

She made her way back to the breakfast room for her letters before going to her room and checking on the little mouse. She popped open the lid and was pleased to see it happily eating away at one of the scraps she had supplied for it.

She slowly reached in the box and gently pulled the mouse out, inspecting it. She could tell by how docile *she* was that the mouse had been handled by humans before. But who exactly?

Agrippina gently patted the mouse's little head before placing her back in the box. She observed her running around the perimeter before curling up under the handkerchief and falling asleep.

She replaced the lid and sat at the desk to finish reading her letters. She smiled to herself as she finished Mr. Mackland's letters, her heart fluttering. Recently there had been a change in them. His language was more feeling, slightly poetic even.

Perhaps she was imagining it, but Agrippina rarely imagined or let her imagination run wild. Would it hurt if she did let her imagination run wild? Her uncle was always telling her to use it.

A creaking noise followed by a shuffling sound behind her made her freeze. She slowly turned her head and looked behind her but saw nothing. The hairs on the back of her neck stood, however, and she couldn't help but feel as if she was being watched.

She rose from the desk and walked to the other end of the room, taking slow, careful steps so as not to make a sound. When she got to the wall, she pressed one ear to it. She heard nothing but muffled air and was about to scold herself for being so silly when two loud bangs reverberated from the wall.

Agrippina let out a small yelp as she fell backward onto her rear, her heart racing with fear. She crawled backward a few feet staring at the wall, her eyes wide.

"What was that?" Janet asked as she rushed in. "Miss! Are you alright?" She ran to help Agrippina from the floor, brushing off her skirts when she was standing again.

"Janet," Agrippina began, trying to take a deep breath to calm herself, "where did you come from?"

"The back stairwell," she asked.

"You were not in the room next to mine?"

Janet shook her head. "No, miss."

"You did not just bang on the wall from the other side of the room?"

Janet shook her head again. "No, miss, I swear it. I've come from the servants' back stairs."

Agrippina moved quickly out of her room and into the

hall, throwing open the door to the adjacent bedroom. She moved through the room, throwing open wardrobes and looking under the bed and behind screens before she was satisfied there was no one there.

# 20

AGRIPPINA BECAME PALE WHEN IT SANK IN, AND SHE PRESSED a hand to her forehead.

"Oh, miss! Ya look faint!" Janet gently took her by the arm and guided her to the bed. "Shall I fetch mistress's smelling salts?"

Agrippina swallowed and forced a small smile. "No, thank you, Janet. But, would you mind telling me if you heard it too?"

"It, miss?"

"That banging noise that came from this room."

Janet slowly nodded. "Yes, miss, I heard it when I was comin' up the stairs."

Agrippina closed her eyes for a second, suddenly feeling very tired. She forced another smile, however, and stood. "Thank you very much for your help, Janet. I am feeling much better."

"Oh, do let me get ya a tea, miss," Janet insisted. "You still look rather pale. I would hate for ya to faint all alone up here."

"Tea sounds lovely, but I think I am going to make my

way to the library." Agrippina cleared her throat. "Would you mind accompanying me?"

Janet offered a friendly smile and nodded. "Aye, miss. I was going that way myself."

Agrippina appreciated Janet's small lie as they walked silently down the hall and to the main staircase. Agrippina gripped the railing hard as she descended, needing to feel what was real so she could remind herself what was not.

*Witches and ghosts are a figment of the human imagination. They were only created as a means to explain unexplainable events and/or catastrophes.*

She nodded to herself as she relayed her new motto to herself over and over.

"Please make yourself comfortable, miss," Janet said, opening the door for her. "I shall bring ya your tea shortly."

"Bring two cups, please, Janet."

She curtseyed before scurrying off.

Agrippina moved toward the window and peered out onto the landscape of the backyard. It was rather flat in the back with a patch of woods several yards away. Too far away for the woman in black to have slipped into them without being seen. The grass was also not tall enough to hide in.

She looked to the left and right and noticed a few small bushes she had not seen in the dark of last night. It is possible she could have hid behind one of them. Did she even look away long enough for anyone to run that far without being seen?

"Here ya are, miss," Janet said a few minutes later, carrying a tray. She placed it on the table. "Shall I pour it for ya?"

Agrippina shook her head, leaving the window. "No, thank you." She poured the first cup. "How do you take your tea, Janet?"

"Me, miss?"

"Yes, you. Do you prefer sugar and cream? Just sugar? Just cream? Neither?"

"Oh, I like a little cream, but I am a little heavy on the sugar too. Mistress has scolded me more than once."

Agrippina reached for the sugar dish. "Is that two or three scoops then?"

"Not quite three, I suppose."

Agrippina scooped in the sugar and poured in some cream, giving the cup a good stir before handing it to Janet who looked genuinely surprised.

"Ya made a cup for me?"

"I did not ask you how you took your tea out of general interest, you know?" She pointed to a chair at the table. "Please sit."

Janet's lips twitched into a small smile. "No, of course not. It is just, no one has ever made me tea before. Well, no, that's not entirely true. Uncle Frank used to when I was a little girl, but that was a long time ago."

"Your Uncle Frank is Mr. Arter?" Agrippina asked, pouring her own tea.

"Yes, he raised my brother and me."

"What about your mother?"

Janet shook her head. "My mother died when I was still a baby. My uncle said she never fully recovered from childbirth."

"Your mother was his sister?"

Janet nodded. "Half sister. They've different mothers. Uncle Frank's mother died not long after he was born. I think that's why he took such great care of us. He knew what it was like to grow up without a mother."

"And your father?" Agrippina sipped her tea.

Janet blushed and looked down, shaking her head. "I don't know who my father is. I have tried askin' before, but

152

my uncle says I'm better off not knowin'."

"Your uncle seems to be a harsh but fair man," Agrippina ventured to say. "If that is how he feels, I am sure he has his reasons."

Janet shook her head. "I do not blame him for not tellin' me. I know it's because he's protectin' me." She smiled lightly. "He might seem harsh to other people, but he never raised a hand to me or said a mean word."

"You and Alex are very lucky to have an uncle who cares about you so much."

Janet looked up at the sound of her brother's name. "Yes, well, my brother might feel slightly different. Uncle Frank was always a little harder on him than he was on me. But he was still just and fair. Alex was just more difficult than I was growin' up."

Agrippina nodded as Janet talked, watching her over the rim of her teacup. "Was Alex the man I saw you arguing with yesterday morning?"

Janet colored again. "Ya saw that?"

"I apologize. I just happened to look out the window when I woke up. I did not mean to spy on you."

She shook her head and sighed. "It's me who needs to apologize. I should not have done that outside your window, but I had pulled him from the music room, which is right below yours, and when I saw what he had been doin' and with who, I couldn't believe it. Oh, how shocked I was when I—" She grew crimson, realizing she was saying more than she should. "Forgive me. I've been told to forget it." She took a nervous sip from her cup. "Uncle did say to leave it be."

"I will never mention it if it gives you pain."

Janet sighed in relief. "Thank ya kindly, Miss Greystone." She took one last sip of her tea before placing it back on the tray and standing. "I should get goin'. I've still work to do." She curtseyed. "Thanks for the tea."

Agrippina smiled and nodded. "Thank you for keeping me company, Janet."

"Good day, miss."

Agrippina took one last sip of her tea before getting up and walking through the aisles of books. She was hoping the calming presence of the books would help her shake the residual uneasiness she felt after the incident upstairs. She trailed a finger along their spines as she took in the scent of musty paper and their leather bindings.

Most of the books were historical, business, or farmers' almanacs, with a small section of novels and poetry. She turned the corner of one aisle and began her way discovering it when a book fell from a shelf in front of her with a loud 'thud.'

Agrippina froze, staring at the book on the floor. She took in a ragged breath, rolling her shoulders to give herself courage to move forward.

"Witches and ghosts are a figment of the human imagination. They were only created as a means to explain unexplainable events and/or catastrophes." She took a step forward. "Witches and ghosts are a figment of the human imagination. They were only created as a means to explain unexplainable events and/or catastrophes." She took a deep breath and took a few more steps. "Witches and ghosts are a figment of the human imagination. They were only created as a means to explain unexplainable events and/or catastrophes."

She stepped forward, pausing in front of the book. She inspected the shelf that it fell from, gently tapping on it to make sure it wasn't loose. From the empty spot where the book was placed, she could see to the other side of the shelf where she had already been.

Perhaps the book was recently used and not pushed back in all the way. Therefore, all the vibrations Agrippina caused while walking down both aisles caused it to fall.

She nodded, half satisfied with her answer, but somewhere in the back of her mind, she heard her uncle telling her to use her imagination. She let out a huff of air as she bent over and picked up the book, brushing it off as she read the title.

*Plants of Herbal, Medicinal, Euphoric, and Even Poisonous Means.*

"Oh! 'Tis you, miss!"

Agrippina looked up with a start to see Kitty.

"Seems I've a habit of scarin' ya. Thought I were in here alone dustin' when I heard a noise and a voice."

"Were you dusting the books?" Agrippina asked slowly.

Kitty shook her head. "No, miss. I were by the window." She pointed to the other side of the room. "What were it you was chantin' just now?"

Agrippina cleared her throat, suddenly feeling silly. "It was something my uncle used to tell me when I was a child, and something frightened me."

Kitty smiled softly at her. "'Tis strange. When we're children, we're often scared of silly things like the dark. It's not 'til we're grown we realize it's people we should be afraid of. Even then, it catches us by surprise."

"That is a rather bitter sentiment, but I cannot find fault with it," Agrippina replied quietly.

Kitty curtseyed. "Enjoy your book, miss. Somethin' like that would be eye openin', I assume."

Agrippina looked down at her book. "Can you read, Kitty?"

She was answered by empty air and the echoes of the maid's footsteps on the wooden floor.

# 21

AGRIPPINA STARED DOWN AT THE BOOK NOW SITTING ON HER writing desk in her room. She stood a couple of feet away contemplating its title as she rubbed a finger across her lips.

Mrs. Bolten did not strike her as someone who enjoyed the outdoors; Richard she knew did not care for such a subject; Cecelia, bless her, was evidently not a great reader; and Mr. Bolten—she wasn't sure about Mr. Bolten.

She shook her head. It had to be a coincidence. And yet she knew it was not. She took a deep breath, sat down, and opened the book, the spine already well-creased with use. She flipped through a few pages, skimming the words, her finger tapping furiously on the desk as she read.

Would anyone have read this book? By the condition of the pages, it was apparent the book had been read, studied, and bookmarked. Some of its page corners were folded, marking the interest of the reader.

Some of the plants marked were Rue, Callamint, Savine, Morning Glory, Cherry trees. Why these? Rue, Callamint, and Savine were used as—

"Miss?"

Agrippina was pulled from her thoughts with a gasp. "Janet!"

"Oh, miss, I'm so sorry to've startled you. I did knock, several times."

Agrippina shook her head. "Forgive me. I was deep in my thoughts. Is it teatime?"

Janet shook her head and smiled a little teasingly. "No, miss. You've visitors."

"Visitors? As in more than one?"

Janet nodded excitedly. "They're in the parlor."

"Thank you, Janet. I will be down directly." She stood from the desk and straightened her skirts. She then picked up the book and placed it in a drawer of the desk where she stored the shawl and ribbon before making her way downstairs.

Agrippina opened the door to the parlor and blushed upon seeing her first visitor and then started when she saw the second. They were not a pair she ever would have guessed, and she stammered for a moment.

"M-Mr. Mackland, Uncle Henry," she began, trying to regain her composure. "What are you *both* doing here... together?"

Her uncle, an average, fair-featured man who always looked out of place in his illustrious clothes, smiled lightly. "Agrippina, I am glad you are looking well. Though, perhaps, a little tired under the eyes."

Agrippina blinked back her annoyance.

"Miss Greystone," Mr. Mackland said with a bow, his tone soft, but his features seemed grave.

She looked from one man to the other waiting for either of them to speak. She moved closer, trying to catch Mr. Mackland's eye again, but he had turned his attention out the window. "Is something the matter?"

Her uncle waved his hand. "No, no! Everything is just fine!

I have—or I guess 'we'—since Mr. Mackland insisted on tagging along—have come with good news."

"Oh?" Agrippina replied cautiously.

Henry held his hands out, palms up. "You are engaged! Congratulations, my dear!"

Agrippina blanched before turning red. "I beg your pardon?" Again, she looked at Mr. Mackland who seemed determined not to look at her. "I was not aware someone had asked and that I had accepted."

Her uncle chuckled. "You always had a strange sense of humor. I," he patted his chest, "made all the arrangements for you. I am bringing you home to Ipswich where you will be married within the month."

Agrippina angrily gaped at him, too confused and blindsided to respond. Finally, Mr. Mackland met her eye; his somber expression telling her he was not the one of whom her uncle spoke. She huffed and shook off her confusion. "And, pray, who is this unfortunate fellow with whom you made this ridiculous deal?"

Her uncle laughed. "I have forgotten how funny you can be."

"I was not being funny," she replied dryly.

He ignored her comment. "It is a step down from your situation, but I know you care little for such things. You will still be a lady, so I had no qualms agreeing to it."

"Oh, no, of course not! Why should you have qualms about accepting a proposal of marriage on my behalf?"

Her uncle, finally catching her tone, frowned. "The Viscount Haderleigh will make an excellent husband."

Agrippina scoffed. "The Viscount Haderleigh? Unless there is a new Viscount Haderleigh I was unaware of, he is over seventy years old!"

"Yes, and with any luck will only live long enough for you

to give him an heir. Then his whole estate will belong to you and the child."

Agrippina's stomach churned at her uncle's words. "If that was supposed to be an argument *for* the arrangement, I have missed the point entirely for that only makes me more against it." She shook her head. "I am extremely sorry that you came all this way to tell me of this farce of a proposal, but I do not accept."

A small smile cracked Mr. Mackland's lips apart.

Anger flashed across her uncle's face. "Mr. Mackland, I must ask you to leave while I talk some sense into my niece."

"No!" Agrippina said defiantly. "I must insist that you stay, Mr. Mackland. We shall have a good laugh at my uncle's expense later."

Her uncle fumed. "Insolent girl!" he shouted. "You are nearly three-and-twenty and unwed. I daresay no one shall have you! No one of worth, that is, for who should want an old maid? And I don't know who shall keep you after Alfred dies!"

Agrippina's breath caught in her lungs and tears singed her eyes. "An old maid is preferrable to the wife of a decrepit old man with a sordid history of late wives who all died mysteriously."

"You will do as you are told and marry him!" her uncle commanded.

"You have no power over me, Uncle Henry. Uncle Alfred made sure of that long ago."

"You are my niece, and an orphan, and as your guardian, I have full power over you," he replied through his teeth, his fists clenched, and face speckled with red.

"No." Agrippina shook her head indifferently. "If or when I choose to marry, it will be to a man whom I choose." She turned to Mr. Mackland who was failing to suppress a smile.

"Walk with me, will you?"

"I am your guardian, Agrippina!" her uncle shouted. "You shall do as I say!"

Her glare hardened. "I have not seen you in over three years! And every time I have ever visited you, you never made me feel welcome, but an inconvenience. You care no more for me than the laces on your boots. I was a duty, not your niece."

"I am still your guardian! I can take you to court and have your inheritance taken away!"

She smiled slightly. "You *were* my guardian. I am of age, uncle. I came into my inheritance and shall do nothing you say." She slipped her hand through Mr. Mackland's arm and allowed him to lead her outside.

She trudged across the grounds of the estate fueled by anger. Neither of them said anything, their silence broken once in a while by an angry huff from Agrippina followed by a shake of her head.

"Three years!" she finally exclaimed. "I have not seen my Uncle Henry in almost three years and then he shows up out of nowhere to tell me he has agreed to marry me off to a septuagenarian old man." She shuddered. "Give him an heir! How mortifying!"

Mr. Mackland gave a single nod.

"I am sure the act of making a child would give him an apoplexy!"

Mr. Mackland coughed back his laughter.

"The ridiculousness of it all! This is certainly the work of his odious wife as a means for her to climb the social ladder. *Her* father certainly had no title, so to marry an earl was certainly a win for her." She scoffed. "I would still be a lady! How—how—"

"Ridiculous?" Mr. Mackland ventured, trying not to laugh.

"Quite ridiculous! I have never been so infuriated in all my life!"

Mr. Mackland nodded. "He had no right to accept a marriage proposal for you. Being furious is the only sensible reaction."

She bobbed her head and sighed heavily before pausing. "What are you doing here?" she abruptly asked, looking at him.

Mr. Mackland blushed, clearing his throat. "Well, uh, I—I came to see you."

"I suppose that is obvious," Agrippina replied slowly starting to walk again. "But how did you come across my uncle? And how did you both know I was here? I cannot imagine you received my letter already."

He shook his head, a soft smile spreading across his face. "I was bored with Blindburn and thought I would make a trip to London for the season. I stopped in Cambridge to call on you and your uncle—Doctor Greystone, that is—and he informed me you were here. Dr. Greystone invited me to stay the night, and your other uncle arrived while we were supping."

"Did he tell Uncle Alfred what he wanted to see me about?"

"He did. Dr. Greystone laughed himself into a coughing fit and said you would never agree to it."

Concern fell over her face. "Coughing fit?"

"He is well. We left him in good spirits."

She nodded and they continued walking in silence for a few seconds. "You know, at first, I thought Uncle Henry was talking about you."

Mr. Mackland looked down, a little overcome. "You did?"

"Well, yes. I was not sure why else you would accompany Uncle Henry on such a mission if you were not a concerned party. Though I must say, I was quite furious with you until I realized you were not the man about whom he spoke."

Mr. Mackland stopped walking, allowing her arm to fall from his. She turned to look at him, confused.

"Why should you think that I would not be concerned, or why should you be angry if I were the man your uncle referred to?" he asked, his voice sounding a little strained.

Agrippina sputtered for a second. "I have offended you." She shook her head trying to regain her thoughts. "That was not my intention." She pressed a hand to her forehead suddenly feeling awkward. "I was merely trying to convey my disappointment that had you been the man of whom my uncle spoke," she bit her lip and took a deep breath through her nose, letting it out a huff, "I would have preferred you coming to me first." She blushed and let out another huff of air. "It has become quite warm, has it not?" She began fanning herself with her hand, turning from him.

Mr. Mackland smiled, his heart full. He reached out and gently took her other hand, hearing a small gasp escape her lips. "I would never dare go to anyone before you about anything."

"Anything? I am rather far away, you know, so the thought that you would not on *some* things would just be—"

"Miss Greystone," he interrupted her with a smile. "Just accept it, please."

She smiled and nodded, allowing him to tuck her hand back into the crook of his arm as they resumed walking. "You looked rather upset when I first saw you. Did you think I was going to go for my uncle's odious plan?"

Mr. Mackland chuckled a little nervously. "Honestly, I was more hopeful you would not. However, I was unsure how much weight your uncle's opinion carried."

"On what? My decisions?" She shook her head. "Wrong uncle."

He smiled and placed his other hand over top of hers.

"I must confess, I am rather glad you are here," Agrippina ventured slowly.

He looked over at her, a small smirk on his lips. "Are you? I am glad to hear it. I, uh, I have missed your company." He cleared his throat. "Would you think me too forward is I asked you to call me James?"

A smile spread across Agrippina's face, and she let out a small laugh. "I just sent you a letter asking the same thing of you. Not for you to call me James, of course."

He nodded singularly chuckling. "Of course."

"But Agrippina, or even Aggy."

"I would like that very much."

Agrippina felt her heart flutter, briefly turning away to hide her blush. "May I confess something, Mr. Mackland?"

"James," he corrected with a smile.

She let out a small laugh. "James." Her skin tingled as she said it. "There is something rather strange about this place. Did my uncle tell you why I am here?"

He nodded. "Yes, some strange activity and possible witchcraft?"

"Well, I will not agree to the witchcraft, but there is certainly something very strange going on. I daresay, I feel a little bit out of my league."

Mr. Mackland, James, stopped and turned to her. "You are going to tell me that the great Agrippina Greystone feels incapable?" He shook his head. "I refuse to believe it."

"That I think myself incapable or that I am so?"

"Both!" he replied fervently. "Aggy."

Her breath caught when she heard her name on his lips.

"You are the most capable person I have ever met. And most confident. Your confidence is the first thing I noticed about you. Do you not remember the first time we met?"

She looked up at him questioningly. "Of course I remember."

"My dogs Hubert and Angeline charged after you. You bellowed for them to stop so confidently, and sternly, they did not dare to question your authority." He laughed and shook his head. "Most people would have tucked tail and run. They would not have gotten very far, but they would not have stood their ground as you did."

She smiled as she remembered, her skin flushing. The large Irish wolfhounds barreling toward her, barking, while James ran after them, his dark hair bouncing about his face, jacketless with his shirt slightly unbuttoned. Unbuttoned enough to see a subtle patch of chest hair and glowing skin.

"That is what I first noticed. Your confidence. Do not tell me you have lost it just because you are having some difficulty figuring out a puzzle."

She shook her head. "No," she replied, the smile still plastered on her face. "It wavered for a moment, but I heard what I needed to firm it back up."

James took her hand from his arm and held it, turning to face her. "Miss Greystone, Agrippina, Aggy," he took a deep breath and let it out slowly, "I did not accompany your uncle so much as shared a carriage with him. Whether he came or not, I wanted to see you." He cleared his throat and rolled his shoulders. "Aggy, you are—"

Somewhere from around the corner came a bloodcurdling scream.

"What was that?" James asked, concern and terror in his voice.

"It is coming from the cherry trees," Agrippina said, running in that direction.

"Where are you going?" James began running after her.

"To investigate the scream!"

"Well, yes, but should I not go first to make sure it is safe?"

Agrippina wanted to groan, but as she was not much of a runner, she tried to save her breath. James quickly outran her, turning the corner as another scream sounded.

"No! Get away from me!"

Agrippina's eyes grew wide as she recognized the voice as Janet's. She picked up her pace, her lungs burning and her side throbbing as she pushed through it. She was only a few yards from the trees when she saw Janet running out from one of the rows, shielding her face.

She saw James catch up to her and place a hand on her shoulder to make sure she was alright. Janet pointed back into the trees, hiding her face with her other hand. James rushed in the direction she indicated.

By the time Agrippina got to Janet, she was out of breath, her side cramping, and her forehead sweating.

"Are you alright, Janet?" she asked between gasps for air.

"Oh, miss! She nearly got me!" Janet cried, falling onto her shaky knees as she sobbed. "I was just enjoyin' a few minutes of fresh air, and she came out of nowhere!" She shook her head. "But why would she come for me? I've done nothin' wrong!"

Agrippina knelt beside the crying girl, placing an arm over her shoulder. "It is alright, Janet," she said softly. "You are safe. She cannot get you."

Janet shook her head again. "Yes, she can! She is after everyone! No one is safe here!"

James returned a few minutes later shaking his head and shrugging. "I could not find anyone."

"No, you would not," Agrippina replied softly.

"What has happened?" Mr. Arter yelled, running from the music room door. His face was full of concern for his niece, and he fell on the ground beside her. "Are you hurt?"

Janet shook her head. "I saw her, uncle. I saw her! The woman in black!"

Mr. Arter looked up at Agrippina and James who both shook their heads. He gently shushed his niece and helped get her off the ground. "Come now, child," he told her gently. "Let's go make you some tea."

"I saw her, uncle," Janet repeated. "I saw her come out of the ground!"

"It's alright, my dear. She will not hurt you. I promise."

Agrippina and James watched as Mr. Arter led his niece inside.

"Who is the woman in black?" James asked slowly.

Agrippina laughed through her nose. "That is the same question everyone wants to know." She turned and moved toward the trees, touching a few of them as she walked by.

"Is she a ghost?" James was right beside her inspecting the trees and ground.

She shrugged. "If the family would be believed, it is the vengeful spirit of a woman who was falsely accused by one of their ancestors of witchcraft for which she was executed." She shot James a glance. "She cursed the family with her final words, and this is her seeing her curse through to the end."

"Ah, that is rather impressive, if you ask me." He frowned. "Though quite contradictory. If she was not a witch, how did she have the power to put a curse on the one who falsely accused her?"

"Hmm. You see one of the conundrums I have come across." She smiled as she inspected a low-hanging branch. "Mr. Bolten says the hatred and anger she felt upon being executed gave her the power and she sold her soul to the devil after the fact. Or, something to that effect."

James chuckled. "That is a rather convenient explanation."

Agrippina nodded, agreeing. "What is it you were going to say earlier?"

James cleared his throat and shrugged. "I, uh, uh—when?"

She frowned at him. "Right before we heard Janet scream."

"Oh, uh, I, uh," he shook his head. "I have forgotten."

"I am sure you will remember later."

He forced a small smile and nodded.

Something caught her eye, and she creased her brow. She leaned in closer to inspect the trunk of the tree, reaching out her hand to touch it. There on the trunk were missing pieces of bark and scratches into the flesh of the tree.

"What are you looking at?" James asked, coming to stand behind her.

"Someone stripped some of the bark off this tree," she said.

"Could be a male deer rubbing his antlers on it."

She shook her head. "I do not think so. It looks too precise. But why would someone want to strip the bark off a cherry tree?"

"Maybe in order to make a tea out of it?"

Agrippina took a deep breath and nodded. "In small doses it could be considered medicinal." She peered down the row of trees and saw a patch of bark gone from several of them. "But in larger doses it could kill you." She pulled a small knife out of her boot and chipped away a piece of bark for herself.

James chuckled. "Do you normally carry a knife with you?"

"Ever since Blindburn I do." She brought the bark to her nose and sniffed tentatively. It, of course, smelled like cherry, but there was a strange undertone—a hint of something else. She sniffed again and the blood drained from her face.

Bitter almonds.

# 22

"MISS GREYSTONE!" RICHARD SAID, HIS ARMS OPEN IN WEL-come as she and James entered the house. He cast her a knowing glance, causing her to blush, before turning his attention to James. "I have already met your uncle so I presume this to be Mr. Mackland." He bowed.

"James," Agrippina blushed deeper as Richard's brow arched and his lip curled into a not-so-subtle smirk, "this is Mr. Maddox."

James bowed. "It is a pleasure to meet you, Mr. Maddox."

Richard waved his hand. "Please, you can drop the 'Mister.' Any friend of Miss Greystone's is a friend of mine. You are most welcome. I have already had a room prepared for you."

James bowed again. "Thank you. I will not trespass on your hospitality for too long."

Richard shook his head, his brows creased. "You could not trespass on it long enough." He indicated a servant with his hand. "Mariah here will show you to your room. I am sure you will want to freshen up for dinner. Lord Greystone—" he turned to Agrippina, "jolly fellow, by the way—" he turned

168

his attention back to James, "told me you left at four this morning. Good heavens! You must be tired."

James thanked him again before shooting a smile at Agrippina and following the maid up the stairs. Richard turned to watch them as they ascended before smirking at Agrippina who tried to avoid his eye.

"*That* is whom you have been blushing for?" he asked, raising his brows. "Bravo, Miss Greystone. Bravo."

Agrippina cleared her throat. "Do you have a moment to talk?"

His expression fell, turning serious. "Of course, this way." He led her into the library and shut the door behind them.

She shuddered for a moment when she remembered the book falling from its shelf.

"Are you cold?" Richard asked her.

She shook her head. "No, it is not that." She took a deep breath. "Do you know if your household uses wild cherry bark often?"

Richard lifted his brows in question, slowly shaking his head. "I could not tell you."

"In small doses, it can help suppress coughs and soothe a sore throat. In larger doses, however, it can be used as a poison."

Richard's face turned white. "Why would you be asking if someone in my household would use that?"

Agrippina explained the stripping of the bark on the wild cherry trees. "There are several trees where bark has been removed." She shook her head. "Perhaps, you could say it is a male deer stripping his antlers, but I doubt a deer would be so particular that he would use the same row of trees."

Richard rolled his tongue across his teeth. "And, what, you think someone in my family or members of the staff are poisoning people?"

She shook her head. "No, I believe the intended victims are already dead."

He stared at her for a moment, before the realization sunk in. He pressed a hand to his mouth and lowered himself down to a chair. "You believe someone poisoned Anna Brown."

She shook her head. "That, of course, is still possible. But I have nothing to solidify my suspicions there. I am talking of the Browns' cows."

Richard gaped at her, confused. "The cows?"

Agrippina nodded slowly. "Do you remember what Mr. Brown said about the strange smell the cows emitted?"

"Uuuh." He shook his head. "Not particularly."

"Bitter almonds." She took out the piece of bark she cut from the tree and proffered it to him. "Smell this."

He took it tentatively and brought it to his nose, sniffing. He shook his head after a moment and sniffed again. "I don't smell anything except for cherry."

Agrippina frowned and took the bark back, smelling it. "It is clearly there. Try it again."

Richard did as she said but shook his head again. "I am sorry, but I don't smell what you're smelling. Perhaps your sense of smell is better than mine."

"Perhaps," she replied quietly.

"What does this do for the cows? Why would they be poisoned?"

Agrippina studied the bark for a moment. "Less blood."

Richard looked confused. "Less blood?"

She sighed mildly exasperated. "Yes. The cows were dead before their necks were cut. If the heart is not pumping, then blood is not flowing through the body. The cow is fed the poison, it dies, its throat is opened, what little blood flows out is captured in a bucket, and moved away from the scene, making it appear as if the cow was drained of blood."

Richard nodded slowly still trying to catch up. "So killing the cow first makes for a cleaner scene since the blood would not be—" He stammered, trying to find the right word.

"The blood would not be spraying all over, but flowing a little more gently."

"Ah." He nodded. "Of course."

Richard let out a puff of air. "Someone has put a lot of planning into this scheme."

"Yes."

He cleared his throat. "And you are sure Miss Brown was not murdered as well?"

She shook her head. "I am not sure. I have just not found evidence proving she was. My suspicions given the circumstance in which she was found is not enough."

He rubbed his chin a moment, looking deep in thought. "Is there any reason you might think she would be killed? I cannot imagine anyone harming that sweet girl."

Agrippina thought for a moment about whether she should tell Richard about the pregnancy. She wanted to preserve what dignity the poor girl had left, but knew Richard was her ally and withholding information with him could be foolish.

Agrippina stood straighter and rolled her shoulders. "I am sure Miss Brown was sweet, but however innocent she may have been was lost before her death."

Again, Richard took several seconds to absorb the information he had just been given. His eyes grew wide with shock. "Are you saying—Are you trying to tell me—" he ran his hands through his hair. "Are you telling me Miss Anna Brown, the shy girl who blushed so hard when I would look at her you would think she was on fire, was with child at the time of her death?"

THE CURSE GROWS STRONGER STILL

Agrippina nodded.

Richard stood and paced the room taking deep breaths and sighing. "What is the connection here?"

She sighed. "Anna Brown and Maven Rupert got into a disagreement before all of this happened over a man. A man who seduced both of these girls. A man who possibly got them both with child."

Richard sat down again, his eyes distant and horrified. He pressed a hand over his mouth as he stared at nothing.

"Mr. Maddox?" Agrippina said softly, bringing him back to the present.

He blinked as he looked up at her. "What does this have to do with the woman in black?"

Agrippina shook her head. "That is what I need you for. There was another sighting of the woman in black earlier. Janet saw her amongst the cherry trees. Soon after, Mr. Arter came running outside from the house. Where were you half an hour ago and who were you with?"

He thought for a moment. "I was in the parlor with your uncle. Aunt Lucy and my uncle came in not long after and began speaking with him." He shook his head. "Cecelia," he paused, "I am not sure. She was writing a letter to her fiancé, I believe."

"And last night? When your uncle and I saw her outside the library window?"

"Ah, I was again in the parlor with Cecelia. Aunt Lucy was—huh. I cannot remember where Aunt Lucy had been."

"Was she out riding?" Agrippina suggested.

Richard laughed. "Aunt Lucy riding?" He shook his head. "Aunt Lucy hates horses if they are not connected to a carriage."

Agrippina remembered back to the night before, sure that she had heard Cecelia say her aunt had gone riding.

Mrs. Bolten had even confirmed it when she came down the stairs. Why would they have lied?

"I am not sure she told me what she was doing. I remember she came into the parlor to greet Cecelia, I left for a few minutes to talk to one of the staff and when I returned, I think she had already left."

"I am sure she was in the house somewhere."

He nodded and stood, moving toward the table with the decanters. Agrippina saw they must have been filled since last night. He poured two glasses and brought one to her.

She shook her head. "Oh, no thank you."

"You have to at least try it," Richard pressed. "My uncle only buys the best port." He held it in front of her.

She shook her head again when she caught a whiff of it. "Is that the same port he always drinks?" She took the glass from him and held it under her nose as she inhaled.

He blinked at her. "Yes, I think this is all from the same cask. It was only opened a few days ago."

"It does not smell the same." Agrippina sniffed again. "The other day, after the incident in his study, I sniffed his glass of port and it," she shook her head, taking another sniff, "it smelled different than this. It had a more earthy, spiced smell to it."

Richard's face fell. "Do you think someone has been poisoning my uncle too?"

"I am not sure."

He paused for a moment, looking down into his glass when he abruptly turned and left the library. Agrippina, surprised by his sudden movement, followed suit. He pushed his way into his uncle's study to the far side and picked up the decanter from the table. He sniffed it tentatively before smelling the glass in his hand.

"Come." He held the decanter out for her.

She walked over slowly and took it before smelling it. She shook her head as she exhaled. "No, that is not it either."

Richard let out a relieved sigh. "Perhaps you are wrong or thought you were smelling the port when really you were smelling something completely different."

She gave him a stern look. "I might not drink, Mr. Maddox, but thanks to Professor Hartley, I know exactly what port smells like. And what I smelled was port mixed with something else."

Richard put the decanter back down and took a few sips from his glass.

"I need to know, Mr. Maddox. Who stands to benefit from your uncle's demise?"

Richard rubbed his face with one of his hands and shrugged. "Me! I am his heir. He has left everything to me. My aunt will be taken care of, naturally, but she does not get the house or the money."

"He does not have any business rivals? Someone who could bribe a servant to lace his drinks with something and dress like the woman in black to scare him?"

He shook his head fervently. "I do not know." He creased his brows. "No. No, I do not believe he does. He is an honest businessman. I know when the Boltens first made a name for themselves, a lot of our money was made through smuggling, but that has not happened since before my grandfather or even great-grandfather's time."

"If it is not someone unconnected with the family," Agrippina stated slowly, "then it is someone in the family."

Richard shot her an angry look. "No! My uncle is loved and respected by his family. He raised me and my sister when my father died leaving my mother with practically nothing! He is a good man. I cannot imagine anyone who would want him dead."

There was a clearing of the throat and they turned to see Mr. Arter.

"Forgive the interruption, Master Richard, but dinner has been served."

Richard nodded briskly. "We will be there shortly."

"Did my uncle stay for dinner?" Agrippina asked hesitantly.

Richard chuckled softly. "My aunt invited him to stay the night."

# 23

Mrs. Bolten smiled proudly as Lord Greystone praised the food. She had never had an earl in her house before and was glad she had ordered an illustrious dinner on a whim.

"Miss Greystone did not tell us her uncle was an earl," Cecelia said, a little in awe at their guest.

This brought a tinge of red to Lord Greystone's face. "Yes, she does not normally capitalize on her connections. Neither does my brother. They are a strange lot, the two of them. With all the money the two of them have, they could be living in a house not much smaller than this one." He sighed as he cut into his meat. "But they choose to live in this dreadfully small house with barely an acre of land."

"We live modestly," Agrippina commented, trying not to let her uncle aggravate her. "Living below your means is certainly better than living above them."

"Modesty is a virtue. No one would fault you for it," James said in her defense.

They locked eyes for a moment, a soft smile spreading on both their faces.

Richard tapped on his wine glass for a refill.

"A virtue!" her uncle laughed into his wine. "The Greystones are an ancient family. We can afford other virtues that do not embarrass the name." He nodded his head in Agrippina's direction. "Had my brother spared a little money on Agrippina's education, she would not always be dressing like a drab governess. She would have been more fashionable and even married by now."

Agrippina could feel her face burning with fury and her spine stiffen with pride. She took a calming breath and laid her fork down on her plate before opening her mouth to talk.

"If I am not mistaken, Lord Greystone," James said before she could, "*Lady* Greystone's father was the earl before you, and you only took over the title after his unfortunate death."

Everyone slowly turned their attention to Agrippina.

"And even after the death of the ninth earl, you still only acquired the title after Dr. Greystone, the brother you talk about with so much disdain, *gave* it to you."

Lord Greystone's face turned crimson.

"So the modesty that you have been sneering about 'embarrassing' your family, is the only reason you have the title yourself, is it not?"

Richard tapped on his glass for another refill as everyone at the table returned their attention to the earl, but Agrippina could not take her gaze off James whose eyes sparkled right back into hers.

Lord Greystone recovered, however, and cleared his throat. "Yes, I suppose you are right. I should be grateful my brother and niece do not have grander ambitions." He glanced at Agrippina and, following her gaze, realized she was looking at Mr. Mackland with ardor. "I do still have certain expectations of my niece. Marrying a lord of some sort as her station requires. Anyone else would just be," he locked eyes with James, "a shame."

Agrippina had had enough. She dropped her fork on her plate, making an obnoxious clattering sound. "How dare—"

"Nothing your niece would ever do could be labeled as 'shameful,' my lord," James said, again coming to the rescue. "Perhaps, if you saw her more often and spoke to her, not at her, you would see her for who she is."

Richard grinned into his wine as he watched the scene, while the rest of his family gaped from Lord Greystone to James.

"She is more than just the beautiful woman you see," James continued. "She is intelligent—most likely the most intelligent person you know. She might not wear the most expensive or most fashionable clothes, but a true man of substance would never be concerned with something so frivolous." He turned his gaze to her. "Any man would be so lucky to call you his own."

"Here! Here!" Richard exclaimed, raising his glass. "Well said, Mr. Mackland. We are surely glad to have her and her brilliant mind here to help us out with our little fiasco." He took a sip. "Are we not?" He looked at each one of his family members.

Lord Greystone raised a brow in Richard's direction. "Fiasco?"

"Oh, did my aunt and uncle fail to tell you?" Richard began, his words slightly slurred.

"Richard," Mrs. Bolten said, half laughing. "I hardly think now is the time. Perhaps we should all finish eating before we begin such a serious subject."

Richard shook his head, taking another sip. "No, no! Why would we not talk about it?" He looked over at the earl. "It is rather an intriguing case. One with witches, curses, ghosts, poisonings!"

"Poisonings?" Cecelia repeated, looking over at her aunt with concern.

"Did you not hear?" Richard continued. "The Browns' cows were poisoned before their throats were slit."

Silverware clattered on plates as a few gasps filled the room.

"Something about less blood," Richard droned as he took another sip.

"Mr. Maddox!" Agrippina called out in alarm, her face full of panic.

"What?" Richard said with a shrug. "Why should we not tell them?"

Agrippina was looking for a way to stop him from talking, the panic she felt for the case increasing the more Richard spoke. Telling everyone everything she knew would devastate the plans she had. She looked over at James, her eyes wide.

"In fact," Richard continued, "why should we not tell them everything we know? Like the fact that Miss Brown was wi—"

Before Richard could finish his thought, James fumbled with his own wine glass causing it to spill all over Cecelia who screamed and pushed away from the table, her own glass spilling as she flailed her arms.

"Oh, I am so sorry, Miss Maddox!" James proclaimed. "I am such a klutz! I hope I did not ruin your dress." He tentatively shot Agrippina a glance and winked.

Agrippina could not help but smile and she knew in that moment, she truly loved James Mackland.

## 24

RICHARD POLISHED OFF ANOTHER TWO OR THREE GLASSES OF wine after his dinner display and a scolding from Agrippina. She had gruffly pulled him into the hallway as everyone began to disperse to the parlor for cards.

"We do not talk about the case with those not involved in the investigation!" she had hissed at him. "Are you trying to ruin all of the work I have been doing?"

He had shrugged her off, a little deflated.

"If you plan on telling everyone the secrets of the case, then I will keep you in the dark."

He had huffed, but nodded, waving his hand as he moved toward the library. "I promise! I will no longer interfere, but I cannot sit in that room and play games with everyone as if everything is perfect."

The next morning, he was late to rise, and completely absent at breakfast.

Agrippina and her uncle breakfasted first, the tension still thick between them as they sat as far away as they could from one another. For several minutes, all that could be heard were the clinking sounds of their silverware moving across their plates.

Lord Greystone cleared his throat. "Mr. Mackland seems like a very decent man."

Agrippina shot her head up in his direction.

"He owns a great deal of land in Blindburn, I understand."

Agrippina nodded. "Yes, he is the majority landowner."

Her uncle nodded. "Hmm. But no title?"

Agrippina gritted her teeth and swallowed. "No, he does not have a title."

"Hmm. Pity. He has a lot of gumption and spirit. Some lords lack that." There was a pause as he continued to eat. "He might do well in parliament. I could talk to some of my constituents and get him in."

Agrippina sighed lightly. "I do not think he wishes to join parliament, uncle."

He looked over at her. "Have you ever asked him? Perhaps he has just never voiced it to you. You do live rather far away from one another, do you not?"

"Yes, but we write to each other almost every day."

"Every day?" He lifted his brows. "How do you keep track of all those letters?"

She smiled. "We have a system. We copy the letters we write to each other, date them, and number them. In the letters with the number one at the top, we are currently discussing the war in France and the influence the peasant uprisings could have here in Britain. In the letters with the number 2, we are discussing our opinions on novels we are reading together. In letters with the number 3, we are just passing random ideas back and forth to each other and giving our opinions and advice as to how those ideas could be executed."

Her uncle blinked, seemingly surprised.

"We have," she paused to count, "ten conversations

running between us."

He took in a deep breath and sighed. "I, uh, I want to apologize."

Agrippina froze, her fork hovering in the air as she turned to look at her uncle.

"I came here believing I was going to find a silly girl with no direction or thoughts for the future." He shook his head. "But Mr. Mackland was correct. You are more than the pretty woman I see before me."

"Uncle Henry," she said softly.

He held up a hand. "You were correct too. I came here with the expectation of obedience in a woman whom I have not seen or written to in three years. I was embittered and enraged when you balked at my wishes." He locked eyes with her. "My display at dinner last night was not much better. Mr. Mackland humbled me, and I am sorry if I embarrassed you."

Agrippina's heart twinged a little. All her life, her Uncle Henry treated her as a duty to fulfill, an obligation. But here he was, a man who never cared to know her before, apologizing to her. She did not know how much she had needed to hear him apologize until he did.

Her lips curled into a small smile. "Thank you." She blinked back an unexpected tear as a realization hit her. *When Uncle Alfred finally passes from his illness, Uncle Henry will be the only family I have left.*

He cleared his throat again. "I will cancel your engagement as soon as I return to Ipswich. I would also love for you to come and visit. The children have grown so big, I hardly know where the time went." He looked a little embarrassed and he took a moment to look away. "I think I will even extend an invitation to Mr. Mackland."

Agrippina's heart swelled and a lump grew in her throat.

"Do you know if he hunts?"

She shook her head. "No, he is not very fond it. But he does like to fish."

"Ah, well, you know I can accommodate him there."

There was a brief pause.

"Uncle, did Uncle Alfred tell you he is sick?"

Lord Greystone nodded. "It is what prompted me to seek out the proposal. I wanted to make sure you were well taken care of." He smiled weakly. "Though I understand you are highly capable of taking care of yourself, making your own decisions."

She bobbed her head. "Thank you. Even if I did not appreciate the mode of your actions, I do appreciate the sentiment of them."

He nodded again, giving his breakfast a little more intention.

"Are you heading home today?" Agrippina asked, taking a bite.

He shook his head. "I am going to meet Juline and the girls in London. Fanny is out this year."

"Is she?" Agrippina said. "I know she must be very excited."

"Yes, yes! Excited to spend my money on as many dresses as she and her mother deem possible." He smiled softly at her. "I will leave as soon as I can say my farewells to the family."

Agrippina stood and walked over to her uncle, planting a kiss on his cheek. "I would love to visit you in the fall, if that is alright. I miss Ipswich in the fall."

Her uncle laughed through his nose. "Fall is my favorite time of year at Ipswich."

"Then that is when I shall come." She said goodbye and turned to leave the room when her uncle stopped her.

"Aggy."

She faced him again.

"Do you think there is room to add me as a correspondent?"

She smiled at her uncle. "Of course." She left her uncle in the breakfast room just as James was coming down the stairs, a satisfied smile on his face. His eyes sparkled as they met hers.

"Good morning."

Agrippina, having in so many words just received her uncle's blessing to marry whomever she liked, smiled just as satisfied. "Good morning."

"Have you already broken your fast?" he asked as he met her on the landing.

She nodded.

"Would you like to take a walk?"

She frowned for a moment. "Would you not like to eat first?"

"I have been up for hours and have already eaten."

He offered her his arm which she gladly took, allowing him to lead her outside. The cool spring air rushed over them as the footmen opened the door and Agrippina happily breathed it in.

"There is a slight chill to the air," James said. "Do you want to go in for a shawl?"

"No, I find it rather refreshing," she replied, taking another deep breath. "I actually prefer—" she stopped herself. James's mention of the word shawl reminded her about the shawl she had found in the cherry trees.

"What do you prefer?" James asked when she did not finish her thought.

"What?"

He laughed. "I believe I lost you for a minute."

"Oh, yes, I remembered something about the case." She shook her head. "There is something I am not seeing or understanding. Someone is not being altogether truthful."

"How can I help?"

She smiled up at him. "We could go through my notes together. Perhaps you will see something that I have yet to discover."

He laughed. "You put too much faith in my observation skills."

She shook her head. "It is not your observation skills I am interested in but how you might interpret something. If I am at a dead end and am only focused on going in a certain direction, I will not be able to see a way out. But if I had someone else reading the directions with me, who picks up on certain clues or hints that I have not, then we can help guide each other in the correct direction."

They made their way to the garden and sat on a bench in front of the little fishpond. They watched as the fish teased the surface, their mouths open as they snatched bugs that landed on the water's surface.

Butterfly bushes were starting to bloom, and an array of bugs flitted about it to feed. The breeze carried its scent along with it, giving the air a clean floral accent. Agrippina relaxed into it. Despite everything that she couldn't piece together, she was happy in that moment.

She took in a deeper breath as the breeze blew around her and paused. It was that smell. That smell she had noticed in Mr. Bolten's port the other day. She stiffened as she tried to place it.

Mr. Mackland immediately noticed the change in her demeanor. "Are you alright?'

She turned to him. "Do you smell that?"

Mr. Mackland sniffed the air tentatively. "I am not sure. There are several smells. It is difficult to pick out just one."

She stood from the bench, moving upwind. She stood in front of the butterfly bushes and smelled a blossom but quickly shook her head. She then noticed the morning glory vines beginning to snake their way up the bush. She plucked a blossom and sniffed.

"Morning glories," James said as she handed it to him. He smelled the flower and nodded but was not sure what he was agreeing to. "You know, if you grind up the seeds, it causes a subtle euphoria followed by hallucinations."

Agrippina glanced at him sharply. "Hallucinations?"

He nodded. "I read it somewhere in my travels."

She let out a small laugh. "James! You have no idea what you have discovered. What you have helped me with."

James looked surprised. "Oh? You are welcome. I am, of course, always happy to help."

"Oh, James! I could kiss you!" She immediately blushed and cleared her throat. "I mean, I—I apologize. I did not mean—" she cleared her throat. "What I meant to say was—"

James put a hand on her waist and pulled her to him, gently pressing his lips to her. She was tense at first, but soon relaxed into him, letting her lips part ever so lightly against his.

They were both a little flushed when they pulled away, their hearts pounding in their ears.

"I apologize," James said after a moment, almost breathless. "I should not have done that without your permission. I had just—"

Agrippina, with a fist full of James' jacket in her hand, pulled him to her again, their lips locking once more. One of his arms wrapped around her while his other hand cupped her face.

After a minute's embrace, she pulled away, her brain a little hazy.

"There," she told him, her voice slightly distant. "Now we are even."

He nodded slowly, a smile plastered on his face. "Yes, I believe we are." He laughed through his nose and shook his head. "You find different ways to amaze me without even trying, Aggy."

Her blush deepened.

"I came here to tell you that."

She creased her brows. "To the garden?"

He laughed. "No, I came *here* to Essex. I came here to tell you that I am not lonely in my house in Blindburn because I fill it with ideas of *us*."

Agrippina quietly gasped.

He took a deep breath and let it out in a huff. "I have admired you since the moment I met you, and I do not ever foresee me admiring anyone more than I admire and care for you."

"James," she almost whispered.

"Aggy." He took her hand and kissed it, pressing her palm against his face. "I—"

"Miss Greystone! Miss Greystone!" Janet was running in their direction, waving her arms furiously.

"No, no, no!" Agrippina moaned softly. "Please do not stop. Finish telling me what you have to say."

He smiled softly, giving her hand a final squeeze before letting it drop. "It is alright. It can wait."

"Miss Greystone!" Janet repeated as she got closer. "You've a visitor!"

Agrippina exchanged another glance with James before answering her. "Another visitor?" she repeated, a little confused.

"Yes! Mrs. Rupert has come to see you, but she said she can't stay long as she's needed at the farm."

Agrippina nodded. "I shall come directly." She cast James a longing glance as she followed Janet back to the house.

# 25

AGRIPPINA WAS SHOWN INTO THE PARLOR WHERE AN ANXIOUS Mrs. Rupert was pacing by the hearth. She looked relieved when she saw Agrippina walk through the door, her large doe eyes wet with tears.

"Mrs. Rupert, is everything alright?" Agrippina asked, sounding concerned.

Mrs. Rupert nodded, releasing another tear that rolled down her already tear-stained cheek. "Everything is as good as it has been, miss, I thank you. And I thank you for the tea and Mr. Maddox for the cuts of meat." Her voice wavered a bit. "It was most kind of you to think of me after the way my husband threw you out."

Agrippina shook her head. "Your husband was only doing what he thought necessary to protect his daughter. I cannot blame him, and I certainly would never blame you for his actions."

A weak smile brightened her face. "You are very kind, Miss Greystone."

"How can I help you?" She gestured for Mrs. Rupert to sit, but the woman quickly shook her head.

"No, I thank you, but I cannot stay long. I just wanted to bring you this." She pulled a book from her bag and proffered it to her.

Agrippina took it gently, running her hand over the dark green leather cover, a silver rose embossed on the front. "What is this?"

Mrs. Rupert swallowed. "That is Maven's journal. I found it last night while I was straightening her room." She coughed and sniffed, wiping her nose with a handkerchief. "We sent her to live with one of Mr. Rupert's sisters for a few weeks. She was so upset by your visit. I just went into her room to look around and feel her presence." She shook her head. "She's never been away from me for more than a day and never this far. So I was missing her." Her eyes welled with tears.

"It is alright, Mrs. Rupert. I am sure she will be perfectly safe at her aunt's house."

Mrs. Rupert shook her head again. "It seems we could not keep her safe in our own house!" she cried, burying her face in her hands.

Agrippina shifted, uncomfortable and unsure what she should do.

"I did suspect something, but I thought—" She shook her head and took a deep breath, trying to smile. "I know now I was lying to myself."

"What do you mean?" Agrippina asked gently. "What did you suspect?"

Mrs. Rupert swallowed hard. "Her courses had never been regular, but they stopped for a few months and then—" She pressed a hand to her mouth. "There had been so much blood not long after she began seeing the woman in black." She pressed her lips together to keep them from quivering. "Perhaps you might think me a bad mother. That I could

189

allow this to happen to my daughter, but I didn't know!"

Agrippina shook her head. "I do not think you are a bad mother."

"I told myself that she would never go against her father and me like that, but I was wrong. Someone turned her away from us. Had her lie and made her," she burst into tears again, "sin!"

"Can I get you anything?" Agrippina asked after an uncomfortable moment.

"No, no!" She sniffed into her handkerchief. "I am fine. Please forgive my hysterics. It is just," she took a deep breath to calm herself, "I thought I knew my daughter until I found and read that." Her lip quivered again, but she maintained her composure. She cleared her throat and forced a smile. "I thank you again for the tea. If you could keep what you find in that journal a secret, I would appreciate that as well."

Agrippina nodded. "I will be discreet, I promise."

Mrs. Rupert curtseyed. "Good day, Miss Greystone."

"Good day."

Mrs. Rupert rushed out of the parlor, hopping onto an old, tired-looking horse before trotting off.

A yawning Richard then entered the parlor. He immediately winced and groaned as the sunlight penetrated his eyes.

"Are you satisfied with your behavior from last night?" she asked him without gazing up from the window.

"Hmm," he replied yawning again. "I believe I might have made a complete ass out of myself."

She glanced at him sideways. "You were rather obnoxious."

He nodded. "I apologize. I possibly ruined the integrity of the case all because I was wallowing in a little self-pity."

"I do not think it is me whom you really need to be apologizing to," she told him. "Your aunt was rather mortified at

your behavior in front of my uncle. The fact that you polished off a bottle of wine yourself was rather—"

"Impressive?"

"—concerning."

He half nodded, half shrugged. "I can see where that could
be an issue." He groaned. "Ugh! Well, it has certainly not
been in my favor this morning. I feel as if an axe is lodged
in my brain." He looked around. "Where is everyone else, by
the way? They are not breakfasting or anywhere else."

Agrippina shook her head. "My uncle left this morning.
So mortified he was by your behavior."

He blanched. "He left on my account?"

She smirked. "No, he just had to get back to London
to his wife and daughters. It is his eldest daughter's first
season out."

"Ah!" He creased his brows after a moment. "Wait. Did
you just try to tell a joke?"

She shrugged. "Yes."

He chuckled. "You have been around me for far too long,
Miss Greystone. I am starting to wear on you."

She lifted a brow. "I doubt it."

He laughed. "Where is your man then? Did he leave with
your uncle?"

A deep blush spread over her face. "Uh, no. No, he is out
in the garden. I think. At least, that was where he was when
I left him."

He smirked and lifted his brows. "The garden?"

"I just had a visit from Mrs. Rupert," Agrippina said, trying
to shift the subject.

Richard gently shook his head. "You're only a few days into
your stay and already have had more visitors than I get in a
month. More letters, more visitors! You are quite popular."

Agrippina held up the journal. "She gave me her daughter's

private journal."

He walked toward her, his hand outstretched to take the journal, but Agrippina held it away from him, her other hand gently pushing him back.

"You do not honestly think I am going to give it to you, do you?"

Richard scowled down at her.

"I promised Mrs. Rupert I would not let anyone else look at it."

"What? You cannot be serious? Why tell me about it if you are not going to allow me look through it?" He made a pass for the book again, but Agrippina took a step back.

"I will read it myself and then I will divulge the information I feel you are privy to."

Richard scoffed, reaching again for the journal, barely missing as Agrippina stepped to the side.

"Will you stop!" she told him sternly. "You are behaving quite like a spoiled child."

"You are the one who accused my family of having some part in all of this," he replied. "If that journal helps absolve them, then I want to know about it!" He reached again, this time taking hold of her wrist.

Agrippina squealed. "Let go, Mr. Maddox!" She placed her other hand on his chest, pushing away from him as he tried pulling her closer. "Stop it!"

"This would be less difficult if you just gave me what I wanted!"

Agrippina stomped on his foot. "I said no!"

"Aaaah!" Richard growled through his teeth. "That was not nice, Miss Greystone!"

She pulled her arm back to hit him, but as he stepped back to dodge it, he fell backwards, taking Agrippina to floor with him. They both let out a yell as they tumbled, Richard's hand still clutching Agrippina's wrist.

James, having heard the struggle, burst into the parlor seeing Agrippina trying to push herself off Richard who groaned before laughing. Her skirts were bunched up, exposing almost up to her knee.

"Aggy!"

They both gasped as they turned to see James in the doorway his face seething.

"Mr. Maddox! Get your hands off her!" He rushed into the room toward them.

"It is not what it looks like, Mackland!" Richard said. "This is more innocent than you might think on first glance."

Agrippina used the distraction to scramble off him, finally wrenching her wrist from his grasp and planting a slap across his face.

"Ow!" he said rubbing his cheek. "Was that necessary?"

"You are truly infantile, Mr. Maddox," Agrippina scolded him, picking up the journal she had dropped on the floor. She then took James by the arm who looked as if he was ready to kill Richard.

"Never mind, James," she said in a more soothing voice. "It was just a little squabble. It was not as solacious as I am sure it appeared upon first impression."

Richard groaned again as he pulled himself into a seated position, pressing a hand to his lower back. "You are quite heavier than you appear, Miss Greystone."

Agrippina frowned down at him, huffing through her nose. She resisted the urge to hit him again, however, rolling her shoulders and leading James to a different room.

"The nerve of that man!" Agrippina proclaimed, still annoyed by Richard's childish display.

"Might I ask what that was all about?" James asked. "Because it seemed rather—"

She looked up at him waiting for him to finish what he was trying to say.

"—questionable by propriety standards."

"What is not questionable by propriety standards?" she retorted.

He cleared his throat. "Aggy, did he put his hands on you?"

"Well, yes, he grabbed my wrist so he could take the journal from me."

"But he did not try to—"

"James, what are you trying to imply?"

"Did Mr. Maddox try to seduce you or touch you inappropriately?"

Agrippina wrinkled her nose. "Oh Lord, James! No! I can assure you, that has never been his intentions toward me."

"Aggy, he is a man, and you are a very beautiful woman."

Agrippina took a deep breath and let it out slowly. "Without telling you why I believe Mr. Maddox does not see me in that way, I am just going to have to ask you to trust me."

He raised a brow at her. "It is not you whom I do not trust," he grumbled. "It is the other man in this equation. I know how men work, so you are going to have to trust me too."

She smirked. "Is that how *you* work then?" she teased lightly.

James turned crimson, stammering. "No, no, no! Of course not! I am not like that. I merely understand how the mind of a man works, seeing that I am one. We are very similar in one sense but also very different in another."

"For example?"

"Uh, well, some men will chase anything—any kind of woman. They are purely in it for the chase. Woman-crazy, lecherous creatures. While other men, though they appreciate the form and beauty of other women, are only looking for that one special woman." He cleared his throat, visibly uncomfortable with the conversation. "Some men just want notches on their belt and continue to collect them even after they are wed. But men of honor would never dream of it."

"Are *you* a man of honor?"

He looked over at her, a little hurt. "Do you doubt it of me?"

She shook her head. "I do not know. You had me in a very compromising position earlier this morning. My reputation is certainly at stake if anyone happened to see it."

James turned and gaped at her. "Aggy, you must know by now that I have tried on two occasions since I have arrived to—"

She put a finger against his lips. "Perhaps you will need to try a little harder next time." She bit her lip to hold back a smile.

James was not sure if he wanted to kiss her or shake her at that moment, but chose to do neither.

"I appreciate you saving me from the clutches of Mr. Maddox, but I have some reading do," she told him, holding up the journal. "Do try not to attack Mr. Maddox in my absence."

He narrowed his eyes at her. "I will make no such promise." He smiled at her wryly as she left him in the hall.

She smiled the entire way to her room, thinking of the kiss they had shared earlier. She sighed, her cheeks flushing and heart racing. Mr. Mackland—James—shared her sentiments and she could not contain the smile that spread over her face.

She took a deep breath, however, and reminded herself why she was there as she opened the door to her room.

She was startled to find someone within, but calmed herself when she noticed it was the pretty maid Kitty from the day before.

"Forgive me. I've a habit of startlin' ya," she said with a shy smile.

Agrippina shook her head. "There is nothing to forgive. You are only doing your job." She moved to the desk and placed the journal on it.

Kitty resumed fluffing her pillows.

Agrippina smiled lightly. "Might I ask how long you have been working here, Kitty?"

The maid half curtseyed, pleased. "Three years or so, miss. Since I were fifteen."

"And have you witnessed anything," she hesitated, "strange?"

She shook her head. "No, Mr. Bolten's always treated me well. I've no complaints. Though his mother can be right mean sometimes." She pressed a hand to her mouth. "I forget myself. I shouldn't've said that."

Agrippina shook her head. "I will not say anything."

"Oh, thank you, miss."

"What are your thoughts on the woman in black?"

Kitty blinked at her, gently shaking her head. "I've no thoughts. I've heard haunting tales of this house, it being so old, but I've never seen anythin'." She curtseyed again. "Beg yer pardon, miss, but I should be gettin' back to my work."

"Yes, of course. Thank you, Kitty." She took a seat at the desk and picked up Maven's journal

Kitty smiled and moved toward the door. "Be careful, miss. These walls have eyes and ears."

Agrippina whirled around, another question on her tongue, but Kitty was already gone. She stood and moved to the doorway, peering into the hall but there was nothing but cold air.

Agrippina shivered, blinking into the empty hallway. "His mother," she whispered to herself, recalling what Kitty had said about the family.

*His mother can be right mean sometimes.*

She recalled the Bolten family Bible, remembering the entry. Mrs. Eliza Bolten, Mr. Eugene Bolten's mother, died ten years ago.

Another chill ran over her as she shook her head. "No, no," she softly said aloud. "I must have heard her incorrectly. She must have said Mrs. Bolten. I am sure she did."

Shaking off the incident as best she could, she sat at the desk and opened Maven's journal, the adder stone clutched in her hand.

# 26

What a lovely journal I received from Mr. Bolten! It is the prettiest one I have ever seen! Dark green with an embossed rose in silver foil! Oh, how I melted when I saw it! If that was not enough, he bought me a brand new quill to go with it. He often brings little trinkets for us when he goes to London, but this journal has been my favorite!

I was so pleased, I could not wait to run to my room and write in it. Though it took me a week to decide what I wanted to do with it. It's so pretty, I couldn't just write anything. I think I shall make a new habit of writing in it every day!

Wednesday, February 8, 1792

I saw Anna today. Mr. Bolten gave her a new pair of gloves. They are very ornate with lace around the wrist and a beautiful, polished button. I was wildly envious for a moment until I remembered my journal and quill. New gloves would be nice, and they certainly suit Anna, but if I had to choose, I would choose my journal every day of the week.

Thursday, February 9, 1792

Anna sent me a letter today. She says she believes she is in love. She failed to tell me with whom,

198

*but she wrote of his many wonderful attributes. He is, of course, very handsome. I could not imagine anything else with how pretty Anna is. I am sure he is the most deserving of men.*

*Their new farm hand is rather handsome. We have often seen him in church and said so. His smile if directed toward me, would make me swoon. I swear I have seen the two of them staring at each other on several occasions.*

*Friday, February 10, 1792*

*It rained so horribly today you could barely see out the window. I spent the day reading The Romance of the Forest. Oh, how beautiful! If only I could meet a handsome young man to fight for me as Adeline did! I would be his forever. I wonder how Anna met the man she loves. She said she has known him for so long she cannot even remember when they met. It must be the farm hand. She had never mentioned being in love until after he began working for them. I must ask how they fell in love and how she knew she loved him.*

*I want to fall in love too! I want to explore old castles and ruins and be saved from ruffians by a daring, handsome young man who only has eyes for me.*

*I wonder what it must be like to be loved by a man...*

*Saturday, February 11, 1792*

*More rain! I want to soak up the sun and enjoy the last remnants of the cool, crisp winter air. I wish it would at least snow! Rain is miserable in the winter, but snow is romantic.*

*I suppose I should be grateful as a farmer's daughter that it does rain, but I cannot daydream I am being pursued by bandits in the forest waiting to be saved while I am sitting, staring out the window.*

*Though it does give me more time to read my book. I think I might be able to finish it today.*

*Sunday, February 12, 1972*

*I was hoping to see Anna in church so I could press her for more details about who she was in love* with, but she was not feeling well that morning. I suppose she was due for her monthly courses. Oh, I suppose I shouldn't be talking about monthly courses in here. Mother would be appalled.

I was greatly disappointed when Anna was not in church, but I was only able to listen to half the sermon. My mind was too preoccupied with The Romance of the Forest. It ended so beautifully that I cried.

Mr. Bolten must have seen how distracted I was because he asked me what I was thinking about and smiled at me when I blushed. He then asked me about my dear journal. I was so proud to tell him that I have written in it every day.

He then told me I was growing into a beautiful and charming young woman. I hope he is not being polite. I do wish to be charming. But who is there to charm in such a small, silly town?

Monday, February 13, 1792

I received another letter from Anna. She told me she went for a late afternoon walk yesterday and was surprised by her love. She still will not tell me who her mystery man is, so I can only imagine.

It must be the farm hand Mosley. He is very handsome and strong. I caught him watching us when I was there the other day. I hope it is not him for I cannot help feeling jealous if it were. If I could get a man as handsome as he is to look at me...

Tuesday, February 14, 1792

I received a new book today from Mr. Bolten! A Sicilian Romance by Anne Radcliffe. I must have mentioned to him at church how much I had enjoyed The Romance of the Forest and he found me this one.

He brought it over with something for my father. My father was in the fields and my mother was in town, so I sat with Mr. Bolten for a few minutes alone. He is very handsome, and his eyes are so striking.

*I do enjoy when Mr. Bolten comes over. He is not like other men. He actually talks to me as if he wants to know what I have to say.*

*Wednesday, February 15, 1792*

*Mother surprised me with a new dress! She said it was for my birthday in a few days, but she couldn't wait to give it to me! It is the most beautiful muslin dress! It is cream with tiny purple flowers on it.*

*She said Mr. Bolten recommended this design as it is all the rage in London. I cannot wait to show it to Anna on Friday! I hope Mosley will see me in it!*

*Thursday, February 16, 1792*

*It is raining! Didn't we have enough rain last week? I suppose if it should rain, then I would prefer it to rain today rather than tomorrow.*

*I have done nothing of importance today except wallow in my own self-pity.*

*Friday, February 17, 1792*

*Today was magical! I wore my new dress which Anna was wildly envious about! She was still sweet and told me how well I looked in it. She also painted me a forest landscape with a few cows. She is becoming such an accomplished painter.*

*What I really wanted from her though was more information about her mystery lover. She told me it has to be a secret for now since it would not be proper. Which tells me he must be of a different class. It must be the new hand Mosley which disappointed me greatly even if I did get a smile out of him in passing.*

*Another thoughtful gift I received was a purple ribbon that perfectly matches my new dress. I am not exactly sure who gave it to me as there was no name, but there was a little note that read, 'A pretty little thing to add to your beauty.'*

*It came in a pretty little box with the mail. How curious!*

*Maybe I have an admirer.*

*Oh, how magical it is to be fifteen!*

Saturday, February 18, 1792

*I believe it happened! I believe I am in love! It happened on accident while I was taking a walk and I came across—Oh! But I cannot say! I want to shout it out to the world, but I promised I would not say a word. Oh! The agony!*

*I can at least tell the events leading up to what happened and just leave his name out. That will have to do.*

*I was walking, as I said, down the lane when I came across him. He was on his horse, and he stopped upon seeing me asking if I would like a ride. I refused at first, but he insisted. As I know this man rather well, I did not see the harm in it, so he helped me up. He then climbed up behind me and steered the horse through a little path near the woods.*

*We trotted slowly at first, but he soon picked up speed which frightened me. He must have sensed it because he wrapped an arm around my waist and pulled me close to him. In that moment, I was Adeline being saved by her beloved from the bandits. I thought I would swoon right there.*

*After what seemed like a moment and an eternity all at once, he stopped the horse near a clearing and helped me down. He then took me by the hand and led me to the small waterfall in the woods not far from the path. I had only ever been there a few times, but I have never remembered it being so beautiful as it was in that moment.*

*He then whispered in my ear and told me how beautiful I was and how he always thought so. He brushed back a lock of my hair that had fallen out from under my bonnet and asked me if I liked the purple ribbon he bought for me. I could have died of happiness when I heard him say it was he who bought it!*

202

And, then, he kissed me ever so softly on the lips. I felt as though my heart would explode! When he pulled away, my knees were so weak, I could hardly stand. So he took me in his arms and asked if he could see me again, alone.

I believe I must have nodded because he smiled and told me to meet him on the road Monday night and we will have a midnight ride. He then told me, for obvious reasons, I cannot tell anyone about our meeting and that we must pretend nothing has happened while in the presence of others. It is our perfect little secret, he had said.

Oh! I understand but at the same time I am dying to declare my love! Monday cannot get here soon enough.

Sunday, February 19, 1792

I saw my perfect little secret at church. It is so difficult pretending not to love him as I do. All I want to do is look at him and have him look at me the way he did the day before, but we cannot. I promised it was our secret, and our secret it will remain. I will not even tell Anna!

Monday, February 20, 1792

Tonight is the night!! I will not be able to write about it until the morning, but until then, I cannot stop thinking about it.

Will he kiss me again? Oh! I dreamed about that kiss since he left it upon my lips. He is so handsome and perfect in every way. A true gentleman.

He does have one defect that I did not notice until the other day when he held his hand out to me. On his left hand his little finger is significantly smaller than it should be. But it does not matter to me. What is physical deformity in the face of grace and manners? Nothing! He is all perfection.

Tuesday, February 21, 1792

How do I describe what happened last night into the morning? My head is still buzzing from it all.

*He picked me up on his horse as he said he would, and we took another ride through the forest. The air was crisp and a little chilly as we rode along, but the stars were out, and the moon was bright.*

*He wrapped his free arm around me and held me close. I felt so safe.*

*When we arrived at the waterfall, he brought me down from the horse and led me to a little patch of grass where he laid down a blanket. We sat and talked for a few minutes until he kissed me again.*

*My whole body tingled as I leaned into him, his hands trailing my face, my body. My breath still catches in my mouth as I remember his lips on my skin, his hand up my skirts.*

*I am blushing as I write this and am wishing for more. I was nervous last night, but I am no longer. I cannot wait to meet him again.*

*Wednesday, February 22, 1792*

*I do not think I will see him today and my heart aches without him. He is everything that I think about. His eyes, his lips, his hands, his voice, his smile! I close my eyes and I see them.*

*Reading about romance is nothing to living it, but I shall have to amuse myself somehow until I can meet my perfect secret again.*

*Thursday, February 23, 1792*

*I have received a note from him! He says he misses me and cannot stop thinking about me. He wants to meet again tonight! I can hardly contain myself!*

*Friday, February 24, 1792*

*Last night I gave myself fully to him. He said that the only way we can fully be together right now is if I did so. He said he will think of other ways to ensure our future together, but it had to start there. The perfect moment where we became one.*

*Oh, how romantic and beautiful it was. He was so gentle and patient with me while I was so scared and unsure. It hurt at first and I am still a little sore, but he assured me that it will be even more pleasurable the next time.*

*I have sighed a thousand times today thinking of him and wondering if he was thinking of me too.*

*I love him! I love him! I love him! A thousand more times, I love him!*

Saturday, February 25, 1792

*I walked along the lane today, hoping I would see him again, but, alas, he did not come. I was not expecting him to, but I was hoping. Hoping he would come and sweep me off my feet again.*

*I know I should not expect it. He has told me he has several responsibilities and there will be days where I will not see him or hear from him. My heart aches when I think of it. To not see or hear from my love for days? Is there any agony worse than that?*

*I will go to Anna's tomorrow and then I can finally tell her that I have a secret love too. How shocked she will be!*

Sunday, February 26, 1792

*My perfect little secret was not in church today. I wondered if he was out of town, and it made me sad to think he should not tell me he was leaving. Nothing seemed to be amiss as I did not hear anyone mention his name after service.*

*Anna seemed just as distracted during church as I was. Perhaps she was thinking of her love just as I was. How does one function when they are in love? My mind is hardly where it should be.*

*Anna came over after church for tea. I could tell her mind was somewhere else there too. I wanted to tell her my news, but we hardly got a moment to ourselves. So, I told her I would call on her tomorrow.*

Monday, February 27, 1792

*Oh, you should have seen Anna's face when I told her that I had a secret lover too. She was so*

205

jealous that she was no longer the only one that had someone to love and who loved her.

She, of course, begged to know who he was, but I was true to my perfect little secret and denied every hint. Besides, she still has not told me who her mystery man was. She would only tell me that he was not in church yesterday. I couldn't help but notice that Mosley was not in church yesterday either. I, in turn, told her the same thing. She merely grumbled at me.

As I was leaving, she appeared to receive a letter from her mysterious lover because as she was handed the note, her eyes sparkled and she gave me a hasty goodbye before rushing back inside. Can Mosley read and write?

When I returned home, I received a letter as well. It was from him. He wanted to meet again at our usual spot tomorrow night!

Tuesday, February 28, 1792

I finished A Sicilian Romance! I think I shall read it again and again until I die. I cannot wait until Miss Radcliffe's next book. What adventures she takes you on. It is the only thing I have to pass the time until I meet up with him. Really, it is the only thing that makes time pass while I am waiting.

Being in love is such a beautiful torture! How strange...

Wednesday, February 29, 1792

Last night was just as beautiful as the last. I can still hear him whispering "Oh, Maven!" in my ear and it sends a shiver of pleasure through me.

I shall be thinking of nothing else today!

## 27

Agrippina was interrupted by Janet who found her in her room reading Maven Rupert's journal.

"Forgive me, miss," Janet said with a little curtsey. "But lunch is ready."

Agrippina nodded, closing the journal.

"Everyone's eating out in the garden. 'Tis such a beautiful day. Would ya like to join everyone or have it brought here?"

Agrippina smiled lightly. "I think the fresh air will do me good. Thank you, Janet." She stood from the desk and followed her down the stairs. "Have you recovered from yesterday?"

Janet glanced at her sideways, looking a little ashamed. "Was just the stress I suppose. I think with everything that's been happenin' I must've imagined the woman in black. Hysteria can be catchin'."

Agrippina frowned. "I do not understand. Are you saying that or is that what you were told to say?"

Janet did not reply as she continued to lead Agrippina out to the garden.

"Janet, do you know what is going on here? If you do, you

need to tell me."

Janet turned to face Agrippina, a scowl on her face. "I beg your pardon, miss, but I'm rather offended you'd think such uh thing. I've given ya no reason to think poorly of me or to doubt my word."

"Forgive me, Janet. You are very right. I should not have questioned you," Agrippina replied though she was still skeptical.

Janet nodded, looking a little more confident. "Thank you."

She resumed leading Agrippina outside where an elaborate table was set with cold meats and seasonal fruit. They were seated near the koi pond where James and her had shared a kiss earlier that morning.

She blushed subtly, looking up to lock eyes with James who was standing by a chair waiting for the ladies before sitting. He smiled at her, giving a single nod. She stood next to him and their fingers brushed against each other causing her blush to deepen.

"Where have you been hiding yourself away to this morning?" Cecelia asked seated next to her. "I was going to ask if you wanted to join me in a ride to town, but Richard said I would be wasting my breath. That you are far too busy to keep me company while I frolic through the milliner's shop."

"Oh, I suppose he is right. I am not one to frolic through any shop."

She laughed. "You are so literal sometimes, Miss Greystone. I am not really going to frolic. I just want to pick out a few new dresses for the season. It will be my last one and Henry did not want me to miss out. I am to spend it in London with his sister and mother. He, of course, will join us later, but it will just be us three women for a few weeks. I do love my future sister-in-law. She is the most darling thing. And this is her first season so it will be extra special!"

Richard laughed. "Cece, take a breath when you talk. I am sure Miss Greystone does not care about your new dresses or your last season in London."

"Oh la, Richard!" she exclaimed. "Do not spoil my excitement!"

"I remember when I was first out," Mrs. Bolten said. "It was the most glorious time of my life. The dresses, the music, the dancing. Everything seemed so magical."

"You met uncle during a dance, did you not?" Cecelia asked.

Mrs. Bolten nodded. "Yes, during my second season. I had a few offers the year before, but I was not interested. They were too boring and lacked something I desperately wanted."

"And what was that, aunt?" Cecelia pressed.

She looked over at her husband, a subtle smile on her face. "A man with spirit, or a certain sense of life." She shook her head. "I cannot describe exactly what I was looking for, but I knew Eugene had it the moment we locked eyes."

He lifted his glass to his wife. "And you are just as beautiful as the day we met, my love."

Cecelia turned to Agrippina. "Have you ever spent the season in London?"

Richard laughed again. "I cannot imagine Miss Greystone parading around town like a prized peacock."

Agrippina raised a brow in Richard's direction. "Male peacocks are the ones who 'parade,' Mr. Maddox. And though I might not have made a lasting impression on everyone while in London, I most certainly had a season there."

"Oh! Did you?" Cecelia asked, intrigued. "You are so pretty; I dare say you did not even need the most expensive dresses and materials to shine. Did you have many dance partners? Or," she gasped, "did you have any proposals?"

The corner of Agrippina's mouth twitched into a smile. "I believe I was popular until most of the men realized I was significantly smarter than them."

"That does not surprise me," Richard started, laughing. "What does surprise me is you agreed to a season."

She shook her head. "It was suggested that I should by my uncle."

"Your uncle the earl? He is a rather fearsome character," Cecelia said.

Agrippina smile gently. "No, by my other uncle. The one who raised me. He thought if I did not have at least one season, I would regret it." She half shrugged. "He was not wrong. It was rather interesting observing the ridiculousness of it all. The mating rituals of humans are not that different to the peacock if I am not mistaken."

Everyone at the table chuckled.

"You do bring rather interesting conversation to the table, Miss Greystone," Mr. Bolten said. "I wonder, have you been able to figure anything out about what has been going on?"

Agrippina nodded. "I have pieced together a few things."

"There is a fair chance she is about to piece together more," Richard continued. "Mrs. Rupert found her daughter's journal."

Mr. Bolten dropped his fork, the sound of it clattering onto his plate interrupting Richard. "Excuse me," he said, clearing his throat. "A journal, you say?"

Agrippina glanced over at Richard. "Yes, sir. I have read some of it, but it has not given me as much information as I have hoped. Though I still have a little ways to go."

Mr. Bolten coughed and scratched his neck. "And, uh, what have you found so far?"

"The ravings of a mad girl, I am sure," Mrs. Bolten

interposed, looking into her glass of port.

Agrippina shook her head. "She is very lucid and well written so far, but only time will tell. There are also a few pages that have been ripped out, so I hope they are of no great import."

A gush of wind caught the party by surprise and Cecelia— who had rushed out of the house without securing her bonnet to her head—let out a squeal as her bonnet was blown swiftly away. It tumbled to the ground and caught the wind, threatening to fall into the koi pond.

"Oh no!"

James stood to try and catch it, but before he could get out of his chair, Alex Mosley stepped from his post and was able to grab it before it fell in.

"Ah! Oh, thank you!" Cecelia exclaimed with a clap. "I thought my bonnet was surely ruined!"

Alex bowed, holding it out for her to take. As Cecelia took it, Agrippina noticed that the little finger on his left hand was significantly smaller than it should be. She pushed back on her chair so hard as she stood that it fell backward to the ground.

Everyone stopped and looked at her, confused by her sudden movement, but she didn't notice; she was busy looking at Alex Mosley's hand.

"How well did you know Maven Rupert, Mr. Mosley?" Agrippina asked, causing a blush of confusion to fall over Alex.

He shook his head, confused at her direct question. He looked up at Mrs. Bolten.

"Is this really the time, Miss Greystone?" Mrs. Bolten asked her. "We have only begun to eat. Can it not wait?"

"No, no. Answer her, Mosely," Mr. Bolten ordered.

Alex shifted his gaze uncomfortably. "I saw 'er sometimes

when I worked for 'er father and maybe at the Brown's farm when I were there, but that 'twas all. We barely spoke."

"Then how did she know about this?" Agrippina grabbed his hand and held it up, displaying his dwarfed little finger.

Richard gaped, frozen; Cecelia pressed her napkin to her mouth, stunned; Mrs. Bolten's eyes grew wide; Mr. Bolten's face lost all its color.

Alex took his hand back. "I don't know what yer talkin' about, miss," he said taking a step back. "Miss Rupert's a nice girl, but I know me place. I'd never dare to overreach it."

"Miss Greystone," Mr. Arter said, appearing as he usually did out of nowhere and taking his nephew by the arm. "Is Alex bothering you? I will have him assigned to a different duty if he is. But, for now, please sit and enjoy your lunch."

Agrippina snapped back to where she was, realizing she had made a display of herself. She stammered for a second before clearing her throat and shaking her head.      "No, I would like to question Mr. Mosley right now. I have been delayed enough. Take him to the kitchen and I will meet you there," she said sternly, stepping away from the table and righting her chair. "Forgive me, everyone, for the small outburst. Ja—Mr. Mackland, would you care to join me and Mr. Mosley in the kitchen?"

James nodded as he took one last bite of his food and wiped his mouth with a napkin before he stood. He bowed to everyone at the table. "Lovely set up. Thank you." He bowed again and followed after Agrippina who had already begun to move toward the house.

"Do you care to fill me in?" James said as he caught up to her. "Why are you so offended by that servant's hand?"

She glanced over at him as she continued to walk. "Someone with an unusually small little finger on their left hand was intimate with both Maven Rupert and Anna Brown

212

just before they began seeing the woman in black." She took a deep breath and let it out in a rush of air. "I believe both girls were with child around the time the sightings began."

"You think this servant, Mr. Mosley, could be that man?"

"I do not think that Mr. Mosley's hand disfigurement is common," Agrippina told him. "Do you?"

He opened his mouth for a second before rethinking what he was going to say. He then shook his head. "No, I suppose I have never seen something like that before and I have been a few places."

"Exactly," Agrippina said. "Mr. Mosley could be the key to figuring this out, or at the very least, he could be the person who killed poor Anna Brown."

# 28

"MISS GREYSTONE, I DO BELIEVE YOU ARE MAKING SOME sort of mistake," Mr. Arter said when they entered the kitchen. "Alex does not know anything about what you are investigating. He has no involvement whatsoever."

Agrippina ignored Mr. Arter's pleas. Instead, she asked for a pot of tea. He looked rather annoyed by her request but eventually nodded and moved to order another maid to get it done.

Alex looked a little nervous as he rocked on the balls of his feet.

"Mr. Mosley," Agrippina began, "might I ask why you were watching me the other day in town?"

Alex blinked down at his feet and shook his head. "I don't know what ye mean."

"In Halstead. I stopped by there with Richard a few days ago. We went into a tavern and from across the street, I saw you staring at me. Why?"

Alex cleared his throat. "Yer pretty enough to look at, I guess," he mumbled. "I didn't see any harm in it."

Agrippina narrowed her eyes at him. "That is not the truth,

is it? Why will you not tell me? Or can you not tell me?"

Alex coughed and shifted where he stood.

"You do not have to stand, Mr. Mosley," Agrippina told him. "Please, sit."

Alex, though still uncomfortable, sat at the little table for staff across from Agrippina and James.

"How did you get to town that day?"

Alex sniffed and shrugged. "I rode up with the driver of the carriage."

She looked surprised. "So you rode with us to Rupert farm?"

He nodded. "I rode to the Brown farm too."

"Were you told to keep an eye on Miss Greystone, Mr. Mosley?" James asked.

Alex didn't answer; instead he turned his head, ignoring the question.

"I believe that is a 'yes,'" James said looking over at Agrippina.

Agrippina sighed. "On the same morning we went to Rupert farm, I saw you and your sister Janet arguing about something. What was that about?"

Alex tensed slightly.

"Janet told me she caught you in the music room."

This time, Alex's face became red, his ears burning. "She weren't supposed to say nothin'," he replied angrily.

Agrippina shook her head. "She did not tell me anything really. I saw you both from the window that morning and I asked her about it. She only mentioned the music room."

Alex frowned. "She best not have said anythin'! If uncle or Mrs. Bolten find out they will be very angry Janet mentioned it."

"Mrs. Bolten knows then whatever it is you did?" she asked, catching onto his mistake.

Alex began to get flustered. His face once again reddened, and he rubbed his hand nervously across his mouth.

Agrippina tapped a finger on the table. "Were you intimate with Maven Rupert and Anna Brown?"

He glared at her. "No! I've never touched neither of them girls. They'd never look my way even if I wanted to."

Agrippina lifted a brow. "Are you sure? Maven mentions you enough in her journal. She calls you handsome."

He shrugged. "I never sought after them girls. Maybe a flirtin' glance once in a while, but I never touched 'em!"

"And what about your finger?" She held her hand out indicating the appendage in question.

Alex pulled his hand under the table and shrugged. "What about it? Why not ask my father. I'm told it is hereditary. Passed down through the generations."

"Alex!" Mr. Arter half yelled, his eyes wide, holding a tray of tea.

Alex bowed his head and stared down into his lap looking like a scolded dog.

"This interview is over," Mr. Arter ordered. "Go and see if you are needed outside, boy."

"I am not done questioning him!" Agrippina protested.

Without a word and before he could be stopped, Alex shot up from the table and scrambled out of the kitchen.

"What right do you have to interfere with Miss Greystone's questioning?" James asked, heated. "You are a servant here. She has been given permission by your master to investigate."

"Mr. Maddox is not the master of this house yet," Mr. Arter informed them. "You are here as a courtesy to him, but that does not mean your antics will be tolerated."

"My antics?" Agrippina frowned. "I am trying to find out who wants to get rid of Mr. Bolten, and solve the possible

216

murder of Miss Brown. I feel as if everyone, save Mr. Maddox himself, is hiding something from me!"

Mr. Arter narrowed his eyes at her. "Some secrets are best left buried, Miss Greystone. With all of your intelligence, one would think you might understand that." He turned and left the kitchen leaving a seething Agrippina in his wake.

Agrippina scoffed. "Can you believe the insolence of that man?" She huffed, angrily splashing cream into her tea. "With all of your intelligence!" she said mockingly. "I dislike that man exceedingly."

James cleared his throat. "Do you think it possible that Alex and Mrs. Bolten are having an affair?"

Agrippina let out a small laugh. "That is one way to get me out of my sour mood." She took a sip from her cup.

He shook his head. "I am being serious."

Agrippina regarded him for a moment. "What would make you think that? She is married and nearly forty and he is perhaps nineteen, maybe twenty?"

James shrugged. "She is still a very attractive woman."

"Oh?"

James chuckled. "I am not vying for her, but I am not blind."

"But what would make you think that?"

He nodded his head at her cup. "Finish your tea. The kitchen may have ears."

Agrippina took another long sip before putting her tea down and following James through the breakfast room, into the foyer and down the hall to the study. James made sure no one was outside in the hall and closed the door.

"I sometimes have trouble sleeping at night," James began in a low tone. "And last night was one of those nights. So, instead of rolling around in bed, I got up and walked around the house. It always helps me clear my head when I am home. As I was making my way downstairs, I heard a noise coming from the music room."

A slight draft in the room caused a few papers on the desk to flutter. One fell to the floor and Agrippina picked it up, placing it back neatly on the desk.

"What kind of noise?" Agrippina asked innocently.

James cleared his throat. "I was not sure when I first heard it, but as I got closer, I realized it was a moaning sound. The door was cracked, so I peered through it, and I saw two people engaged in," he hesitated, unsure how to word it, "in a very intimate act."

"You can say intercourse, James, I am not a child," Agrippina told him. She shivered as another draft filled the room.

"Right." He cleared his throat again. "Intercourse. I did not see either of their faces as it was rather dark, but I did hear the woman say 'Alex.'"

She shook her head. "But why do you think it was Mrs. Bolten?"

"Something in the voice." He paused for a second. "During lunch, she appeared to be looking past me, her eyes lost somewhere distant, yet smiling. I realized that was where Alex was standing."

Agrippina thought for a moment, watching the papers rustle on the desk. "But if that is the case," she sighed, "what about Anna Brown and Maven Rupert? Are you saying he seduced all three of them?"

"I do believe earlier I mentioned how some men just like to add notches to their bedpost, did I not?"

"And Mrs. Bolten? Why would she allow herself to be taken in by such a young man of low means? Perhaps if she were a lonely widow, I would understand, but she is still very much married and very proud of her station."

James coughed to hide a chuckle. "Your morality is encouraging, but not everyone feels the same way about certain things."

Agrippina shook her head as another piece of paper fluttered to the floor. "What is going on with this family?" she whispered in a harsh tone moving to the window to secure it. She stopped when she saw that it was tightly closed.

"What is wrong?" James asked, seeing her confused expression.

"Where is that draft coming from?" She walked to the other window further down the wall, but it too was securely fastened.

James shook his head. "I do not know. I have not noticed anything."

Agrippina and James moved about the room, even trying the door to find the source of the draft but found nothing. James tried the windows again, thinking the seal was old and leaky, but something about this room had always nagged at Agrippina.

She let out a frustrated sigh, missing her uncle. If he were there, he would tell her to walk away from what was bothering her. *Take a moment to gather your thoughts without letting your emotions get in the way.*

She shook her head. That was not the advice she wanted at the moment. What was it her uncle's last letter had said? She was sure he must have said something about using her imagination or being openminded. There was something else though.

*If a door will not open, sometimes you must break through a wall.*

She laughed at herself for a second. That is not the metaphor she thought she needed currently, but she then remembered what the maid Kitty had told her.

*These walls have eyes and ears.*

Agrippina stopped, thinking of the possibility. Her uncle would tell her that didn't matter. Even if the odds were low, there were still odds. She walked over to the far wall with the tapestry and paintings, and where the personal bar was. She began tapping on it, her ear pressed against it.

"What are you doing?" James asked, curious.

"I think there is another door along this wall. A secret door," she told him, continuing to tap and listen.

James nodded. "Alright." He began to mirror her, starting on the far end of the wall. Six feet from the corner, and right along the tapestry, he paused. "Aggy, I think I found something."

She quickly walked over to him as he lifted up the tapestry. Along the seam of the wallpaper, just concealed by the tapestry, was a puff of air.

"I knew it!" Agrippina exclaimed excitedly. "I knew this room was too small." She began to feel along the seam, trying to find a way to open it.

"What would they need a secret door for?" James asked as he pushed hard along the seam. A small portion of the wall, smaller than a regular door, slowly swung open.

Agrippina's heart raced with excitement and trepidation as she looked down into a dark stairwell that descended into darkness. "Richard himself told me the Boltens used to be smugglers. I am sure they had this built to help move and store their product."

James looked down the stairs and nodded. "I suppose we will need candles?"

She nodded. "But we cannot right now," she told him. "There is no way to tell how far down it goes or how extensive it is. They will notice we are gone for too long."

He let out a huff. "So, instead of exploring this dark

cavernous hole in the ground during the day, you wish to do it during the night when it is extra dark?"

Agrippina blinked at him.

"Oh, yes, of course, that is exactly what we are going to do. You are right." He coughed. "Perfect. This will be perfect. Not strange or uncomfortable in the least bit."

Agrippina was still silently watching him.

He shook his head. "You staring at me is not helpful."

"Are you scared, James?" she asked quietly.

He half shrugged, half shook his head. "Scared is not the word I would wish to use." He coughed. "Um, uneasy comes to mind." He bobbed his head.

"Well, you do not have to come with me if you do not want to."

He shook his head. "Want is also not the word I would use. I will go down there with you, uh, because I feel I should help you. I want to help you more than I do not wish to go down there."

"Would you prefer to go now?"

He cleared his throat. "Yes, but it makes more sense to go when we will not be missed. So, uh, when everyone is supposed to be sleeping is the best time to do it."

Agrippina reached out and took his hand. "I appreciate your support, James. With my uncle unable to be here to help guide me, having you here has been a great comfort."

He smiled, pressing her hand to his lips.

She let her hand linger in his a moment longer. "We should close this before anyone comes."

James nodded and quickly pushed the door back into place, fixing the tapestry so it looked untouched. They left the study for the parlor, finding Richard staring out one of the windows. He was startled for a second when he heard the door, but bowed silently upon seeing them.

Agrippina frowned, noticing the sullen expression on his face. "Mr. Maddox, is everything alright?"

He didn't respond right away; he just lightly swayed back and forth on his feet. "I no longer wish to proceed with the investigation," he told her blandly.

Agrippina gaped at him, unable to speak for several seconds. "I do not understand. What do you mean? Why?"

Richard turned to face them. "I realize bringing you here was a mistake. There is nothing going on here and I made a big hullabaloo about nothing."

"But how do you explain the woman in black? And everyone seeing her, including myself?" Agrippina pressed. "Or everything else that has happened including Anna Brown's death?"

Richard cleared his throat. "Anna Brown's death was unfortunate, but hysteria can sometimes be catching."

Agrippina blinked, stunned that Janet had said almost the exact thing only a couple hours before. Her confusion soon turned to anger as she narrowed her eyes at Richard.

"Hysteria?" James repeated. "You think all of this is because of hysteria? That is the most ridiculous thing I have ever heard."

Agrippina put a hand on James's arm, stopping him from saying anything further. "I do not believe you think that at all, Mr. Maddox, but if it is your decision to stop pursuing the answers to your problems, then I have no choice. I have no authority here and will leave. So poor Anna Brown, who you said was such a sweet girl and did not deserve her fate, will receive no justice."

Richard looked ashamed. "It is regretful, but you said yourself there is no proof she was murdered. I am sorry to have wasted your time. There is no rush to leave. We of course are not so ungrateful as to expect you to leave today, but tomorrow the carriage will be ready for you."

Agrippina scoffed. "How kind you are." She left the parlor, steaming with fury.

Mr. Mackland cleared his throat. "I am going to venture to say that what Mr. Maddox said has no bearing on us exploring that deep, dark pit we found, and despite him having said he no longer wants you to investigate you are still going to use the last few hours you are here to figure this whole thing out."

Agrippina's anger eased and a mischievous smile sparkled in her eyes. "It does make it a little more exciting, does it not?"

"Is this the kind of thing you find exciting?" He lifted a brow at her. "Should I be concerned?"

"I shall see you at midnight," she whispered, ignoring his questions, making her way up the stairs and to her room. She made it to the door just as Kitty was slipping out into the hall.

"Miss," she greeted, bowing her head as she slipped into the service stairway.

Agrippina entered her room surprised to find a candelabra fitted with fresh candles.

# 29

*I nearly fell asleep in church this morning and was scolded by my mother who has now forbade me from staying up all night reading. But that was not the reason I was so tired.*

*I met my perfect little secret again. It has been four months since I have given myself to him and I have never been happier. I even hum while I do my chores now! Though, he has told me once we are able to fully be together, I will never have to lift a finger to do anything ever again. He said if I wanted to read all day, I could. I would just have to be available for him at night.*

*That would never be an issue. I would make myself available to him at any time of the day.*

Wednesday, June 6, 1792

*I received another little present from my love! A basket of oranges! I told him the last we met how much I love oranges and he listened! I have to share with my mother, of course, so she does not become suspicious, but I am so pleased!*

*He truly is wonderful!*

Friday, June 8, 1792

I am in utter agony! I have been crying for the past several hours and am inconsolable! To think this could be possible is almost laughable! I cannot believe it! I will not believe it!

I was at Anna's earlier, and she was showing me the newest gift she had received from her lover. It was just an array of marzipan, nothing special, but the note! Oh, the note!

I had to stop writing I was crying so hard and am still crying now! How could something hurt so much? It is as if there is knife in my chest!

I don't and cannot understand what all of this means!

The note was in his hand! He is her secret, mysterious lover! Her lover and mine are the same! Oh, it is as if I have been stabbed in the heart! I cannot believe he would do this to me after he said he loved me, after what I have given to him!

I feel as if I shall die from heartbreak!

Monday, June 11, 1792

I have not seen him since Thursday night and have spent the last several nights crying myself to sleep. My mother believes it is because Anna and I have argued. And we did. Neither of us could believe that the man we loved could ever love someone else.

She called me an envious liar and said I made the whole thing up because I could not bear to see her happy. But I did not imagine it! I know that what he and I had—have—is real.

I shall write him a note today, begging to see him.

Wednesday, June 13, 1792

Is there no end to my pain? My love has denied me! I confronted him about Anna and he has chosen her over me! I have given him everything and he has denied me! I want to scream until I

225

no longer feel the pain coursing through me.

I hate them both! I HATE them!

I have been lied to. All of the beautiful things he has said to me were lies! He is not the man I thought he was. He portrays himself as loving, caring and kind, but he is wicked!

Wicked, hateful, deceitful, awful man!

# 30

AGRIPPINA AND JAMES MET OUTSIDE THE STUDY A LITTLE after midnight, both of them holding candelabras and walking on tip toe. They pushed through the door, closing it silently behind them.

James moved over to the tapestry and pushed on the seam, the 'whoosh' of the air that escaped from the door causing his candles to flicker. Agrippina was beside him, looking down into the dark stairwell. She took a step forward, but James held his arm out, stopping her.

"I cannot allow you to go first," James whispered. "I should lead."

Agrippina opened her mouth to tell him she did not need a display of bravado, but she knew it was more for his pride than for her. She nodded and took a step back allowing him to go first down the stairs.

James moved slowly down the curved staircase, his candles illuminating the half-rotted stairs that creaked and groaned with every step. He paused, almost stumbling when he saw a broken stair, the wooden plank dangling by a single nail.

227

"Be careful," he whispered over his shoulder to Agrippina. "There is a step missing."

He waited at the bottom of the stairs for her, holding his hand to help her down the last step. She took it gratefully, squeezing it lightly as they shuffled further into the underground room.

They both looked about them in awe at its vastness.

"This looks as if it is as large as the upper house," James said, touching the stone foundation and tapping the wooden planks that lined the ground.

Agrippina nodded as she tentatively stepped forward, the floorboards creaking under her. "I believe this must have been built first and the house was built to conceal it."

"They must have had one very big smuggling operation to need this amount of space."

They moved through what appeared to be a hallway with partially rotted doors on either side marking rooms. Agrippina cautiously pushed a door open, flinching at the creaking sound it made. She peered in, holding out her candelabra, but the room was empty.

James chose a door on the other side of the hall; its door having fared better over the years. There were a few wooden crates, but they too appeared to be empty. The third room no longer had a door though the rusty hinges still hung to the frame. This room had an old desk with little bottles and jars next to a mortar and pestle.

The two of them exchanged glances as they entered.

Agrippina picked up one of the bottles and held it close to the candelabra so she could read the label, but the writing had been smeared. She picked up another, this label being more legible.

"Rue," Agrippina breathed, putting it back and taking another. "Savine." She picked up another. "Calamint." She

228

looked over at James who was holding a jar, but stopped in his observations to look at her.

He shook his head. "What are they for?"

Her head spun as she recalled what she had read in *Plants of Herbal, Medicinal, Euphoric, and Even Poisonous Means.* "They are abortifacients," she replied feeling a little overwhelmed. "They are used to get rid of unwanted pregnancies." She looked over at him. "What are they doing down here?"

"Do you think Alex was making them for the girls?"

She shook her head. "Alex might be charming, and not as simple as his uncle wishes me to believe, but I doubt he has the knowledge to correctly concoct something this dangerous without killing the one who consumed it. No, Alex did not do this."

"Is that not what happened?" James asked. "Did not one of the girls die? Could this not have been what killed her?"

"I am not sure. There is no evidence to prove it," Agrippina said picking up another bottle and tentatively smelling it.

"What did she die from then?"

She took a deep breath and let it out slowly. "In my opinion, Anna Brown was strangled to death after she was hit over the head with something heavy." She cleared her throat. "Or, she fell and hit her head and was of a weaker constitution than previously believed. She died and fell into the river."

"Hmm. In other words..."

"Yes, I know. I am," she paused, "guessing."

James shook his head and bent over to try to opening one of the desk drawers. "Well, let us go along for a moment with your first 'guess' and say she was murdered."

"Yes?"

He pulled the first drawer open with a grunt. "Why would

one of the girls be killed but the other one spared?" The drawer held empty jars that clattered and tinkered about as the drawer moved.

Agrippina sighed. "That is what I am trying to figure out. If I can figure out why Anna died over Maven, then maybe I can settle this."

"What if," he grunted as he pulled harder on the next drawer that seemed to be stuck, "her death had nothing to do with all of this? What if she snuck out of her house and met with some sinister person who is wholly unconnected, and he killed her?" He pulled harder again, the drawer creaking open about an inch.

She considered what he said and shrugged. "I suppose that could be a possibility. But it makes more sense that the man whom she was seeing did it. Reading through Maven's journal, she snuck out multiple times to meet with her mystery lover in the middle of the night. I can only imagine Anna was doing the same thing especially since it was the same man."

"You mean Alex?" He grunted again as he pulled, breaking the drawer as he did so. He held his candelabra over it, just making out something in the back. He knelt down and stuck his arm in, trying to reach for it.

She sighed again. "Now, I am not so sure. I was convinced when I saw his finger, but perhaps there is another man with the same deformity seducing young girls not far from here. His father perhaps. Though I have no notion of who that is."

"Ah!" James said grinning. "I got it!"

"What is it?"

"Feels like a book or something." He let out a small hiss of pain.

"Are you alright?" she asked in concern. "What happened?"

"No worries. It is just a splinter." He wriggled his arm out, pulling with it a black, leatherbound notebook. He observed each side of it before flipping through its pages.

"Well?"

He shrugged. "Looks like a journal of some sort." He handed it to her.

She took it a little greedily and flipped through it, frowning. "I do not understand. What am I looking at?"

She flipped toward the middle of the book, holding it in the light so she could read it. On the left margin there appeared to be columns of initials next to a year. Across from each initial was a number ranging from fourteen to twenty. Further across from that were certain words: good, very good, perfect, bad, and awful. Further down was the last row which listed three groupings of two letters: LI, WC, AO.

Each page was similar though some were more descriptive than others. Agrippina blinked down at it, lightly shaking her head.

"It appears to be a catalogue of something."

James cleared his throat as he looked over her shoulder. "That book is a bedpost, and those initials are notches."

She looked at him, still confused. "A bedpost? What are you talking about a bed—" She stopped when the realization sank in. "This is a catalogue of women someone has been with."

James nodded, taking the book from her. "Dating all the way back to," he flipped to the first page. "1768."

"Twenty-five years." She shook her head. "That is before Mr. Mosley was most likely even born."

"Look at this." He held open the last page. "The last entry was 1792. 'MLR, 15, found out about AMB, became confrontational, LI.'"

Agrippina pressed a hand to her mouth and reached out with her other one to take the book back. "MLR, Maven Rupert. AMB, Anna Brown."

"Then Mr. Mosley was not the one who seduced them."

She tapped the line with Anna's initials, seeing WC. "What do you think LI, WC, and AO mean?" she asked, flipping back to the first page. "Has to be some sort of code."

"I am not sure."

She scanned the initials stopping at one listed over twenty years ago. "CPM, 17, good, WC. These are the initials on the shawl I found."

"What is scrawled right there next to it?" James asked, pointing.

Agrippina squinted at the tiny scrawled note. "'Gave rue but would not take. Sent away.'" She gasped. "WC stands for with child. The first column is obviously the year he began the affair, followed by the woman's initials. The next is the number of times they—" She trailed off. She scowled, disgusted. "Why would he need to know that?"

James was unconvinced and shook his head. "I believe it is their age when the affair began."

"But that would make some of these girls only fourteen when—" She huffed, even more disgusted, but continued. "Their age, followed by—well, I think we understand it is a basic grading system on their performance. The last is why he ended the affair."

She trailed her finger down the last column. "Look at the WCs. Some of them have extra notes next to them that say, "Gave rue."

"What is this one here?" James pointed to a line with two initials.

"'1773, LHB (nee LHL), 19, very good, AO/WC, given rue five times.'" Agrippina thought for a moment, something Mr.

Arter had told her running through her mind.

*She was Miss Lowry back then.*

"James," she whispered, almost breathless. "This is Mrs. Bolten."

"What? Why would Mrs. Bolten take an abortifacient?"

She looked at him, horrified. "What if she did not know she had taken one?" She shook her head. "Something Mr. Bolten had said a few days ago gave me the impression he did not want children. He did not want the family curse to continue but to end with him."

"With as many women as he had relations with you would think that was the opposite."

"Yes, but bastard children do not bear the father's last name, so he must not think there is anything wrong with it."

He shook his head. "It would be awful to think he forced his wife to take something that would get rid of her child, or he put it in something, and she had no knowledge of it."

"My guess is he did the latter," Agrippina said, though a little distantly. "It was quite obvious Mrs. Bolten wanted children." She pointed again at the initials 'CPM.' "I want to know who this person is."

James looked over her shoulder again. "I think I saw another CPM but more recently. On the page where you discovered the girls."

Agrippina flipped through to the last page of the list and found it. "'1787, CPM, 14, very good.' There is no reason he stopped the affair."

He shrugged. "Maybe they have not stopped it yet."

A horrible sinking feeling grew in Agrippina's stomach as she thought back on the past few days. Her heart began to race as all the information she gathered coursed through her head. She snapped the book shut, observing the cover and spine. She froze when she saw the initials EGB on the side.

"I know what is going on," she breathed shaking her head. "I know what has been happening to a certain degree." She put a hand to her mouth. "Dear God, James."

"What is it?"

Agrippina opened her mouth to answer, but the creaking of wood near the stairs stopped her. James held up a hand. He placed his candelabra on the desk and slowly crept back out into the hallway.

She waited for what felt like several minutes, her heart pounding, before James slipped silently back into the room.

"Someone is coming down the hall."

Agrippina's mind raced. "We should hide."

James reached for a candelabra, but Agrippina stopped him.

"They will see the light. Leave them."

"Should we not snuff them out first?"

She shook her head. "They will only smell the smoke. Either way, they are about to know we are down here. If we leave the candles, they will not know where we are, but we will be able to see them."

He nodded and took her hand, leading her to the doorway. He peered out into the hall for a second before pulling his head back in.

"They are in another room down that way," he said indicating with his finger. "I can see the glow of their candle illuminating from it."

Agrippina tightened her grip on his hand, allowing him to lead her into the dark hallway.

"Stay as close to the wall as possible," James told her. "The boards are less likely to creak."

They moved slowly along the wall, feeling their way through the dark until they came to another room, its door half open. James gently pulled Agrippina into it taking tentative, feeling steps to make sure there was nothing to trip on.

A shiver came over her and she gently pulled her hand out of James', rubbing her arms for a moment. A strange urge to run enveloped her, to see who had come down the secret passage.

Agrippina took a deep breath and let it out slowly.

"What are you about to do?" James asked suspiciously.

"What? I am not going to—I am going to see who that is."

"Aggy, no!" he whispered harshly. "We are not supposed to be down here. What would it solve to go and spy on whoever that is?"

She hesitated in her response but only for a moment. "Everything." She slipped back out the door before James could take hold of her hand again, her back pressed against the wall as she made her way to the room where the candlelight was flickering.

She heard a small shuffle beside her and realized James had decided to follow her. She smiled to herself.

"You are insane, Agrippina Greystone."

If it had not been so dark, she would have shot him a small glare, but as it was, she kept her focus on taking as light of steps as possible. She began to hear someone humming softly which just barely covered up the small sounds of squeaking.

Agrippina was finally close enough to peer around the doorframe inside the room. She paused, took a deep breath and held it as she leaned her head enough to look. Her heart lurched when she saw a woman, dressed all in black holding a little white mouse in her hand.

She felt James's hand take hold of hers and she grasped it, but she could not tear herself away from where she stood, watching, waiting for the woman to turn around. She watched as the woman reached into the box on the table before her and pulled out another mouse. She made clicking noises at them both before placing them back in and putting a lid over them.

Agrippina leaned a little closer into the doorway, but as she did, she brushed against the door, causing it to creak open a little more. The woman froze and slowly turned her head to look, but James had pulled Agrippina back into the hall before she could see her face.

He pulled her across the hall to another room, once again being enveloped by darkness. They both looked into the hall, hiding on either side of the door frame as the woman stepped out, holding a single candle, her face obscured by a veil.

A surge of emotions and energy rushed over Agrippina as she stepped out of the room in direct view of the woman.

"Stop right there!" she demanded. "Who are you?"

The woman stumbled backward for a moment before taking off, running down the dark hallway, the light from the candle holding on for dear life as it fluttered helplessly along, casting wild shadows on the walls.

Agrippina, despite James calling after her, took chase, running hard. She gained on the woman and grabbed her arm, causing her to spin around. She ripped off the veil and gasped as the candle illuminated the face before her.

"Cecelia!" she breathed. "But what—how?"

Cecelia narrowed her eyes at her. "You should not be down here," she growled. "You should have left well enough alone!"

"I want to help," Agrippina told her. "I understand now. I saw your uncle's book."

Cecelia's eyes grew wide with surprise and pain before they flashed with anger. "You will never understand!" She pulled a hand out of her pocket and blew a powder into her face.

Agrippina coughed and stepped back, blinking hard as whatever it was landed in her eyes.

"The woman in black will have her revenge," Cecelia said as she ran off into the darkness and disappeared.

# 31

"Aggy!" James called out. "Aggy!"

"James?" Agrippina replied, rubbing her eyes. She could barely see James' candelabra floating toward her, her vision slightly blurred from whatever Cecelia had blown into her face. She stood, pressing her back against the wall as she waited for him to reach her.

"Are you alright?" he asked, inspecting her face.

Agrippina thought she nodded, but she couldn't be sure. "I believe so."

"Why would you run like that?" he asked her, his voice full of anger, concern, and relief all at the same time. "Are you hurt?"

She shook her head which seemed to be growing heavy. "She blew something at me, but I—" She sniffed, smelling the powder that was lodged in her nose. "Oh no, James. It's morning glory. She must have grinded up seeds or something in her pocket." She could feel herself beginning to panic.

"It is alright, Aggy! They will not kill you," he told her calmly, taking her hand. "You are only going to hallucinate.

You are going to be just fine."

She took shallow breaths through her nose as she shook her head.

"Did you see who she was?"

"It is Cecelia!" she replied half screaming. "The woman in black, one of them, is Cecelia."

"One of them?" He shook his head. "It does not matter right now. We need to get out of here."

"She went that way," Agrippina said pointing.

"I believe the study is the other direction," James said, looking from one end to the other. "That end looks as if it goes on for a long time."

"We need to follow her," Agrippina said a little sternly.

"We need to get out of here."

Agrippina gasped, flinching. "Did you feel that? Something fluttered by me." She let out a small squeal. "There it was again."

"Look at me," he said in a soothing voice, gently pressing her cheek. "It is not real. It is just the morning glory. There is nothing there."

She nodded, her body shaking.

"Good." He tucked her hand into the crook of his elbow, and he began walking into the long dark hallway. "Just stay focused on the sound of my voice. We are going to get out of here. Do you trust me?"

"Yes." She flinched again as the shadows danced wickedly against the walls.    She closed her eyes and laid her head on James's shoulder.

"Are you limping?" she asked quietly. "Or am I imagining that too?"

James cleared his throat. "My, uh, foot fell through a rotten floorboard. It is nothing."

She clung tighter to him, the dark seeming to choke as

she panted. "You hurt yourself trying to chase after me. I am sorry." She swallowed hard. "I let my impatience cloud my judgement."

She felt him shake his head. "Your uncle the earl invited me to Ipswich," James said changing the subject, trying to keep her mind off what was happening to her.

"I told him we would visit in the fall," she replied, her breathing choppy and rapid. "Ipswich is beautiful in the fall."

"You said 'we' as in you and me?"

"Yes, is that not what you want?"

"Do you doubt it?" James could feel her shaking her head against his shoulder.

"No." She gasped, stopping. "What was that noise? Do you hear that crying?"

"It is alright, Aggy. It is not real. It is just the morning glory playing tricks on you."

"There is someone coming!" she yelled, pointing to nothing in the dark. "There is a light coming toward us! They are going to get us!"

"It is just us, Aggy. There is no light ahead."

"Oh, James, I am going mad! I must get out of here." She pressed her other hand to her head. "My head is heavy and," she took a few short breaths, "the light is shimmering in ways I have never seen before. It is both magical, yet terrifying."

James suppressed a laugh with a cough. He stopped walking when he came to a spiral staircase. He held the candelabra toward it to get a better look. The hallway continued to stretch into the dark in front of them, but the stairs could get them out faster.

"Let us see where this leads," he said, gently pulling her along.

She gripped his hand tighter. "I feel as if my heart will explode."

"Keep holding my hand," James told her. "I will get you out of here."

"The light is following us!" she yelled, tripping as she tried to scramble faster up the stairs.

James pulled her back up. "Remember. It is not real, Aggy."

She began to whimper as they continued up the stairs that seemed to spiral into an eternal darkness with each step bringing a different horrifying sensation. She flinched with every creak, the sound turning to screaming in her ears. The warm draft that wafted down was fingers reaching out to touch her. Even the darkness, which the candelabra barely abated, hid faces that smiled and bared their teeth at her, laughing at her fear, feeding off it.

James stopped when they came to a small platform. He held the candelabra up looking for a seam.

"There could be a door here, or we also have the option to continue going up." He moved the light to show the continuing staircase in its upward spiral.

"Please find a door," Agrippina begged.

James was already feeling along the wall, pausing when he felt a small draft.

"James, hurry!" Agrippina said, beginning to panic.

"I almost have it. Just take deep breaths, Aggy. We are getting out of here."

His hand finally found a small knob and he let out a relieved 'ah' as he turned it, his heart leaping with joy when he heard the click. He pushed open the door and led Agrippina into the music room of the main house. The room was full of moonlight, which, after the blinding darkness, seemed almost as bright as the sun. He helped her to a chair before securing the secret door, breathing a sigh of relief as he pushed it closed.

"James," Agrippina whispered in a heightened voice.

He turned sharply toward her.

"Please tell me she is not real." She pointed to a dark figure sitting at the piano who slowly began to rise.

James stood in front of Agrippina, shielding her. "It is alright, Aggy," he soothed.

"I had Mr. Arter put on some tea," came the voice of Mrs. Bolten as she faced them. "It will not completely counteract the morning glory, but it will help settle your nerves."

Neither James nor Agrippina spoke.

"Cecelia burst into my room and told me what happened. She told me how you found your way to our smuggler's den. You should have seen the panic she was in. I had to give her a sedative before I came down to wait for you."

"How did you know we would come through this door?" James asked.

"I didn't. I had Alex posted in the study and Janet posted in your room, Miss Greystone. They were to lead you here to me."

"Who is waiting in the cherry trees?" Agrippina asked sinking further into her chair. "That is where the tunnel leads, does it not? Perhaps another one leads out by the library?"

"Hmm," Mrs. Bolten laughed. "You are clever."

"The morning glory." Agrippina flinched at nothing as she gripped the arms of the chair tightly. "How long is this going to last?"

She ignored her question. "What, might I ask, did you find down there in the tunnels?"

Agrippina closed her eyes as the room began to spin and shadows melted from the walls. She took a deep breath to ground herself. "It is not real," she said aloud to herself.

Mrs. Bolten seemed to float across the room, her elegant figure swaying in the darkness. "The effects, depending on how much you inhaled, should not last more than an hour. It was wrong of Cecelia to have taken such measures, but you have stumbled onto something you could not possibly understand."

Agrippina swallowed, her throat incredibly dry. She flinched again, shielding her face as Mrs. Bolten's dark robe began to flutter about, reaching for her.

James put a reassuring hand on her shoulder. "Why did you allow your nephew to bring her here?" James asked, his anger rising.

Mrs. Bolten laughed bitterly. "I did not allow him to do anything. I never asked him to bring someone to investigate! He did that on his own."

Mr. Arter came in with a tea tray and put it on a table before standing off to the side. Mrs. Bolten poured tea into a cup, splashing cream in it before offering it to Agrippina who took it eagerly.

"No!" James shouted. "It could be poisoned."

Mrs. Bolten scowled at him. "Do you honestly think me so idiotic that I would kill the niece of an earl in my house! I have more sense than that, Mr. Mackland. And I am rather offended you think I would stoop so low as to poison tea."

Agrippina, unable to bear the dryness of her throat took a sip, immediately soothed by its warmth. She relaxed back into her chair, but refused to open her eyes, still scared as to what she might see.

"Now, I shall repeat my question," Mrs. Bolten said after a moment. "What did you find down there?"

Agrippina took another sip of her tea and tried to control the pounding of her heart.

"With all due respect, Mrs. Bolten, I do not believe this is the time," James replied. "Miss Greystone is not in the state of mind to say anything. She is hallucinating."

"Are you unable to attest to what was seen down there?" Mrs. Bolten retorted, narrowing her eyes at him. "You were down there as well, were you not?"

"He stole from you the one thing you wanted the most," Agrippina said in a dreamy voice. "Not just once, but five times. He gave you rue once he found out you were with child, and made you miscarry. All you wanted was to be a mother and he denied you that."

Mrs. Bolten glanced over at Mr. Arter who bowed his head. She took in a deep breath, letting it out slowly, gently nodding her head. "For years, I thought I was the problem. But there was nothing wrong with me except for the man I married. After Phillip, he stopped visiting me in my chambers. For years, I thought it was because I was broken, but he is the one who is broken." Her last words were riddled with bitterness and anger.

"Are you referring to all the other women?" James asked.

Tears, just visible in the candlelight, glided down her face. "Men of a certain rank have affairs. I always understood that. My father had them, my brother had them. I thought Eugene would be different; I thought he loved me as much as I loved him. But he only loved me as long as I was young." She paused, pressing a hand to her mouth. "I had aged out of his affections."

Agrippina's skin prickled. *Aged out; AO.*

"Since I found his little book, I have wondered why did he even get married? If he did not want children, a normal product of married life, why marry me?" She sniffed. "I realized it was because my husband likes to collect and possess things. Pretty things. And I have been nothing more or less than a pretty thing to him. He has been respectful, save the affairs, but not loving—never loving."

Agrippina took the last sip of her tea which Mr. Arter

immediately collected and poured her another cup. She thanked him, staring down into the liquid as the silence hung around them.

"When did you first discover him with Cecelia?" Agrippina asked in a small voice, disgusted and scared that she had to ask.

Mrs. Bolten inhaled sharply, pressing a hand to her chest as she moved to a chair and sat down.

James gaped at Agrippina before turning his gaze on Mrs. Bolten.

"Two years ago." Mrs. Bolten sniffed and coughed, pulling out a handkerchief. "I do not know why, but I was unable to sleep that night, so I thought to take a walk around the house. As I stepped into the hallway, I saw him, slipping into her room. I could not understand why he would be sneaking into his niece's room in the middle of the night, so I peered through a crack in the door and I—I—" Mrs. Bolten stood and paced the room, trying to control her emotions.

Agrippina slipped her hand into James' for comfort as she watched and waited.

"We practically raised her as our own!" Mrs. Bolten cried angrily. "We treated her like our daughter and he—he—he was violating her. And I did not know. I did not save her from him." She wiped her eyes and coughed, taking a deep breath. "He never did it while Richard was home, and he idolized his uncle too much to see him as anything other than a 'good' man."

"But, Cecelia is to be married and—" James stopped, shocked by what he was hearing and unsure what he wanted to say.

"Henry Rudolph?" Mrs. Bolten said. "He is a good man. Honorable, in need of an heir, and as intelligent as a wet sack of rocks. He will not notice."

"So, you devised this whole elaborate plan with your niece to take revenge upon your husband?" James asked.

"My husband was in need of punishment and the only thing he ever feared was the family curse. We were going to wait and hold off until closer to his birthday, but when Maven Rupert came to me and told me about his midnight meetings with her and Anna, we sped up the plan."

"A girl lost her life because of you," James said.

Mrs. Bolten shook her head. "We had nothing to do with Anna's unfortunate demise. My husband and I were both out of town in Cowden meeting Randolph's family with Cecelia. We did not know she was missing or dead until we returned home a week later."

"What was your final plan then?" He shook his head. "Poison your husband?"

"I admit the morning glory has been used to induce hallucinations and heighten his fear, but I have never poisoned my husband."

"You were just trying to drive him mad until he took his own life," Agrippina chimed in. "Then your revenge would be complete."

Mrs. Bolten smiled as she walked to the window, her profile outlined by the moonlight. With the moon behind her, she almost seemed to glow, and she smiled as she looked down, rubbing her belly which was just beginning to show.

"James," Agrippina breathed.

James' eyes grew wide.

"My revenge will be complete when I bring the newest Bolten into the world. A true Bolten. My husband may not have joined me in my chambers, but his blood will still flow through this child."

"Does Mr. Bolten happen to have a disfigured small finger?" Agrippina asked hesitantly.

Mrs. Bolten nodded. "He often hides it either behind his back or in his pocket. He hates the sight of it."

"CPM," Agrippina whispered. "Janet and Alex's mother. She was the one who refused to take the rue and was sent away. Janet and Alex are Mr. Bolten's children."

Mrs. Bolten laughed through her nose. "You should have seen his surprise when you pointed out Alex's finger to him. To be confronted with his past. To be confronted with what he did to Kitty."

Agrippina's heart skipped a beat and her skin prickled at the name. "Kitty?"

"Catherine Penelope Mosley, or Kitty as we called her, was the purest soul that ever lived," Mr. Arter said from his dark corner. "She did not deserve what Mr. Bolten had done to her. He seduced her, used her, and then threw her away like garbage."

Agrippina shook her head. "I agree Mr. Bolten deserves to be punished, but why like this? Why not expose him?"

Mrs. Bolten laughed. "For as intelligent as you are, you sure are naïve. Mr. Bolten owns half the town. He has enough money to buy off all the officials. He puts on such a perfect face to the world, no one would believe that he is actually a monster."

"That does not give you the right to do what you are doing," Agrippina told her.

"It gives me every right!" Mrs. Bolten shouted, turning and glaring at her. "I have tapped into his greatest fear and will destroy him from the inside out as he destroyed all those women in his wake."

The sound of a gunshot from somewhere in the house made everyone freeze. Agrippina's eyes grew wide as she exchanged glances with James. The shocked look on his face told her she was not imagining what she had just heard.

"Where did that come from?" James asked, his voice heightened.

Mr. Arter, who was the closest to the door, shook his head. "It sounded like it was upstairs."

The four of them ran with Mr. Arter in the lead as they rushed down the hall and up the stairs. Mr. Arter paused a moment at the top trying to decide where to go. Richard was just coming out of his room having been woken by the noise and approached them.

"What in the hell was that?" he asked shocked. "Was that a gunshot?" He then realized the strangeness of the four of them being together at that hour. "What is going on? What are you all already doing up?"

"There is a light coming from that room," James pointed out.

"That is my uncle's room," Richard said as everyone rushed past him. "What is going on?!"

But no one answered as they filed into Mr. Bolten's room, a single candle on the vanity illuminating the scene. Cecelia stood swaying lightly, the gun still dangling from her hand and a vacant expression on her face while her uncle lay gasping on the bed.

Someone screamed, perhaps Mrs. Bolten as she ran to her niece and took her in her arms, the gun falling to the floor. Richard rushed to his uncle's bedside trying to suppress the wound. He yelled for help, his uncle's blood pooling through his fingers.

Servants gathered at the door watching but no one moved to help as Mr. Bolten took his last breath, or as Cecelia's words echoed through them all.

"He will never hurt me again."

# 32

DR. HANSBY ARRIVED JUST AFTER DAWN, SHUTTING HIMSELF in Mr. Bolten's room with Mrs. Bolten and Richard. Richard angrily burst out of the room almost thirty minutes later, running down the stairs and out the front door followed shortly by a calm and reserved Dr. Hansby.

"Suicide is often seen in those ill in the mind," the doctor said as he stopped in the parlor.

James slowly opened his mouth in horror but remained silent.

Agrippina stepped forward to return his journals to him. "How is Cecelia?"

Dr. Hansby nodded taking them from her. "She is in shock. To walk in on your uncle having killed himself would be distressing to anyone." He bowed. "It was a pleasure, Miss Greystone."

Agrippina bowed her head, returning his sentiments as he left.

James shook his head saying in a low voice, "Suicide? Clearly he cannot think that."

Mrs. Bolten cleared her throat from the doorway, causing

them both to sharply look up.

"I have ordered the carriage to take you home," Mrs. Bolten said in her usual, cold tone though her exhaustion was apparent in her eyes. "It should be ready within the hour. I hope you understand. The servants will pack your things, so please enjoy a quick breakfast before you go."

James stepped forward as if he wanted to say something, but Agrippina took hold of his hand, stopping him.

"Thank you, Mrs. Bolten," she said, bowing her head. "We are very sorry for your loss."

Mrs. Bolten sniffed, looking down for a brief moment. "Might I have the pleasure of talking to you alone, Miss Greystone?"

Agrippina exchanged a glance with James before nodding. He paused outside the door of the parlor, keeping his eyes locked onto Agrippina's as Mrs. Bolten closed the door behind him.

"Are you feeling any better?" Mrs. Bolten asked. "Have the effects of the morning glory worn completely off?"

"Yes, thank you."

Mrs. Bolten silently walked further into the room, planting herself on a sofa. She smoothed her skirts for a moment, studying her own movements as she elegantly and deliberately made them.

"It is quite amazing and sad to me that Agnes Steadman had more power in death than she ever could have had in life."

Agrippina said nothing in response.

"In life, she was nothing but a sad spinster, holding onto broken promises of an unworthy man. But in death, she was feared. Feared for over two centuries all because of a few words uttered in bitterness and anger just before she died."

"It sounds as if you admired her."

250

Mrs. Bolten shook her head, her brows slightly furrowed. "No, I pity her." She sighed. "Just as I suppose I pity all the women—excuse me—young ladies my husband seduced." She shifted her gaze to a far corner, her stare distant. "He could be very charming, and he always knew what you wanted to hear."

Again, Agrippina did not respond, but she moved closer.

"Eugene was easy to fall in love with. He was warm and tender in the beginning, but when he was done with you, he was cold and distant. Even as his wife, he was done with me. And after Phillip," she choked slightly on the child's name, "he never visited my bed again." She sniffed and rubbed her lips together. "I thought it was because he was heartbroken and could no longer bear to see me fail at delivering him a child."

"But that was not true."

Mrs. Bolten shook her head. "Recently I discovered it was because I had grown too old." She chuckled bitterly. "I was four-and-twenty, and my husband thought me too old. And now, here I am at almost forty with child again." She rubbed her belly, smiling down at it.

Agrippina blinked at her.

"You judge me for bedding my husband's son."

Agrippina shook her head. "No, in a way, I think I understand. I might not condone your behavior, but certainly do not judge it."

Mrs. Bolten smiled.

"What happened to Anna Brown?" Agrippina asked gently.

Mrs. Bolten shook her head. "I do not know. I swear I do not. I only met with her once when we first planned the whole thing. My husband deserted her, as he did many others, when he found he had gotten her with child. She refused, at first, to get rid of it. She was so sure he was going to kick me out and take her in as his wife." Another bitter chuckle escaped her lips. "Poor child. I used to believe his lies too."

Agrippina furrowed her brows in confusion. "Someone killed Miss Brown, Mrs. Bolten. I do not believe she simply snuck out and died."

Mrs. Bolten shook her head. "I understand that. And as much as I wish to portray my husband as the monster who did it, I cannot. I know we were away when she died."

"If Mr. Bolten was away, who else would have a motive to kill her?" Agrippina wondered aloud. She shook her head. "It does not make sense."

"Life does not make sense, Miss Greystone," Mrs. Bolten simply replied. "Things that should happen never do, and things that should not—" She let her thought trail away, the meaning of what she was saying very clear.

Agrippina felt a flash of anger and disappointment roll through her.

"I know that look," Mrs. Bolten told her gently. "You feel like a failure. You feel as if the whole purpose of you being here has ended in nothing." She smiled softly. "I have to admire your tenacity, Miss Greystone. With all the moving parts involved, you still successfully managed to discover quite a lot."

"You are trying to spare my feelings, hoping I will leave with the most important piece of the mystery unsolved."

"I am trying to keep intact the last of that girl's dignity!" Mrs. Bolten replied a little tersely. "What good would it do to ruin the poor girl's name and her family with it? She has a younger sister whose name will be tarnished if it ever got out that her sister was sneaking out in the middle of the night having relations with an older married man!"

"Is it truly her dignity and good name you are concerned with, or is it yours?"

Mrs. Bolten's cold eyes bore into Agrippina's, unblinking.

"Mrs. Brown is grieving her daughter and deserves to find justice for her."

Mrs. Bolten laughed. "Is that what you think she wants? Justice? Do you think she wants justice airing out her daughter's dirty dark secrets, or do think she wants her daughter to be remembered as a kind, sweet, chaste girl?"

Agrippina remained unwavering and hardened her gaze while Mrs. Bolten softened.

"I do admire you, Miss Greystone. In most of these situations, a large sum of money would will all of this away, but you are not in it for the money. You are in it for the satisfaction of being right. However admirable that is, it is also conceited."

Agrippina started.

"Your desire to be correct—to be deemed as intelligent, to be seen as intellectually superior—has made you blind to the others who could be hurt in the process."

"Finding out who killed Miss Brown has nothing to do with being right. It is the *right* thing to do."

Mrs. Bolten shook her head. "In a perfect world, yes, but we are not in that world. We are in a world where family and reputation mean everything and by finding out what is *right* you will destroy the reputations of three families. You will ruin the future prospects of three young women, Cecelia included, whose fiancé will undoubtedly break off their engagement once he finds out."

"I cannot so easily let go of what I believe to be right."

Mrs. Bolten let out an exasperated sigh. "Right and wrong are not always black and white, Miss Greystone. There are always gray areas. Think of the damage that will come with revealing the truth."

"People want the truth."

"Are you listening to me?" Mrs. Bolten laughed. "No, people want hear what they want to hear. And for the Brown's they want to hear that their poor girl met with an accident and died just as pure as the day she was born."

Agrippina shook her head. "How I am I to let someone get away with murder?" she asked huffing through her nose. "I am already going to turn a blind eye to Cecelia whom we all know killed Mr. Bolten."

Mrs. Bolten sprang from her seat. "And he deserved it! You cannot deny that he deserved everything he got. He was a foul perverted man who spent years hurting young girls and women."

Though she wanted to, Agrippina could not argue with her.

Mrs. Bolten forced a smile, taking a calming breath. "Sometimes we fail, Miss Greystone. It is the human in us." She cleared her throat as she sat down again. "I am not in the habit of begging, but I must plead graciously for you to walk away and allow everyone who suffered under my husband, whether directly or not, to heal." She placed a hand on her belly and rubbed it gently.

Agrippina looked at her hand and then met her eye. "Your husband died without knowing his name will continue, though I am sure he would have been shocked to hear it."

A coy smile curled Mrs. Bolten's lips. "You are right. And in my dreams, I imagined whispering it into his ear on his deathbed." She took a deep breath and let it out in a whoosh. "But I am a practical woman. I know things do not always turn out the way you plan."

Agrippina nodded absent mindedly. "Can you tell me which of my theories about the spoon were correct?"

Mischief sparkled in Mrs. Bolten's eyes. "It was a replica." She nodded. "You put on quite a show. All of you did. Save

254

for Mr. Maddox, and I assume Janet, who knew nothing.

"Janet is a dear girl, but she talks too freely. Luckily, she is not as pretty as her mother was, or she would have been a victim of my husband too. She knew nothing until your antics at lunch yesterday."

"Did Mr. Arter play at the woman in black too?"

"When the occasion called for it. Cecelia and I both had to be in the same room once or twice."

"And the girls just pretended the entire time? They did not see anything?"

Mrs. Bolten shook her head. "They were given a mixture of morning glory to 'help' them 'see,' but they both knew their roles."

"And the cows were killed before their throats were slit?"

Mrs. Bolten smiled. "You are clever." She cleared her throat. "Yes, Alex led them out to the pasture and gave them wilted cherry leaves and bark. After they were dead for a few hours, he cut their throats and carried what blood that flowed out in a bucket, disposing of it somewhere else."

"And then he started the fire in the field? You have reduced the Ruperts to a relative state of poverty. Do you realize that?"

Mrs. Bolten let out a small sigh. "The fire was not his doing. We suggested killing one of the horses. It was Maven who set blaze to the field."

Agrippina was taken aback. "Maven?"

"She thought a horse was not a great enough sacrifice."

"Sacrifice?"

"That is what she called it. I thought it strange as well, but she played her part right and the seeds of fear were sown into my husband's mind."

Agrippina huffed and shook her head. "And what of the silk merchant? Mr. Carver? Your little stunt cost him his life!"

"Mr. Carver was handsomely paid for his participation!" Mrs. Bolten fired back. "He already knew the moths were in the box. The plan was for him to take it to the milliner's shop in Halstead where they would be discovered. But the poor fool died before he made it." She shook her head. "It was an unfortunate coincidence, nothing more."

Agrippina stared blindly across the room. "And that is what you would prefer I say about Miss Brown?"

"There is not much more I can say that I have not already said."

A chill ran over Agrippina filling her with a strange sense of uneasiness. "By doing this," she began hesitantly, "by not continuing my investigation, I will be turning my back on a belief system that I have always clung to."

Mrs. Bolten lifted a brow.

"Truth and justice should always prevail."

A bitter laugh escaped Mrs. Bolten's throat. "Your belief only tells me that you have more to experience in this world, and that it might be time for a new belief system. *Justice*, as you say, does not mean the same thing to everyone."

Mrs. Bolten's words struck a chord, and Agrippina was unsure how to feel.

"I hope you have an uneventful journey home, Miss Greystone." Mrs. Bolten stood, and Agrippina followed suit.

The two women curtseyed, and Mrs. Bolten walked toward the door. "Mr. Mackland is a fine catch, but I cannot say I would not have preferred you for my nephew."

A small smile twitched across Agrippina's face in response. She waited until the door was closed again before she fell back onto the sofa letting a few hot, bitter tears roll down her cheek.

# 33

"Have you come to make sure I actually leave?" Agrippina asked handing the last of her bags to a footman.

Mr. Arter stepped out of the dark hallway into the room. "No," he replied plainly. "I came to apologize for my behavior toward you."

She looked over at him sharply, half surprised.

"It was borderline arrogant, and I was overstepping my station." He cleared his throat, obviously uncomfortable. "Though for a woman of *your* station, you bore it rather well."

She eyed him suspiciously. "My uncle and I have indulged our housekeeper for too long. She often abuses me much worse than you have these few days. I suppose I am used to it."

For the first time, Mr. Arter chuckled, a smile brightening his pale, shadowed features.

Agrippina walked to the desk and opened the bottom drawer, pulling out the shawl and ribbon she had placed there. She stared down at them for a moment before handing them to Mr. Arter.

"I suppose this shawl was your sister's?" she asked watching him gently take it from her.

He nodded, almost smiling down at it. "I gave it to her as a gift one year for Christmas. She had scolded me, saying it was too fine, but I could tell she had adored it." His eyes misted as he thought back on her. "She was so young. Six years younger than myself. She was my half-sister, but I loved her no less for it."

Agrippina bobbed her head. "This might seem a strange question, but do you have another maid here who goes by Kitty?"

He looked up at her, confused for a brief moment, before a smile spread across his face. "No."

She involuntarily rubbed her arm as a chill spread through her.

"You've seen her though, haven't you? My sister."

She met his eye. "Your sister is dead, Mr. Arter. You told me so yourself."

He shook his head. "Gone in body but not in spirit."

She suppressed a shudder.

His eyes twinkled. "I have often thought I sensed her over the years, seen her out the corner of my eye, heard her soft, melodic voice. But I have never fully seen her. Does she seem happy? Content?"

Agrippina stammered a moment. "I do not believe in ghosts. Perhaps one of your other maids was playing a trick—"

"No. No one has been here long enough to have known her."

She shook her head. "Perhaps I misunderstood her name when I asked." She closed her carpet bag and began to walk out the door. "I am done. You can have my bags brought to the carriage."

"Please, Miss Greystone." The pleading tone of his voice made her stop. "I have held onto the guilt of not protecting my sister for over twenty years. Please, tell me."

She took a deep breath and turned to face him. "If it was your sister that I saw, she did not seem bitter or angry." She paused a moment. "In fact, I believe she helped me."

Mr. Arter offered a small smile. "Thank you."

She bowed her head slightly before briskly walking outside to where the carriage was waiting for her. James, who had been pacing the front drive, abruptly stopped when he saw her emerge from the house.

"I thought they were going to make me leave without you," he said chuckling nervously. "Is everything alright?"

She smiled weakly and nodded. "Yes, I am just glad to be going home." She stopped a footman as he walked by with one of her boxes. "Oh! I will take that, please."

He bowed and handed it to her.

"I would prefer this rode in the carriage with us," Agrippina said.

James took it and placed it inside, shooting her a questioning look. "What is in there? It sounds as if something is moving around in it."

She smiled playfully. "Just a little friend."

"Why is that not comforting coming from you?"

She laughed lightly in response.

"Miss Greystone."

They both turned to see Richard walking sheepishly toward them.

"Might I have a word?"

She gently squeezed James' hand and moved toward Richard who shuffled his feet anxiously in the dirt. He took a deep breath, letting it out in a huff, before forcing a smile.

"Do you fancy a brief walk?"

Agrippina glanced over her shoulder at James and the carriage.

"It will not take long, I promise."

She nodded, falling into stride with him as he moved toward the path to the garden. He was silent for a few moments, unsure of what to say first.

"I am sorry for your loss, Mr. Maddox."

He shook his head. "Do not be," he replied in a cold tone. "That man was not who I thought he was." He cleared his throat. "He was—" he shook his head, stopping himself. "I did not know, Miss Greystone. You must believe me."

She nodded. "I do."

He took another deep breath and sighed, his voice becoming shaky. "My poor sister. To hear what she endured, I—" He pressed a hand to his mouth. "I cannot stop the overwhelming anger inside of me when I think of it. And he did it while I was away when I could not be there to protect her." He pressed a hand to his quivering lips.

Agrippina put a gentle hand on his arm. "None of that was your fault, Mr. Maddox. No one would ever blame you, no matter how much you might blame yourself."

He nodded, clearing his throat. "I know. At least I think I know. Perhaps in time I will." He sniffed. "I want to thank you for coming here and trying your best to help my family even though now it seems we are just as lost."

"What will happen now?"

He took a deep breath and sighed. "I suppose Bolten House will remain in a little chaos until my aunt has her child and we can decide the line of succession. If the child is a girl, I will become owner. If a boy, then I will look after the estate in his stead until he becomes of age." He cleared his throat. "I, uh, hope I do not have to ask for your discretion as to the parentage of the child."

"I am rather offended you would think you should have to ask."

He breathed a sigh of relief, his usual coy smile spreading across his face. "I have always liked you, Miss Greystone." He chuckled. "I actually thought of pursuing you once, thinking you would make a fine wife. For me at least."

Agrippina's eyes sparkled with humor. "As flattered as I should be, I know our marriage would only be for you to fulfill the duty of siring an heir. I believe my kind are not to your taste."

He gazed at her, confusion quickly turning to alarm. "You know then?"

She squeezed his arm. "Good-bye, Mr. Maddox. Rest assured that your secrets, all of your secrets, are safe with me." She turned back to the carriage, leaving a smirking Richard behind her.

She smiled at James as he held his hand out to help her into the carriage.

"Everything alright?"

She nodded. "Yes."

He climbed in after her, hitting the side of the coach to announce they were ready for travel. It lurched forward and Agrippina took one last look at Bolten House before pulling the curtains shut.

James cleared his throat, his brows raised quizzically. "Might I ask about the little mouse you have stowed away in a hat box?"

Agrippina smiled. "She found her way to my room, and I decided to keep her. She needs a name, but I have yet to decide on one."

"Would Agnes be inappropriate?"

Agrippina nodded. "Agnes would be very appropriate."

"There is one question that still lingers in my mind."

"Hmm?"

"If there truly is no curse, how is it that the Boltens do

not live any older than forty-five?"

Agrippina sighed softly, exhaustion coming over her as she relaxed back into her seat. "Oh, I figured that out as soon as I saw the family Bible."

He raised a quizzical brow. "And?"

"It is simply explained by some hereditary disease, a heart complaint most likely that affects mostly the men."

James creased his brows. "How would the family Bible have given you that idea?"

A lazy smile pulled at her lips. "For one, most of the women born into the family, and several second, third, or fourth sons did not have their deaths recorded as they married and moved on with their lives. With that, I can assume it is possible they lived past the age of forty-five as there is no evidence stating otherwise. There was also one entry that was overlooked. A Miss Bolten who never married born in 1690 and died in 1745."

"Making her fifty-five when she passed away."

Agrippina nodded. "Curses only have power through the power we give them. The Bolten family line has a weak heart, but in order to make sense of their untimely deaths, they created and gave in to something dangerous. Fear."

"Ah!" James exclaimed, letting out a yawn. "More practical to be sure, but surely not as exciting as a witch's curse."

She sighed, still disappointed at how everything concluded. "Certainly not." She pulled back the curtain and ventured one last look at Bolten House. The curvature of the road brought them to the side of the house, the cherry trees swaying gently in the breeze. Her breath caught in her throat as she caught a figure looking back at her from the room she had stayed in.

Kitty.

She gently shook her head, letting the curtains fall. She

did not believe in ghosts, or curses, or—she no longer knew what she believed. What she knew and what she thought she knew had been shaken to the core. Perhaps, Mrs. Bolten was right. Maybe it was time for a new belief system, a new way of seeing things.

She soon drifted off to sleep as the carriage pulled onto the main road, her mind echoing Mrs. Bolten's words to her.

*Justice does not mean the same thing to everyone.*

# 34

Dr. Greystone, having heard the carriage pull up to the house, greeted his niece and Mr. Mackland with surprise. He pulled Agrippina into an embrace, however, telling her how dull the house had been without her.

"And, so you have solved it then?" he asked as he pulled away.

Agrippina cleared her throat, her glance falling to the ground. "Not quite."

He exchanged glances with James as he bowed shallowly. "Well, let us come in. I will have Abigail make you a plate."

As they stepped out of the darkness into the well-lit hall, Agrippina felt how truly glad she was to be home. She sighed happily as she heard the quick, shuffling steps of Abigail, who flew around the corner with a smile on her face.

"Good evenin', miss, sir," she said with her usual inelegant curtsey. "Might I take yer hat and bonnet?" She shook her head disapprovingly at Agrippina who had worn her hair uncovered the whole journey.

"It is good to see you, Abigail," Agrippina said in response, squeezing the old woman's hand.

"Aye?" Abigail eyed her a little suspiciously. "What's this about?"

Agrippina smiled. "Nothing. Might I have some of your spiced tea?"

A sparkle glistened in Abigail's eyes. "Of course, miss. I shall get right on it."

"Would you," James cleared his throat, "would you walk with me around your garden? I find myself restless after such a long carriage ride, and it is a very fine evening."

"Yes, yes, a very fine evening," Dr. Greystone agreed. "I think some warm tea enjoying the night air would do us all a bit of good. Though I should join you in a moment. I was in the middle of writing a letter when you came."

"If you wait until tomorrow, I can show you the garden in the full sunlight. It is too dark to see anything properly now," Agrippina proclaimed.

"I wish to," James shook his head, "I would like to enjoy the evening a bit longer if you would humor me."

Agrippina looked at her uncle and Abigail who quickly scurried away.

She nodded slowly. "Alright."

She led him to the back of the house where French doors opened to the back. "It is not much to boast about. It is certainly nothing to the one at Bolten House, but it is sufficient and more than enough for my uncle and myself."

He reached the door first and opened it for her, following her out in the dwindling light of the sun. "It is not fully dark yet," he said triumphantly, looking up at the last streaks of color in the sky.

She took a deep breath and smiled, knowing that soon the air would be filled with the scents of her flowers. "The irises will be in bloom soon. They are my favorite. We have several different colors that line the pathway."

She stopped walking when they came to the little fountain in the middle of the garden, its stone recently brushed free of debris and moss by the gardener. Soon it would be full of water that trickled from the top tier all the way to the bottom. She could almost hear it in that moment, the birds chirping about as they bathed in the water.

She glanced over at the apple tree she planted over ten years ago with her uncle and Thomas. She had watched it grow from a doubtful sapling to a promising, fruitful tree. She longed for one of its apples at that moment, a taste of the simpler past.

She turned and looked back at the house and thought how many wonderful memories she had had there. Years full of her uncle's love and kindness. Years of understanding companionship.

She longed to stay in that moment and just reminisce and feel the comfort of a warm memory, but she knew she could not. She loved who she was, but she loved who she was to become. She smiled at James as she realized this and took his hand.

Almost without hesitation, he got down on one knee.

"Agrippina," he whispered in a tone that conveyed more than could ever be spoken, "there are no words sufficient enough for what I want to say to you, and to merely say 'I love you' is not right. I *do* love you, but it is more than that. You are a deep well of cool, crisp water, and I am a poor traveler dying from thirst." He shook his head. "I am rambling. I am trying to say, I will never get enough of you. You are an endless story that I cannot stop reading, or yearning to know what happens next, and I want to be in that story with you." He sighed. "I believe I am not making sense."

The joy that enveloped Agrippina as she watched James make his declaration to her burst forth in a laugh, and she pressed a hand to her mouth to suppress it.

James laughed too, looking up at her in earnest. "I am horrible at this."

She shook her head. "No, you are perfect."

James stood and pressed his hand to her face. "Would you do me the honor of becoming my wife?"

She nodded as she leaned into his hand. "Yes."

He pressed his lips against hers and pulled her closer to him. Agrippina wrapped her arms around his waist and fell into his embrace, laughing joyously as they kissed.

A scream from the house interrupted them. They exchanged confused glances for a moment.

"I believe Abigail might have discovered poor, little Agnes," Agrippina said before erupting into laughter.

James joined her, kissing her forehead. "Perhaps I should go and save her."

Agrippina watched him go back into the house, her heart full of so many different emotions she felt it would burst. She was to be the future Mrs. Mackland and life never seemed more beautiful.

# 35
## (THREE MONTHS LATER)

"Miss Greystone!"

Agrippina turned from the milliner shop window where she was deciding whether or not she wanted to go in. A smile spread across her face as she saw who had been calling for her.

"Thomas!" She curtseyed to his bow. "What are you doing here in Bath?"

"Accompanying my aunt. She thought London much too dull this season and decided to escape. Though I am sure it is only because there is no one left for her to marry off."

Agrippina's eyes brightened. "Did you find your silly girl at last, Thomas?"

He chuckled, slightly blushing. "Did I find the woman I believe is for me? Yes, but I do not think her silly."

"I have heard love is blind."

He chuckled again. "Perhaps I cannot fault that."

"I congratulate you either way," she said. "If you are happy, then I am happy for you."

He nodded, thanking her. "I hear you yourself are soon to

be wed. Mr. Mackland seems a very honorable man."

Agrippina smiled, looping her arm through his. "Walk me home? Uncle would love to see you."

"How do you think I heard of your news?" he asked, obliging her as they turned down the street. "I saw him in the baths this morning. He could not help but gloat about you. He told me about your latest successful venture. You solved another fantastical mystery; this time with witches!"

"My uncle exaggerates, you must know that." She sighed and shook her head. "I must confess I was not completely successful. There was still one part of the mystery I was not able to uncover. However, I have promised to let it go and start afresh. Therefore, do not press me on the subject."

Thomas looked down at her in mock astonishment. "Miss Greystone leaving questions unanswered? That is unlike you. Do you give up so easily now?"

She narrowed her eyes at him. "You are provoking me, Thomas."

He laughed. "I promise you, I am not! I only ask because I might have another mystery to further get this one off your mind."

Agrippina stopped walking, a surge of excitement coursing through her. "Oh?" she replied rather calmly.

He smirked. "I knew you would be intrigued."

"It is a little too soon to assume that," Agrippina retorted. "Tell me what sort of mystery you could have for me and then I can decide if I am intrigued or not."

# EPILOGUE

*The plan we have set seems to be working. Anna has been playing her part beautifully. I have even visited her during one of her 'fits' and I was almost convinced myself they were real. She was always a good actress, however.*

*Everyone believes her to be sweet and innocent. If only they knew who she was behind those pretty, little smiles. I know! I know the true Anna. What one hides from their parents, is not so easily hidden from a friend of the same age.*

*Pretty little Anna has an ugly little secret.*

Friday, August 10, 1792

*I visited Anna again today. We were left alone in her room for a few minutes, and she told me she wanted to run away. She was scared of what her parents would think when they finally realized her secret.*

*I told her it would have been better if she had taken Mrs. Bolten's advice about the rue, but she had confessed she was scared. I remember smiling at this, though I am not sure why.*

She begged for my help. Anna Brown actually begged me for help. The satisfaction I felt in refusing her was undeniably sweet. I walked out of her room a little taller as she cried.

I had a change of heart, however, when I returned home and I wrote to Anna to let her know that I would indeed help her. I told her to meet me at midnight by the crossroads.

Saturday, August 11, 1792

My hands shake as I write. Whether more from fear, or excitement, I cannot tell. I do not know what I had planned to do when I told Anna that I would help her, but I do not think it was this.

I met her as planned, bringing one of my father's horses. She climbed up and we rode to the river. I just wanted to scare her. I wanted her to feel my pain! The pain that has been coursing through me since she stole my love from me!

I dug my heels into the horse, and we galloped across the fields. The whole time, she clung to me, yelling, telling me to stop! But I did not, could not! I only leaned into the horse more, beckoning it to go faster.

She begged me again, a sweet sound from someone so self-possessed that I could not control myself. I wanted her to beg more! I wanted her to cry out and promise anything and everything to me if I should stop.

The sound of her cries was electrifying, exhilarating! I did not want them to stop, and when we arrived at the river, I turned the horse sharply so it would not fall in. The horse must have been agitated because it reared, causing Anna to fall to the ground.

I got down from the horse to check on her. She appeared mildly hurt but nothing serious. I was racked with guilt nonetheless, and quickly dismounted to help her when she began to verbally abuse me. She told me I was a fool, and it was no wonder that Mr. Bolten had chosen her over me.

"Who could love such a plain, silly little thing like you?"

That is what she said to me. I became so enraged that I struck her, but a single hit did not abate

271

*my anger, and I lunged at her, hitting her again. She tried to get up and run from me, but I jumped on her, both of us falling to the ground. She struggled beneath me, but I did not care. I sat on her back and hit her with a rock. I then held her face down into the ground, pushing it into the soft dirt.*

*She flailed against me, but her pathetic attempts to fight me off were just that. Pathetic. I sat like that for what seemed like a lifetime and a split second all at once until she stopped moving, and I could no longer hear her muffled screams.*

*I stood, my head foggy, but my body tingling with life. I rolled her over and stared at her lifeless body, the moon highlighting her fair hair. I looked around me, knowing I would be alone at that time of night, but still feeling a sense of being watched.*

*I then dragged her to the river's edge and pushed her in, watching as she disappeared below the dark waters.*

MRS. RUPERT STOKED THE FIRE, A CHILL RUNNING THROUGH her. She glanced down at the torn-out journal pages, her lip trembling and eyes welling with tears.

"Forgive me, Lord," she whispered. "And, please forgive Maven."

She crumpled up the pages and tossed them into the fire.

THE END

Milton Keynes UK
Ingram Content Group UK Ltd.
UKHW020407021124
450424UK00014B/1474

9 798988 695424